It was all over but the fleeing

None of the group came close to Ryan's keenly honed sense of danger, the unconscious ability to flash-sort through even the tiniest fugitive sensory inputs, to identify the pattern that added up to *threat*.

Out of the corner of his eye, Ryan saw a skinny old man, standing by the side of the road, leveling a single-action Peacemaker blaster at Ryan's head.

But just as the one-eyed man's sense of danger had its limitations, so did his striking-rattler reflexes. He already knew he was nuked, even as his brain sent his body the impulse to dive aside.

The ancient blaster vanished in a giant yellow muzzle-flash, which instantly echoed in a blinding red flash inside Ryan's skull.

Then blackness. Then nothing.

JAMES AXLER
DEATHLANDS®
FORBIDDEN TRESPASS

A GOLD EAGLE BOOK FROM
W✦RLDWIDE®

TORONTO • NEW YORK • LONDON
AMSTERDAM • PARIS • SYDNEY • HAMBURG
STOCKHOLM • ATHENS • TOKYO • MILAN
MADRID • WARSAW • BUDAPEST • AUCKLAND

First edition May 2015

ISBN-13: 978-0-373-62632-8

Special thanks and acknowledgment to
Victor Milan for his contribution to this work.

Forbidden Trespass

Printed in U.S.A.

'Tis not a year or two shows us a man.
They are all but stomachs, and we all but food.
To eat us hungerly, and when they are full,
They belch us.

—William Shakespeare

THE DEATHLANDS SAGA

This world is their legacy, a world born in the violent nuclear spasm of 2001 that was the bitter outcome of a struggle for global dominance.

There is no real escape from this shockscape where life always hangs in the balance, vulnerable to newly demonic nature, barbarism, lawlessness.

But they are the warrior survivalists, and they endure—in the way of the lion, the hawk and the tiger, true to nature's heart despite its ruination.

Ryan Cawdor: The privileged son of an East Coast baron. Acquainted with betrayal from a tender age, he is a master of the hard realities.

Krysty Wroth: Harmony ville's own Titian-haired beauty, a woman with the strength of tempered steel. Her premonitions and Gaia powers have been fostered by her Mother Sonja.

J. B. Dix, the Armorer: Weapons master and Ryan's close ally, he, too, honed his skills traversing the Deathlands with the legendary Trader.

Doctor Theophilus Tanner: Torn from his family and a gentler life in 1896, Doc has been thrown into a future he couldn't have imagined.

Dr. Mildred Wyeth: Her father was killed by the Ku Klux Klan, but her fate is not much lighter. Restored from pre-dark cryogenic suspension, she brings twentieth-century healing skills to a nightmare.

Jak Lauren: A true child of the wastelands, reared on adversity, loss and danger, the albino teenager is a fierce fighter and loyal friend.

Dean Cawdor: Ryan's young son by Sharona accepts the only world he knows, and yet he is the seedling bearing the promise of tomorrow.

In a world where all was lost, they are humanity's last hope…

Prologue

"Wymie!"

At the cry from her sister, Wymea Berdone turned away from the big galvanized tub on the crude counter in the kitchen where she was doing the dishes. Hot water splashed from hands and lower arms reddened from heat and the caustic lye soap her family made from hog fat and wood ash.

The ash they got from the wood they cut in the forests around their house in the Pennyrile Hills near the ville of Sinkhole. The hog fat they had to trade for these days, since Wymie's stepdad, Mord Pascoe, had sold off the last of the pigs to buy hooch at Mathus Conn's gaudy house and bar. It was only one of the ways life had gotten poorer for them since the tree that fell the wrong way had killed Wymie's pa.

"Baby, what is it?" she called, grabbing a rag to dry her hands.

"It's nothin'!" Mord bellowed from his easy chair in the cabin's main room. "Mind your damn business, bitch."

"Blinda?" Wymie asked, ignoring him.

Her little sister, ten years old with her dirty blond hair in pigtails and a rag-doll teddy bear clutched to the front of her ragged linen smock, stared at her with wide sapphire-blue eyes. They were the only trait the two shared in common. Otherwise Blinda was slight and Wymea was strapping, though considered comely by most of the menfolk hereabouts—unfortunately including Mord Pascoe. And where Wymie had hair so raven-wing black it was almost blue falling down over the shoulders of her blue plaid flannel man's shirt, Blinda was fair.

"What happened, honey?"

"It's him," her sister said, without even a glance at the man lounging in the chair with his black-furred belly sticking out the bottom of his shirt, which was closed over his chest by the last few buttons holding out against the strain. The chair was a faded green and overstuffed. His own overstuffing had started the chair's stuffing busting out of seams all over the cushion and back. "He wants me to go outside with him to the woodpile again."

Wymie felt the lower lids of her eyes pushing up in what she knew was a dangerous look. She directed it toward her stepfather.

"I told you not to try that again," she said, managing with effort to keep from shouting. She knew what yelling would cost her ma. As it was, Wymie's defiance would cost the woman at least a couple face punches from those beefy fists.

Through his patchy stubble of black beard, Mord showed a grin that was brown and twisted where it wasn't gaps.

"You could take her place, y'know."

"Try to touch me again, I'll bust your nose like the last time," Wymie said. "If I catch you grabbin' at Blinda anymore, you're lucky if I don't do no more than bust your damn fingers."

She glanced meaningfully at the ax propped by the

door. It took effort she could ill afford, with all the other burdens she carried. But she kept its heavy blade sharp. Her pa had taught her to care for her tools, before the tree took him. And he knew from painful experience that a dulled ax was more dangerous to its user than what he or she might mean to chop with it.

"Don't lie," her mother said, with the flat intonation of someone repeating a chant they'd learned by rote, and long ago forgotten the real meaning of, if they'd ever known it at all. "Lyin's wicked."

Wymie turned a frown toward her mother. Despite her resentment, her eyes lost their dangerous pressure and drooped down at the outside edges, weighted down with sadness. She remembered a time when her mother had been tall and straight, pretty, even.

But the past three years, since her husband died, and especially the past two, since she married Mord Pascoe for no reason Wymie nor anyone about Sinkhole could tell, had shrunk her—shriveled her, almost—to a stooped shadow of her former self. Her glossy brown hair had turned drab and mouse-colored. The flesh of her face had drawn back, making her almost look like a mouse; and the cringing attitude she displayed toward her husband did nothing to dispel the resemblance.

Why can't you stand up for us for once, Ma? Wymie wanted to shout. She wouldn't, though. She knew the answer. If she stood up to Mord Pascoe, he'd beat her down. He might not be willing to lift a finger to help out around the homestead, or even keep the family alive, but he'd heave his bulk out of that chair and raise both hands to hit a woman.

He knew better than to do it with Wymie around. But he also knew—

"Nuke it all, a man's got needs," he whined, giving the lie to her mother's naming Wymie's words a lie. "If his wife can't handle them all, then his daughters should. It's the patriarchal way of things."

A narrow, sly look appeared in his small gray eyes. "And you can't watch over your ma and sis all the time," he said. "Can you?"

She growled.

Ignoring her, now that he'd reasserted his power in the family, he pushed himself up with a great groan of effort. The fumes that belched from his mouth when he did carried clear to Wymie ten feet away. It smelled worse than his pits and feet and crotch did. "Now, enough of this crap. I'm the man in the house and you got to obey. C'mere, you little bitch. *Now.*"

"Now, Blinda," her mother said. "Obey your daddy. You got to do it. It's that patriarch way, like he says."

"No," Wymie said firmly.

As Mord lumbered toward the cowering girl on short, fat-quivering legs, Blinda shot a frightened look at her big sister. Wymie nodded.

Blinda darted away, ducking under a clumsy swipe of Mord's pallid paws. She ran to the open window and leaned on the sill, sticking her face out to breathe in the cool spring-night breeze and watch the early fireflies dance. Her grimy toy bear dangled over the cracked wooden sill.

Mord made to follow, but Wymie put herself between them, her bare, reddened forearms, still steaming from the dishwater, crossed beneath her breasts. She knew that emphasized their heft, but the gesture also helped get her message across. She didn't want to raise a hand against the man unless she had to.

As he said, she couldn't be there to watch over her ma all the time.

But she was here now.

"Not another step," she declared.

"I'm a man," he repeated. It was one of his favorite things to say. It was almost like he thought someone might disagree, or forget it if he didn't repeat it often enough. "I'm stronger'n you, little slut. I could knock you out of the way."

"You could try."

He tried an engaging grin on her. It seemed to work on her ma, but it turned Wymie's stomach. In her eyes it was nothing but a snaggletoothed leer.

"You could take her place," he said. "Help take the edge off for your poor daddy, the way a dutiful daughter should."

"It's not gonna happen."

His eyes flashed and his heavy black brows jutted low and outward above them.

"Why do you act so high and mighty?" he bellowed. The stink of his breath rocked her back on her heels and made her eyes water, but she stood her ground. "I know what a slut you are. Givin' that sweet thang up for every boy in the county, from Maccum Corners clear to the holler!"

"That's a lie and you know it," she said. "No boy would dare touch me with anything they wanted to keep." Again she looked meaningfully at the ax.

Wish I'd gone ahead and struck his filthy hand off when he grabbed me through my skirt that time, she thought. But she had mashed his ugly tuber of a nose for him, as she'd reminded him before.

In return he'd knocked her sprawling with a backhand

and blackened her eye. But that victory was short-lived. She bounced back up right away, and that time she held her ax in both hands. Ready to cut.

"C'mon," he pleaded. "Let me get a little sugar, can't you?"

"Wymie," her mother called from behind him. "You don't be sassing your pa, now. He's right. You got to do what he says. We all do."

"Oh, Ma," Wymie cried, shaking her head and squinting her eyes to try to hold in the hot tears that filled them. "Can't you show some *spine* sometime?"

But she knew the answer. She doesn't dare, she thought. Because I can't protect her. I'm not good enough. Not strong enough. It's all my fault…

She shook her head again, once, fiercely. She wouldn't walk down *that* trail again. Not where it led her.

It had only been the once. But no amount of washing, mebbe not even a dose of straight-up lye, would ever cleanse her of the foul feeling that he had left her with.

"Blinda," she called, "come with me. Let's go for a nice walk in the woods, honey. Get some clean air in our noses for a change."

She turned away from her stepfather. She was afraid he'd rabbit-punch her, but she had to take that risk. She doubted he had the sack to try, anyway. He knew what she'd do to him if he tried a trick like that and failed.

Blinda was slumped over the sill. The dirty soles of her bare feet showed, the toes bowed together against the floor.

"Blinda? Wake up, honey. I know you ain't been sleeping good, but we got to go."

She reached out to take her sister's thin shoulder. She shook the girl gently.

The ragged bear slid from her fingers to the floor. Blinda slid back to follow it.

Horror struck through Wymie like lightning.

Her beloved baby sister no longer had a face. There was only a bloody red gap where her face should have been.

Chapter One

"Wait," Ricky Morales said. "What was that?"

"Probably your imagination," Mildred Wyeth responded. She had stripped off her shirt to work in the humid heat of the hollow in her scavvied sports bra and khaki cargo pants. She straightened from sorting a pile of mostly unidentifiable scavvied tech, mostly metal parts and components J. B. Dix identified as electronics, and drew the back of her hand across her high, dark-skinned forehead. "Heat's making you see things."

But Ryan Cawdor was standing and staring intently at the spot in the brush above the excavation the kid had snapped his head around to look at.

"No," he said. "I think I saw something, too."

He had his palm resting on the grip of the SIG Sauer P226 blaster in its holster. He'd left his longblaster, a Steyr Scout Tactical, in the shade of a rickety lean-to.

He glanced at Jak Lauren, who stood on top of a heap of dirt, rocks, chunks of concrete, and bits and pieces of cloth, plastic and other debris that somehow hadn't degraded into the dense clay soil in the hundred or so years since skydark. The slender, slight young man shrugged. Despite the sticky mugginess he insisted on wearing his camouflage jacket, to which he'd sewn jagged shards of glass and metal fragments to discourage an in-fighting opponent from grabbing him. His adversary would get a further surprise if he grabbed the young man by the collar. Hidden razor blades would cause severe injury. Jak was swiveling his head, long white hair swinging above his shoulders, white-skinned brow furrowed over ruby eyes.

He sensed Ryan's attention and looked toward him. "Check out?" he asked.

"No," Ryan said. "If there's something out there, it knows the area better than we do."

Jak let his thin lips quirk contemptuously. "Could beat."

"Mebbe," Ryan said. "Mebbe not."

The white-haired youth frowned. Though a product of the Gulf Coast bayou country—even hotter and double-steamier than this—he was proud of his wilderness skills. Indeed, his skills at stealth and tracking in any environment—even urban ones, as alien to his upbringing as the dimpled face of the moon. And for a fact, he was good. Those skills had kept Ryan and the rest of his companions alive on many occasions.

"The pallid shadows again?" Doc asked. Doc was a tall, gaunt man with haunted blue eyes and rich silvery hair. Though he appeared to be in his late sixties, he was, in fact, in terms of years lived, in his thirties. Looked at in a different way, Dr. Theophilus Algernon Tanner was almost two and a half centuries old. The whitecoats of Operation Chronos had trawled him from the late 1800s to the twentieth century. When he proved to be a very difficult subject, they threw him into the future, to Deathlands, a prematurely aged husk.

That he had survived was a testament to his intrinsic toughness and drive to live. "Not sure," Ricky said, shaking his head. The kid had been with them for a while

now, tramping the miles and enduring countless hardships with the rest of the companions. He was currently
on watch, squatting at the edge of the sinkhole that had
claimed some kind of small but well-equipped predark
office building. He had his DeLisle carbine across his
knees.

"Can find out," Jak said stubbornly. He hated to stay
still for long, especially doing hard physical labor. He
felt as if he should constantly be prowling whatever surroundings his companions happened to find themselves
in, keeping watch, keeping them safe. And it chafed his
spirit to be forced to do so while there seemed to be enemies about.

"Why don't we wait to see if they are a threat to us,
Jak?" said Krysty Wroth, emerging from the large irregular hole in the rubble that led to the intact, buried
sections of the small predark complex.

As she straightened, Ryan watched her appreciatively.
Like Mildred, she had stripped off the man's shirt she
wore in favor of her halter top. Also like Mildred, she had
substantial need of the support it gave. Ryan never tired
of watching the rise and fall of her breasts as she straightened. She took a handkerchief from her pants pocket and
wiped her forehead. Her glorious red mane of hair was tied
back in a green-and-white bandanna. Its strands stirred
slightly, restless, despite the lack of so much as a sigh
of wind here in this pit in the heavily wooded Pennyrile
Hills. Each individual hair was a living thing, capable of
motion—and of feeling, which made the occasions she
found it necessary to trim it something of an ordeal.

She wasn't just the most beautiful woman Ryan had
ever seen, she was his life-mate. Jak looked at her.

"Want make sure don't," he said. The young man

tended to expend words, especially things like pronouns and articles, as if they were drops of his own blood. The others had enough experience of interpreting his eccentrically clipped speech they could make out what he meant. Usually.

She smiled her dazzling smile. "They haven't tried anything so far," she pointed out. "But why don't you take over for Ricky on watch?"

Jak liked that suggestion. He nodded and scrambled up the treacherous, sliding slope as if he were half mountain goat, half wraith. Ricky was appreciative of the offer and picked his way cautiously back down to join the others beside the hole and their growing pile of the day's bounty.

Ricky was something of an apprentice to J.B., having learned weapons-making skills from his uncle Benito back home on Monster Island, and sharing with the man a special love for booby traps.

The Armorer was bent over the crate with a salvaged chunk of orange Formica on it, where their best swag of the day was piled. He had his battered fedora pushed to the back of his head and was scrutinizing the loot. "Mebbe what you're seeing is what the folks hereabouts call *coamers*," he said, picking up a piece of circuit board and holding it up to the dying sun's light.

"Grave robbers?" Ricky asked a little breathlessly, as he came up to join his mentor. "Could they be what's out there?"

"No one has seen them," Doc said. "They might indeed be our pale ghosts."

Ricky swallowed.

THE PENNYRILE HILLS were a fertile and somewhat secluded region of what had long ago been western Kentucky. The area was an irregular patch of rolling, thickly wooded country, dotted with sinkholes and crisscrossed by streams, roughly forty miles long by twenty across at the widest, set in the midst of a larger stretch of arid limestone plain—a large green oasis amid desolation. Some freak of weather patterns provided it abundant rainfall, and protection from the acid rains that periodically scoured the rest of the surrounding karst country.

Therefore the people of the Pennyrile led a relatively isolated existence, and mostly seemed to like it that way. There were a few small villes, of the sort that boasted a mayor instead of a baron. Most of them were scattered in clans and remote cottages and camps, where they lived by subsistence farming, hunting, fishing, trapping, and cutting firewood and lumber. They generated sufficient surplus, on their own hook and through traders and travelers from outlands who found their way into the area, to make it worth the companions' while to sell the booty they took from the predark trove they had literally stumbled into—thanks to Ricky not always watching where he put his feet—rather than packing the richest haul on their backs and taking it somewhere else.

Ryan was glad the sunken facility had turned up in a sparsely populated area of the Pennyrile. It made sense, of course; if more people lived nearby, odds were that somebody would've found and plundered it decades earlier. But also the locals, while prosperous enough not to be desperate as a usual thing, yet not prosperous enough to attract coldhearts or conquerors, tended to be clannish, insular, and to view outlanders with extreme suspicion.

Still, mutual advantage was a universal language, even though it was one a surprising number of denizens of the postnuke world chose to remain deaf to, for reasons Ryan had long since given up trying to puzzle out. Whatever their misgivings or prejudices toward the tall, one-eyed man and his companions, they were glad enough to trade for the treasures the outlanders dug from the earth.

Conn, the proprietor of a gaudy house outside the ville of Sinkhole, was actually welcoming to outlanders, possibly as a concomitant of his occupation. In particular, Ryan thought, he provided a reasonably safe and clean environment in which to do business and even spend some proceeds of the interactions.

Ryan heaved a deep sigh. He was bone-tired from the day's exertion in the heat and humidity. The sweat ran freely from his shaggy black hair down his face, stinging his good eye—his right one—and tickling when it insinuated its way under the black patch that covered where the other had been.

Sometimes he had to remind himself that if he was this beat, the others had to be dragging themselves along by nothing more than sheer determination.

He walked over to the plunder table, stooped, picked up a clay jug and took a long drink. Then he poured water over his forehead and face. That was one good thing about this area: water was easy to come by. It was another minor wonder the sunken facility hadn't flooded to inaccessibility.

Doc said something about the sandstone cap underlying the soil keeping the water out here, even though the moisture had infiltrated somewhere nearby and scooped a gap in the soft underlying limestone bedrock. That was what led to the sinkhole opening up and eating the small but well-equipped field office complex, although Ryan suspected it had gotten more than a little help from the unnatural wave of monster earthquakes generated by the nukecaust.

"Right, people," he called. "Let's start powering down for the day."

"What have we got here, J.B.?" he asked his friend as he approached their plunder pile.

"Mostly junk like busted old office machinery," the Armorer said. He held up a stapler whose metal parts were almost as red as its hard-plastic shell from rust. "But now that we got down to where their workshop was, we stand to start really finding some prime scavvy."

"Weapons, maybe?" asked Ricky, dark eyes gleaming.

"More ammo, anyway," J.B. said.

They'd found substantial stores of ammunition in a weapons locker in what seemed to be the main office area. As far as they could tell, the structure had been built as a command center for some kind of mining operation nearby, whose nature they hadn't managed to discover, and all traces of which appeared to have been obliterated by earth upheavals and more than a hundred years of weather.

They couldn't use the cans of 5.56 mm bullets, since they lacked blasters that fired them. But there was a cache of 9 mm, 12-gauge, .45 ACP and 7.62 mm ammo that took care of replenishing their stocks for most of the armament they carried.

They found no .38 Special cartridges for the Czech ZKR 551 target revolver Mildred insisted on toting, even though that caliber was relatively common, nor anything for Doc's enormous LeMat. "If we find blasters, will we trade them?" Ricky asked.

J.B. grunted. "Locals favor black-powder blasters," he

said, "mostly single-shot break-action shotguns or even muzzle-loaders. I kind of like the edge our firepower gives us over their smoke-poles, myself."

Ryan nodded.

"They're not that friendly," he agreed. "Anyway, if we find modern blasters, they'll be well worth humping out of here when we shake the limestone dust of this place off our boot heels."

"Not soon, I hope," Krysty said. "The work here's hard, but at least we have a sheltered spot to live while we're doing it."

"Think this would be a good place to put down roots, Krysty?" Mildred asked in a bantering tone.

The taller woman shrugged. "It's always been my dream," she said, a faraway look in her emerald-green eyes. "To find someplace we can make a life."

"Node'll play out soon enough," Ryan told her. "And I don't see us as dirt farmers, anyway."

To his surprise he saw sadness in her face. "Sorry, lover," he said. "I know that's a sore spot for you. Reckon I shouldn't go poking it."

Mildred made an apologetic noise in her throat. "Yeah. My bad. I shouldn't tease you about it, Krysty."

She shook her head, making the beaded plaits in her hair clack together.

"The fact is," she said, "we could all use a break."

"What do you think this is, Millie?" J.B. asked.

She scowled but, for once, couldn't find an appropriate comeback.

"What about our mysterious friends up there?" Ricky asked, uneasily waving a hand.

"They're probably just figments of our overworked imaginations."

She stopped speaking abruptly, gazing upward, her eyes growing wide.

Something grazed Ryan's cheek on the blind side.

"GET DOWN!" KRYSTY heard Ryan shout. She wheeled to see him following his own command, diving to the rubble-choked slope with his SIG Sauer in hand.

"Oh my God, I see them too!" she heard Mildred yell.

That was more than enough for Krysty. She whipped out her Glock 18C with the efficiency of frequent habit and threw herself down, as well. She was glad for the halter top confining her breasts offering at least some protection from the corner of a chunk of concrete that dug into her left one.

The bushes surrounding the pit were thrashing. Rocks and sticks were flying from them, thrown by unseen hands at the group. Unfortunately, despite the trees shielding them from casual discovery, the excavation was approximately the worst possible tactical situation to put themselves into. *Everybody* who knew where they were and wished them harm had the high ground.

Grinning, Jak reached into his jacket. His right hand came out wrapped inside the knuckle-duster hilt of a trench knife. The left whipped one of his butterfly knives open in a blur of precision. He started to move toward the attackers. "Jak, no!" Mildred yelled. "They look too much like you! We might shoot you by mistake!"

The young man froze. Right then Krysty caught a flash of a face peering at her from a gap in the screen of underbrush. To her shock it looked like the bleached-bone white of Jak's face, and the eyes staring at her from beneath matted white locks were the same blood color as their friend's. But Jak, despite the prejudice he frequently encountered—and tended to dispute loudly and forcefully—was no mutie himself, but an albino, subject to a genetic condition that predated the skydark by many generations.

The face Krysty saw, staring at her, was not right, somehow. The nose and jaw seemed pushed too far forward. It was a mostly human visage, but not entirely.

Then it was gone, and she saw other pallid bodies flitting out of clear view behind where it had been.

"What do we do?" J.B. called as a foot-long branch with green leaves still on it bounced harmlessly off his fedora.

A fist-sized stone bounced past Krysty's right cheek. "Blast them!" Ryan shouted.

The head-splitting roar of Jak's .357 Magnum Colt Python was the first response to Ryan's command. As a storm of blasterfire roared around her, the prone Krysty raised her Glock, but she had little to aim at. Doc's "pallid shadows" continued to live up to their name, flitting just outside of clear sight behind the brush or among the boles of the trees around the sinkhole. Especially not knowing whether or when they might face a concerted rush by their unknown foes, she was happy to take single shots as a hint of target revealed itself.

A scream rang out from above to Krysty's right, long, shuddering and unnervingly humanlike. It startled her, but it was no big surprise: plenty of muties were human, for all practical purposes, their "taint" notwithstanding. Some of them were indistinguishable from norms.

Like Krysty, whose mutant traits—with the exception of her sentient red hair—were hidden. As quickly as it began, the barrage of thrown debris stopped. The flitting ghosts vanished. Or at least Krysty abruptly lost all sight of them, even the furtive glimpses she'd been getting since the attack began.

"Cease fire!" Ryan roared. "That means you, Ricky. Don't waste ammo."

"Sorry, Ryan."

"Everybody fit to fight?" Ryan called.

"I'm fine, lover," Krysty said, catching his eye and throwing a wink. The others affirmed they hadn't received so much as a bruise from the pelting.

"So what just happened?" Mildred asked.

Krysty glanced at Ryan. Her lover didn't suffer fools gladly, or at all, and was sometimes inclined to be curt with Mildred when either her sharp tongue or her archaic sentimental notions got on his nerves. And on the surface, the question seemed pretty obtuse.

Seemed. But Krysty found herself unsure, as well. Had they staved off a more serious assault? Had they overreacted? She wasn't too concerned over the latter possibility—if you played pranks on a heavily armed party out in the wilderness, you had no gripe coming if you suddenly acquired a few more holes in your hide.

Ryan shook his head. "No bastard clue," he said. "Everybody try to find a position with halfway-decent cover and stay tight with eyes skinned. We don't know if and when they might be back."

He didn't say "with reinforcements," but Krysty heard the words loud and clear anyway. She knew the others did, too. They'd worked together as a team for a long time and had been in so many similar situations that the words were a given.

BUT NO FURTHER attack came. When half an hour had gone by according to J.B.'s wrist chron, Ryan cautiously called for everyone to stand down. Leaving the rest to keep watch, he went out with Jak to look for signs of the flitting ghosts.

They found some broken branches, and blood spattered on leaves and the grass where the scream had come from. Reassuringly, it was red. What was less reassuring was the fact that not even Jak's keen eyes and tracking skills were able to find any usable trails away from the sinkhole. "Right," Ryan said, coming back to the lip of the sinkhole. The sun started to sink behind the western trees. "We still don't know who they were, what they were, or where they went. But they seem to be gone now. So let's pack up some medium-value scavvy and hump it into Sinkhole."

"How do we know the creatures won't spy on us as we do?" Doc asked.

"We don't, Doc," Ryan replied. "But I don't propose to live out the rest of my days according to what I'm afraid these things we couldn't even get a clear look at *might* do."

LIGHT LIKE THE dancing orange flames of hell threw the shadow of Wymea Berdone, and the limp and lifeless figure she carried in her arms, all distorted onto the bare and beaten ground before her.

Behind her, the only home she knew burned with a bellow like a gigantic, raving beast.

Aside from a butcher knife from the kitchen, its blade reduced to little more than a finger-width by repeated honings, she was unarmed. She had been forced to leave even her father's treasured ax behind in the blazing house, with the chills of her mother and stepfather.

If the bastard cowards who murdered my baby sister come for me, she thought, so much the worse for them!

The rickety roar gave way with a great rumbling and cracking and a redoubling of the intensity of the glare. Without a backward glance, Wymie turned onto a path scarcely wider than a deer track, and, barefoot and grieving, began the two-mile walk to Sinkhole, the nearest ville.

Where she meant to find justice. Even if it killed her.

Chapter Two

"Potar Baggart, back off this instant!"

Ryan lifted the beer mug to his lips.

It was the bartender who spoke, sharply yet without obviously raising his voice. The other hubbub in the Stenson's Creek gaudy, which had risen to a crescendo of happy anticipation when Potar tried to pick a fight with the grubby group of outlanders, abruptly died.

Potar was a big man, with a clenched red fist of a face beneath blond hair that would have been described as "dirty blond" had it been clean, which it wasn't. The general smell wafting from him suggested to Ryan that neither it nor the rest of him had been clean in a long time. Ryan sipped his beer. It was good; the landlord was proud of his skills as a brewmaster, and so far as the one-eyed man was concerned, he was entitled. Ryan hadn't risen from the chair where he'd been sitting at a table in the gaudy's darkest corner with his friends when the lummox Potar came over and started making suggestions of a distinctly unwelcome kind to Krysty. But though the big man didn't back off at the whip-crack command, Ryan saw the tension go out of him like the hammer of a blaster being returned gently down with a thumb.

So he let his own hand slip from the hilt of the his panga, with which he'd been preparing to gut the huge man like a fish when he made the move he was so clearly working himself up for.

The bartender, a middle-sized, prematurely balding man whose name was Mathus Conn, and who also happened to own and run the gaudy, also seemed to notice the big man's reaction.

"Now step right back from there, you hear?" he said, his tone softer, but barely. "Now. You don't want me to reach under the counter."

Though sitting in a half sprawl in the chair as if solidly at his ease, Ryan watched the man-mountain narrowly through his lone eye. He knew an aggressor usually had to get himself worked up to actually launch an attack. It was just human nature. But he also knew that in some men that could happen with frightening speed.

But apparently he didn't want to see what the gaudy owner had under the counter. Instead his raised his ham-slab hands placatingly toward the bar as he shuffled away across the dried-grass-covered floor.

"I wonder what he *does* have under there," Ricky said beneath his breath.

"Sawed-off double-barrel 10-gauge muzzle-loader," J.B. said softly, "if I had to guess."

"Sorry, Mathus," Potar said. "Just funnin' a little. You know I didn't mean nothin' by it."

"I know no such thing," Conn stated crisply. "But I do know *you*. And you know I don't put up with trouble inside my place. So I reckon it's time for you to leave."

The huge man looked around. The gaudy was filled with faces lit yellow by smoky oil lamps. None of them looked sympathetic. Potar turned and strode out, head high, as if leaving was his idea.

"He's the town bully over to Sinkhole," Conn told the companions.

"We figured," Mildred replied.

"I think he just wants acceptance."

"The kind of big lunk who has no real harm in him, huh?" Mildred said acerbically.

Ryan cocked a disapproving brow at her. The gaudy owner was their main and best customer for their scavvy. He saw no point in letting Mildred sour a perfectly profitable business relationship.

Conn laughed without much real humor. "Oh, there's plenty harm in him," he said. "It just happens to stem from him not being able to find a place in the world, is all."

Ryan looked around at his friends. With his head turned so no one else in the gaudy could see but them, he inflated his cheeks and blew out an exaggerated sigh between pursed lips.

Krysty winked at him.

Stenson's Creek's gaudy was much like any other, if cleaner than most. That made it different from the nearby ville of Sinkhole, which was something of a dump. It seemed to be run-down more from a sense of comfortable complacency than from the pervasive despair that defined much of the world outside the Pennyrile district. The gaudy was a sprawling roadhouse in the woods, east of Sinkhole along the creek that provided its name. It was mostly solid postnuke construction, fieldstone and timber. The bar was polished local hardwood. The tables and chairs had a crude look to them, as if they'd been made with little concern for appearance. But they were sturdy. The place didn't offer much by way of decor, but that wasn't what Conn was in the business of selling, and his customers didn't seem to mind.

"Hey, big boy," a dispirited-looking gaudy slut asked a man at the table nearest Ryan and company, "looking for a good time?"

She wore a ragged skirt, a blouse whose neckline hung almost as low as her breasts did and a sort of scarf around her neck made of interwoven rags. It was apparently meant to suggest a feather boa. What it did suggest was a mutie hybrid of an actual boa constrictor and a weasel with the mange.

The man she was talking to looked cast from a similar mold to the departed Potar, but of a shorter, wider, flabbier model. He had a neck bulged out thicker than his head, into which a succession of chins blended seamlessly as he slurped at the foam on his own beer mug with an intensity single-minded enough to suggest to Ryan that it just about maxed out his capabilities in the mind department. He didn't so much as flick his vacant brown eyes the slut's way.

She ran her fingers down the burly shoulder left bare by his grime-, sweat- and man-grease-mottled singlet, and leaned down so far Ryan could see the full pendulousness of her breasts from ten feet away without trying to, much less wanting so. Putting her painted lips close enough to his ear to risk leaving red marks, she purred, "Mebbe you didn't hear me the first ti—"

He shoved her away, and she went down on her not-so-well-upholstered fanny so hard her tailbone cracked against the floorboards like a knuckle rapping on a table.

Scowling, Conn put down the bottle of shine he held and started around the bar, reaching under the counter as he did so.

The woman jumped to her feet. "What the nuke, you fat slob?"

"Back up off the triggers of them blasters, everybody," a deep voice boomed from another corner of the room.

It was naturally arresting. Everyone stopped—even Conn himself, whom Ryan had observed in their previous visits was the unquestioned master in his own house.

The speaker wasn't tall, but he was wide. A black man, the gray in his short, tightly curled hair showed him to be in middle age. And while he had a bit of a gut bulging out onto his thighs as he sat nursing his brew, Ryan suspected there was more muscle than flab. He was surrounded by four men and two women, most of whom showed a family resemblance, though it was far less pronounced than in the three largely chinless, large-foreheaded types who accompanied the meatbag.

"Don't take it to heart," he said calmly. "You're new in these parts and don't know. Them Sumzes don't ball nobody more distantly related than first cousin. And Buffort, there, ain't the sharpest tool in the shed."

"It's a family turdition, Tarley," said a skinny red-headed Sumz with ears like open wag doors. "Dates back to the dark times. That's how us Sumzes pulled through."

Buffort guffawed and pounded a beefy fist on the table. It happened to be the one clenching the handle of his mug. Frothy brown beer slopped forth.

Ryan could smell him and his brothers from twenty feet away. The Sumzes were turpentiners, he knew—they made the stuff from the resin of loblolly pines growing around the valley where they made their home. Its astringent, piney smell overwhelmed even the body reek wafting from the group, and the fresh-sawdust-and-old-vomit stink that even the best-kept-up gaudy sported. It was even noticeable over the odor of the lanterns, which like most of the lamps hereabouts burned a blend of the pine oil with wood alcohol.

"You tell 'em, Yoostas!" the huge fat man crowed in a surprisingly shrill voice. "Family that sleeps together keeps together!"

Everybody laughed. Even the gaudy slut, though she looked as if she wasn't clear as to the *why*.

A couple of husky young men, one dark-skinned, one light, had appeared near the scene. They were local youths Conn employed for odd jobs, including bouncing the occasional rowdy patron. They looked now to their boss.

He sighed, but he was already withdrawing his hand from underneath the bar. He used it to smooth back his thinning seal-colored hair instead.

"Right," he said. "Keep a tighter leash on your boy, there, Yoostas."

"Aw, c'mon, Conn. There ain't no harm to him."

"I know," Conn said, moving back to his accustomed spot and picking up his bottle again, as if he meant to use it for its original purpose instead of cracking heads. "That's why y'all are still here."

He looked at the girl, who was trying to untangle her arms and upper torso from her ratty makeshift boa.

"Go take a break, Annie," he said. "Catch a breath, pull yourself together."

"But my take for the evening—"

"I said, take a break. I won't jam you on the take. Don't bleed when you're not cut."

She bobbed her head and vanished toward the back, where the few cribs were. Like a lot of the more respectable gaudy-house owners, Conn allowed a few women, usually down-on-their-luck locals, to rent time and space to ply their sexual wares rather than keeping them in greater or lesser degrees of slavery, as most did. Ryan had also noted he treated his workers the way he did trading partners: politely, calmly and driving a hard bargain but a fair one.

He didn't cheat too much, which made him a Deathlands paragon.

Ryan turned his attention back to his friends. He saw them all easing their hands back from their own blasters. Handblasters only; Conn insisted longblasters be checked at the door. That chafed J.B.'s butt a tad, but Ryan went along with it, meaning the Armorer and the others did, too.

Ryan was willing to rely on Conn's unwavering insistence on keeping an orderly house.

And if that failed, it wasn't as if Ryan and his friends weren't packing enough heat to burn a way to the little cabinet by the door where their longblasters were.

"There are worse places," Mildred said with a shrug.

J.B. showed her a hint of sly grin. "You still got your mind on settling down?" he asked.

She shrugged her shoulders. "We've been in way worse locations, is all I'm saying."

"Indeed," Doc said. He was leaning forward, staring down at an angle at the tabletop with an unfocused look in his blue eyes. Ryan couldn't tell for sure if he was agreeing with Mildred, or with some randomly remembered person from his past, like his long-lost wife, Emily, or even their children, Rachel and Jolyon. The predark whitecoats and their malicious time-trawling had done more than age him prematurely. Sometimes Doc lost touch with the present and wandered off through the fog of his own reminiscences.

The others couldn't help but fear that sometime he might just wander off inside his own skull and never come back. But he always had, and lately things seemed to be getting consistently better. In any event he always snapped right to when the hammer came down.

Jak was frowning.

"What's the matter, Jak?" Krysty asked gently.

The albino's scowl deepened. But he didn't snap back at her, as he sometimes could with his male companions. He just pressed his scarcely visible white lips together so hard they vanished altogether, and shook his head briskly.

"Don't gnaw your own guts over not being able to track those stick-throwing white things," J.B. said. As was his custom, he didn't raise his voice. If he had something to say, he said it calmly. If he had something to do, he did it without hesitation or qualm. "They know the lay of the land better than even you can, most likely. And they probably have some kind of lairs nearby they can duck into."

Though the gaudy chatter had resumed its normal volume, Ryan could hear Jak growl low in his throat. It wasn't a gesture of hostility but a sign of his own dissatisfaction with himself.

"Listen, Jak," Mildred said helpfully. "There's always someone better than you."

That got her a red-eyed glare.

"Mildred," Ryan said dryly, "stop helping."

The door burst open.

For a moment all that poured inside was darkness and the sound of crickets, audible because the dramatic opening had quieted the small talk again. It wasn't necessarily in anticipation of an equally dramatic entry; people here-

abouts, like most places, were just that starved for something a little different from the day-in, day-out routine.

But they got the drama anyway. A young woman came
through the door, half striding, half staggering under a
burden of deadweight and fatigue. She carried a body
in her arms. It was apparently a child, a girl by the long
hair that hung down from the intruder's right arm, and
she was dead, from the lifeless swing and dangle of her
small, bare arms.

But the young woman's head was high, black hair falling in waves around broad shoulders, one bared by her
half-torn-open flannel shirt. Her deep blue eyes blazed
with rage.

"My baby sister's dead!" she cried in a vibrant voice.
"Blinda's been murdered, and I saw who done it!"

A number of patrons had jumped to their feet. "Who
did it, Wymie?" one asked.

She fixed Ryan with a laser glare. "Those stoneheart
outlanders there!"

That silenced the rising murmur as though cutting it
off with an ax. Immediately whispers started up again:
"Oh, holy shit, her face."

Ryan saw that it was missing. Something had taken
much of the bone from brow to lower jaw along with
flesh and skin.

Ryan heard Krysty gasp. Doc made a strangled noise.

"You can't be talking to us," Ryan said, as evenly as
he could.

"I saw you! You *bastards*!"

"You didn't see us," Mildred said. "We were working
at the claim until late. Then we came right here."

"Tell us exactly what you did see, Wymie," Conn
told her.

The black-haired young woman stooped and eased her burden onto the floorboards. Blood began to trickle outward. Behind her Ryan could see a number of others with anxious, angry faces. Plenty held weapons, from hoes and axes to a muzzle-loader shotgun or two. Slowly, Wymie straightened.

"I looked out the window, soon as—as it happened," she said, brushing back a lock of crow's-wing hair sweat had stuck to her face. "I seen a white face lookin' in at me. White hair. *Bloodred eyes!*"

All eyes turned to Jak, who sat with his mug halfway raised to his lips and a thunderstruck expression on his face.

"Where's your ma and stepdad?" Tarley asked.

"Chilled, both. I had to burn the house down as I got away. I couldn't tell if one of you devils might've crept inside!"

"We're all here," J.B. said. "So that didn't happen, either."

"You callin' me a liar? With the body of the child you murdered lyin' right here at my feet?"

"We're calling you mistaken," Ryan said.

He stayed sitting. He decided that standing up might be taken as provocative, both by the frantic young woman and the retinue she'd evidently picked up on her personal trail of tears from her burning homestead. If he had to, he could stand up plenty quick.

He was afraid he might have to. The people out in front of the gaudy had clearly not followed the young woman carrying her chilled and mutilated sister here looking to party. And the other patrons inside the house were starting to shoot barbed looks their way. Things were no more than a hair away from getting bloody.

"It's a terrible thing that's been done to your sister, but we didn't do it."

"I saw what I saw." Her voice was as low and deadly as a slithering copperhead.

"Ask yourself," Krysty said, "why would we *do* such a thing?"

"You're outlanders! From out *there*!"

Her hair whirled as she snapped her head left and right, looking at the stunned crowd inside the gaudy.

"You know what they call the rest of the world out there, outside the Pennyrile, don't you? They call it *Deathlands*. Well, I reckon they call it that for a reason. People out there, or what pass for 'em, they just as soon chill you as look at you. Even if you're just a tiny girl who never hurt a fly!"

"But these are plainly just regular folks," Tarley said, "even if one is an albino. And *he* looks like a good puff of wind could blow him away. How could they take her face off like that, all at once?"

"Mebbe used an ax."

"Don't look like no ax," said the black bouncer, bending slightly toward the corpse, as if wanting to see better but not too much better. "Got bit clean off, if you ask me."

"Mebbe it was, Tarley. Mebbe he bit it off."

"'Bit it off'?" Ryan echoed incredulously.

"Mebbe he's a—a werewolf or somethin'! We all know there's monsters out there!"

Tarley shook his head. "Wymie, Wymie. Listen to yourself. We can't go lynchin' strangers because they might be werewolves. Not without some kinda evidence they are. Or that werewolves exist, even."

"People say there's all kind of weird muties, out in the Deathlands," one of the men standing on the stoop behind

Wymie said. "Like little rubber-skinned bastards with suckers for fingertips, can rip the hide clean off you!"

"That part's real," Ricky said. "Those are stickies. They're bad news."

"I've seen stickies," Tarley stated. "They're pretty much what you say. But stickies didn't do this, and I see no reason to believe these folks did, either."

"You takin' their part, Tarley Gaines?" Wymie shrieked. "Of outlanders who murder our own?"

"Nobody's takin' anybody's part," Conn said, his voice level and as unyielding as an anvil. "Not tonight. Not in here. Except the truth's, mebbe."

"I know the truth!" the young woman yelled.

"You got precious little to show for it, Wymie."

"I know what I saw!"

"And mebbe what you saw wasn't what your mind's made of it. Fact is, these folks have been right here a good past hour, half an hour spent hagglin', half an hour eatin' my venison, stewed greens and beans, and drinkin' my brew. They came in without a dot of blood on them, wearin' clothes they'd double clearly worked in all day. And their hair isn't wet enough to be from anythin' but sweat, so they didn't clean themselves up after doing murder. The albino in particular—blood'd show up pretty clear on him."

Wymie was looking around, but from the slump of her strong shoulders Ryan could see that, while the anger and even hate were still there, still smoldering, sheer exhaustion and emotional reaction had damped her fires. She had nothing left.

Not now, anyway.

"You out there," Conn called past the suddenly befuddled-looking woman. "Burny Stoops. Walter John.

Get in here, pick this poor girl up off my floor and take her to Coffin-Maker Sam, over to the Hole. He'll see she gets a decent burial."

"I can't afford to hire a hole dug for her," Wymie said, sounding more sullen now than raging. "Much less a box to bury her in."

"Tell Sam I'll cover the expenses," Conn said. "But you got to leave now, Wymie. Find a place to stay. Don't make any more fuss, now. It won't do poor Blinda a speck of good."

"But—"

"We'll get it sorted out. When the sun comes up, we'll go take a look at your old place. We need information, and that's a thing we haven't got."

"I know all I need to," she said, the spark of anger flaring again.

"The rest of us don't," the gaudy owner said, with just a bit of edge to his voice. "Mrs. Haymuss!"

After a moment a stout brown-skinned woman emerged from the kitchen. She was wearing a much-stained apron and wiping her hands on a rag. She was evidently the cook.

"Take this poor girl and see to her. Get her settled with Widow Oakey. She's close and likes to take in strays."

"But, Mr. Conn, the kitchen—"

"Kitchen's closed," the gaudy owner said. "Nobody's got an appetite left now. And if they do, I'm not minded to feed them, right now."

The woman walked forward, encircled Wymie's shoulders with a brawny arm and began alternately clucking and cooing at her. Ryan couldn't make out what she was saying. Or even if it was words.

The black-haired woman made as if to push her off.

Then she turned, buried her face at the juncture of Mrs. Haymuss's neck and beefy shoulders, and began to cry uncontrollably.

The two men Conn had called on came in past the two to gingerly pick up Blinda's body. Mrs. Haymuss steered Wymie back out into the night. They followed, struggling to carry what a single woman had brought here on her own.

"The rest of you out there," Conn called, "move along. It isn't polite to stare."

Whatever passions Wymie's trek had excited in the locals who had collected to follow her to the gaudy house, they had vanished, as well. Shuffling their feet, not meeting one another's gazes directly, they broke up began to go their separate ways.

Conn watched them for a moment. Slowly, those inside the gaudy who had jumped up at the spectacle sat themselves back down.

"I'd wait to make sure they all get headed in the right direction, just in case," Conn said to Ryan. "Then you might want to clear out of here."

"Much obliged," Ryan said.

"Thank you for your help," Krysty said. "Do you think we did it after all?"

Conn shrugged. "I don't know what to think. Somebody did this, and that somebody needs to pay. But if I thought it was you, I never would've said what I did. Fact is, I don't see how you could have done it."

"But that big-titty girl still thinks you done it," Yoostas Sumz said. "Sure as shit stinks double bad."

Chapter Three

"What do we do now?" Mildred asked.

The faces gathered around the little campfire mirrored the concern and uncertainty she felt. Except for Ryan's. He sat off a little apart, knees drawn up, facing off to the side. His chin was down and he was clearly brooding.

Jak was nowhere to be seen. Ryan would have had to physically restrain him to keep him from prowling the perimeter of their camp to scout for signs of watchers or intruders—and look for signs the elusive white shadows had been there. Crickets and tree frogs trilled in the night. A few late fireflies danced.

"Can we stay here?" Ricky asked.

"Don't see as how we rightly can," J.B. said. He sat across the fire from Mildred, face turned toward the flames. The yellow underlighting brought out the strong bone structure of his face, and turned his eyeglass lenses into disks of flame.

"The place has gotten too hot for comfort, I reckon. It's time to shake the dust of it off our heels."

Mildred pressed her lips into a line. She hated to contradict J.B. She loved him. More, she *respected* him.

"Let's not overreact."

Mildred's eyes widened in surprise.

She glanced at Krysty. The tall, statuesque redhead sat beside her brooding man. It was she who had spoken out as Mildred opened her mouth. Looking back at J.B., she saw a quick furrow of his brows as he glanced at Krysty.

On him, that was the equivalent of a full-on scowl. He was usually as expressive as a stone statue.

But Krysty said what she wanted, and not just because Ryan was her partner. Everyone could speak his or her mind.

"'Overreact'?" Mildred repeated.

"We have a good place here," Krysty said. "A comfortable camp, the cave is good shelter, and we have running water. The dig has a lot more scavvy to be unearthed. You yourself said it looks as if we're just getting down to the good stuff, J.B."

"Jack's worth squat," J.B. replied, "if you don't live to spend it. So Trader used to say."

Mildred frowned. J.B. did not tend toward the dogmatic, but when the quotations from his and Ryan's old mentor were trotted out, that meant he was settling into his groove of thinking.

"He also used to point out you tend to make jack in direct proportion to the risk you run," Ryan added without looking around.

"Why, Ryan," Doc said. "I thought you of all people would urge caution."

Ryan shrugged. "Looking to look at the whole situation before I make up my mind," Ryan replied.

"Looks straightforward to me," J.B. said. "We've got two packs of enemies on our tails. That's beyond bad odds."

"But, J.B.," Ricky said, almost desperately. "Think of the stuff that might be down there! The tech—the weapons!"

The Armorer shook his head. He took a half-smoked

black cheroot from a pocket of the brown leather jacket he wore, struck a spark from a butane lighter he had found in the last redoubt they'd jumped to and puffed the smoke to life. He cast a swift glance at Mildred.

The woman repressed a grin. His apprentice knew his soft spots, for sure.

His occasional smoking didn't please her as a twentieth-century physician, even one who preferred research to hands-on doctoring—before she got wakened from her cryosleep into a brutal, desolate world where "healing" was her number one marketable skill, that is. But she'd long since lost the heart to chide him for it, other than a slight frown.

Realistically, she didn't count on *any* of them living long enough for cancer to take them. In Deathlands, sudden death wasn't just a constant possibility. It was an immediate reality.

"Right now," Ryan said softly, "we've got no evidence I can see that anybody's on our tails. Here, anyway."

"But those pale shadows know where our dig site is, certainly," Doc stated.

"Yeah. But they haven't shown up around here, yet."

"Yet," J.B. echoed.

It was Ryan's turn to shrug.

"We're not on the last train west yet, either. Even if the locals are after us, too, they don't know where either place is."

Ryan had chosen a campsite a mile or so from the sinkhole that had swallowed the predark trove. It was a fine site, as comfortable as it got sleeping rough—and better than a lot of buildings they'd bunked in, Mildred knew all too well. The cave provided shelter from the frequent rains as well as from casual observation. A little stream ran along the base of the sandstone outcrop that formed their current home. And even though it was a pain humping back and forth each day to the excavation, the separation ensured that even if one location was compromised, the other wouldn't be.

As the fact that the pale shadows had found the dig but not this place—as far as they could tell—attested to. Though with Jak on the job, she wasn't concerned they might be under covert observation. Just because even he couldn't track them here on their home range— whatever the hell-on-earth they were—didn't mean he wouldn't be able to spot them if they came creeping around here.

But now something was eating at her, too, in spite of the fact that she, like Krysty, badly wanted to stay here as long as possible. Even if this wasn't going to be a final, permanent safe haven—unless of course they left their bones here in the Pennyrile—they were all riding the ragged edge of exhaustion. Not so much the physical sort, but the kind brought on by constant stress.

The stability they'd enjoyed for the week or so that they'd worked the sinkhole had visibly restored them all, despite the hot and arduous labor every day brought.

"If the locals think we're murderers," she pointed out, "how can we stay here? I mean, we need somebody to trade with."

"We can conceivably work the excavation for a few more days," Doc said, "until, as Ricky observes, we get to the most valuable relics. At that point we can pick the most portable and valuable items, and then head out of the area. It's not as if we have not done that a score of times already."

"But Conn," Ryan said, "the man we've been mostly

trading with, seemed triple far from convinced we had anything to do with that girl's murder."

"But the girl's sister was certain we did it," Krysty added. "And she did manage to convince some of the locals that we were guilty."

That was another thing about Krysty. She had her druthers, same as everybody—in particular, the longing for stability—but she was wise to the bone, as well. She saw both sides to every coin, and she spoke the truth as she saw it, always.

At least to her friends. She could lie with the best of them to an enemy, as all of them could. And did.

"And Conn poured cold water on that."

"Not Wymie," Krysty said.

"No. She's got her heart set against us. But Conn managed to get some doubts in other people's minds. I don't think we got the whole county roused against us."

"Yet," J.B. said. It was becoming a theme for the evening. "But she'll get around to coming and hunting for us, and that's a triple lock for sure."

"She in all probability will not come alone," Doc said. "She showed herself to be quite persuasive, in her vengeful wrath."

For a moment they sat in silence. A bat fluttered just outside the mouth of their cave, chasing the insects drawn by the firelight. A distant screech-owl trilled mournfully. The night smelled of moist earth and cooling, sunwarmed rock, along with the more acrid smoke of their fire.

"Then we should find evidence to clear ourselves!"

Everybody turned and looked at Ricky. His brown eyes were wide. His round cheeks showed a decidedly red flush on top of their usual olive color.

"S-sorry," he stammered. "I didn't mean—"

"Kid," J.B. said, "haven't you learned by now, that if we let you run with us, we let you speak your mind?"

"When there's mind involved," Mildred said, "and it's not just a matter of words popping into your head and rolling right out your mouth." She liked the youth, well enough. He was a solid companion, a surprisingly good fighter and painfully smart. But he was still working on developing any damn *sense*, in her view.

"Ease off," Ryan said without heat. "Clearly you got something in mind, Ricky. So let's hear it."

"We know we're not guilty, and it's a fair bet these albino creatures are what killed Blinda," Ricky said. "After all, what she described seeing, that made her think of Jak—that looks just like what we saw."

"What little of them we saw," J.B. added. "But true enough."

"So we need to find evidence it was them who did it, and not us! And then this Wymie will shift her hate off us and onto them."

"People don't always let go of that kind of anger easy," Ryan said. "Even when there is evidence. Anyway, what evidence did you have in mind?"

"Well, we chill one, and take in the corpse. That'll show them. And I bet even Wymie will admit these things are more likely to have murdered her little sister than we are."

"Right you are, lad!" Doc exclaimed.

"But there's a problem," J.B. said. "We know we hit one of the things back at the dig. Chilled one, mebbe. Mebbe even more, but we found nothing but the blood trails."

Ricky shrugged. "Maybe there's other evidence we could find."

"Or mebbe we could do a better job chilling one and keeping hold of it," Ryan said. "Rather do that than cut stick and run, on balance."

Krysty smiled. After a beat, Mildred joined her. Her friend knew her man well. You could tell Ryan had just made up his mind—if you knew the signs to look for.

The others knew them, too. "So we do us some hunting, too," J.B. said. He tipped his fedora back on his head a few degrees. His thin lips quirked slightly at the corners.

That was his equivalent of Ryan's wolf grin. He loved the prospect of a hunt as much as any of them. As long as there was action to take he was well satisfied, so long as it was meaningful, with a proper chance of payoff.

"The only question is, how?" Doc asked. "If they manage to elude even our master tracker, Jak."

"Try again." They heard the albino's soft voice from right over their heads, perched on a ledge above the cave. "Catch next time."

"Mebbe," Ryan said, but he was nodding, acknowledging the possibility. "They're good. They know the country. But they make mistakes, double sure."

"And they don't know Jak," Mildred said.

"What are we looking for, exactly?" Krysty asked. "I mean—what are those things?"

"That one local yokel thought werewolves," Mildred replied.

"We have seen werewolves," Doc said. "It is just as well young Ricky didn't choose to share that fact with that distraught young woman. It might quite have swayed the case against us."

"He wasn't with us when we were down in Haven, Doc," J.B. said gently.

"Ah. So he was not. My apologies. Time…my time is all out of joint, it appears…"

"Still good," Ryan said. "But I'm not willing to jump that far quite yet. The baron and his lady down there were special cases."

"Muties?" Ricky suggested.

"Albinos not—" Jak began, with quiet heat.

"We know, Jak," Ryan said. "Albinos aren't muties. But we also know some muties are albino."

"We lack sufficient facts to speculate," Doc said.

"Speculation doesn't load many magazines," Ryan agreed. "What interests me is, you shoot these things, they holler and bleed. Meaning also, you shoot them enough, they die."

"So you want to stay here, in the Pennyrile," Krysty said carefully, making sure her wishful thinking wasn't making her read more into Ryan's words than he meant to put in them, "and look for evidence even Wymie will have to accept."

"Go hunting," J.B. stated.

"Bull's-eye," Ryan said. "Fact is, it's not like there's anywhere really safe in Deathlands. Shy of the grave."

"That crazy chick in the gaudy was right about one thing," Mildred said. "They don't call these Deathlands for nothing."

"Got a plan, Ryan?" J.B. asked.

"Go scout around. Keep our eyes skinned. We know they hang out around the dig site, so we can inspect the area around it triple close. Better than we did this afternoon. See if we can cut sign on a second pass."

"And if we don't?"

Ryan shrugged again. "Widen the search, I reckon. There doesn't seem much point in continuing with the scavvy operation until we figure out who these hoo-doos are and how to keep them off our necks anyway, the way I see it. We can head off the local folks from doing anything rash, so we won't have to ventilate a power of them."

"Now?" Mildred asked. She yawned. It wasn't an attempt to back up her question—not consciously. She was that beat.

It had been a long, hard day *before* they'd had to face down wild murder accusations and a potential lynch mob.

"Mildred, the way our asses are dragging, we'd be in double-deep shit if we ran into any of the shadowy bastards. If Jak couldn't follow their tracks in the daylight, we bastard sure aren't turning up anything now."

He straightened and stretched.

"Tomorrow," he said.

Chapter Four

"What a mess," Mathus Conn said, shaking his head.

The ruins of the Berdone house still smoldered, drooling dirty brown smoke into a mostly cloudless blue morning sky. The sweetish smell of overcooked meat spoiled the freshness of a new day's air. It even overpowered the stink of still-burning wood.

"You didn't expect it to be pretty, did you?" his cousin and chief lieutenant, Nancy, said.

He grunted and rubbed his chin. "Just funny how it always turns out worse than you expect."

"I always hear tell of how your imagination makes things worse than they really are," Tarley Gaines said. "But then the reality usually sucks harder."

The three, along with a few of Tarley's kinfolk and half a dozen or so well-disposed or just curious ville folk from Sinkhole, had trekked out to the Berdone location to see for themselves what could be learned from the site. It was clear that Wymie had been telling the truth.

At least so far as she knew it.

"So who set the house afire, I wonder," Conn said.

"Don't see as we'll ever know for sure," Nancy replied. "Mebbe the outlanders did it. Mebbe Wymie did it in hopes of trappin' some of whoever chilled her family inside."

"Speaking of which," Tarley said. "Yo, Zedd. Find any chills in there?"

"Two," came back the voice of one of his nephews from inside the gutted house. Like many established homes in the Pennyrile, the outer walls were stoutly built of fieldstone, not scraped-together scavvy and newly sawn lumber the way villes like Sinkhole tended to be. Wymie's great-grandfather, a man remembered only as "Ax," had built the house with the help of his sons, after setting up a successful wood-cutting claim in the area.

And now it's gone to ruin overnight, Conn thought, shaking his head.

"Reckon we'd best go see for ourselves," he said.

"NUKE THAT MATHUS CONN!" Wymie exclaimed, slamming her fist on the breakfast table in the boarding house Widow Oakey ran. The assorted crockery clattered and tinkled. "I can't believe he stuck up for those outlanders like that!"

"Now, Wymie," the widow said, tottering in from the kitchen holding a steaming pot of spearmint tea on a battered tray. "You got no call to be pounding around raising a fuss like that."

Wymie judged the old lady had to have seen her. She was deaf as a rock, unless you hollered in her face. At that there was no telling how much was lip-reading rather than any kind of hearing.

Widow Oakey was a tiny woman, who seemed to consist entirely of a collection of dried hardwood sticks bundled up in what had most likely started its existence as a gingham dress, but now seemed mostly made up of roughly equal amounts of soaked-in seasoned sweat and patches, all topped off by a bun of yellowish white hair.

She seemed frail and so bound by arthritis and rheumatism that her joints barely functioned at all. Yet Wymie knew she chipped her own kindling like a pro, and her cooking was better than passable good.

It was her housekeeping that fell by the wayside.

"Why are you wishin' death and devastation on Conn?" asked Garl, one of her fellow lodgers, from across the table. A few fragments of scrambled egg dribbled from the side of his mouth and cascaded down his several chins toward his belly, which kept him so far back from the table his comically short-seeming arms had trouble reaching his plate. He looked as if he went straight from being a baby to being a vast, gnarled, weathered, grizzly baby, without passing through the intervening stages of childhood and adulthood.

"How dare he stick up for outlanders who chilled my baby sister?" she asked hotly. "Cannie coldhearts. The worst thing! Worse than muties, even! I saw it with my own eyes!"

"Now, are you sayin' you saw them all in the act of chilling your sister, Wymie?" the other boarder at breakfast asked. "Because that sounds double crowded to me. They'd all be gettin' in each other's way. Not to make light of a terrible thing, or nothin'. Still, it don't seem practical."

Duggur Doakz was a middle-aged black man with a fringe of gray hair and not a tooth in his head. A gifted silversmith, he could have been a rich man—an important tradesman to some important baron. But that would take him far off beyond Pennyrile, and he hadn't chosen to leave the place where he was born. He kept his hand in and his body out of the ground by being a tinker and general repairman.

Wymie scowled furiously into her own plate. It was bare except for a few crumbs of biscuit and near-invisible scraps of egg. She had eaten like a ravenous wolf. She had a hearty appetite at the best of times. For some reason the onset of the worst had made her even hungrier.

Or mebbe it's because I ain't et since yesterday, she thought.

A cat jumped as if on cue onto Wymie's shoulder. She started to swat it off, but refrained. She was a guest in the oldie's house, after all. And her pa had seen her raised right as to politeness to one's elders. She in turn had passed that on after he died to— Her eyes drowned in hot, stinging tears.

The cat jumped to the floor, then rubbed against her leg and purred.

Wymie didn't like cats. She couldn't trust a creature that looked only after its own interests and never after hers. But Widow Oakey's rickety-seeming predark two-story house was overrun with the wretches. Mebbe a dozen of them.

The whole place reeked of cat piss and shit, which at least kept down the smell of dust and mold. The house was a crazy quilt of scavvy furniture, decorations and ir-regularly shaped lace doilies apparently made by Widow Oakey herself, without apparent skill, and strewed hap-hazardly over chairs, tables and bric-a-brac alike to pro-tect them from…something.

"I saw one of them," she muttered fiercely. "The mutie. I saw the white skin and white hair, plain as day. And the eyes. Those red eyes…"

"Now, now, Wymie," Duggur said. "Albinos aren't hardly muties."

She raised clenched fists. But becoming vaguely aware

of Widow Oakey hovering fragilely nearby with her tray trembling precariously in her hands, she refrained from smashing them down on the piss- and grease-stained white damask tablecloth.

Someone knocked on the front door. Widow Oakey set down the tray, spilling about half a cup of tea out the spout of the cracked pot. She tottered off to answer.

Before Wymie could reach for the spoon to ladle out a second helping of eggs, she came back with a trio of locals.

Her cousin Mance Kobelin immediately came to her, spreading his arms. She rose to join in a wordless embrace. She felt the tears run freely down her face, moistening the red plaid flannel of his shirt beneath her cheek.

"We heard what happened, Wymie," intoned Dorden Fitzyoo, hat in hand, as Mance released her. He had doffed it per Widow Oakey's stringent house rules, revealing a hair-fringed dome of skull that showed skating highlights in the morning sun as filtered through dusty, fly-crap-stained chintz curtains. "It's a terrible thing."

Wymie nodded thanks, unable to speak. Dorden, who made and milled black powder on the far side of Sinkhole, had been a close friend of Wymie's mother and father. He had been driven somewhat apart from the family after Tyler Berdone's accident. Like so many others. Wymie still thought of him as a kindly uncle.

He had already sweated through the vest, which didn't match the suit coat he wore over it, straining to contain his paunch. "What happened to your parents, then, child?" the third visitor said in a cracked and quavering voice. "We heard they're dead too."

"They got chilled," she said.

"Ah. How horrible that you had to witness that." He

shook his wrinkled head, which showed even more bald skin that Dorden's though, as if to compensate, his hair stuck out in wild white wings to both sides. "Only the good die young."

So long as you're talking about Blinda, she thought. I wonder if you'd say that if you knew how often Mord talked about grabbing you some dark night and hanging you over a fire till you spilled the location of that fabled stash of yours.

But Wymie's stepdad had never acted on his gruesome fantasy, and never would've. Though this man's hands shook like leaves in a brisk breeze most of the time, they steadied right down when he gripped a hammer or other tool. Or a handblaster. He was still the best shot for miles around with his giant old Peacemaker .45 revolver.

Wymie had a hard time believing the stories that oldie Vin Bertolli had been the western Pennyrile's biggest lady-killer in his prime. But that was decades ago: he had lived in and around Sinkhole for over half a century, since arriving as a young adventurer in his twenties who'd been forced to seek a quiet place to settle by a blaster wound that'd crippled his left hip some.

"The outlanders did it," Wymie said. "I saw the white face and red eyes of the murdering son of a bitch myself. I could almost reach out and touch him! But that taint Conn sticks up for them!"

"You got to do somethin' yourself then, Wymie," Mance suggested. "I'll help."

"Obliged," she said.

The older visitors exchanged uneasy glances.

"Mathus Conn's a good man," Vin said. "A good man is hard to find."

To her surprise, Wymie found the stuffy air inside the

boarding house could smell worse than it already did. The oldie ripped a thunderous, bubbling fart. Her knees actually weakened as the smell hit her.

A black-and-white cat rubbed against the wrinklie's shins, purring loudly. It's like the little monsters are applauding him for out-stinking them, she thought.

"How can he be good if he shields murderers of little girls?" she demanded.

"I hear tell he wanted evidence that what you saw was really one of them outlanders, Wymie," Dorden said.

"I saw him with my own eyes!"

"You saw an albino," Dorden corrected her, "just like Shandy Kraft was. There's likely one or two more in the world than just that skinny kid with the outlanders."

"Are you defendin' them, too? Whose side are you on?"

He raised his hands. "Yours, Wymie. We're not blood kin, but I allus been close to your family. But Conn's a good man, like Vin says. Always dealt square with everybody. Dealt square with your ma and your pa, while he was alive."

He didn't mentioned Mord Pascoe. He didn't need to. Wymie's late stepdad never dealt square with anybody. And once the gaudy owner had caught him trying to cheat him one too many times, he refused to deal with him at all.

"More'n that," Dorden said, "he protects himself double good. And if anybody pushed Conn too hard without good reason, Tarley Gaines and his clan would step up to back him. And that's a bunch nobody wants to mess with."

"If aidin' and abettin' little-girl-murderin' outlanders isn't good enough reason, I don't know what is!" Mance declared furiously.

"Words are like birds," Vin said. "They fly away."

Everyone stopped and stared at him for a moment. He seemed unfazed.

"Fact is," Dorden went on deliberately, "more people here around Sinkhole reckon Conn's got the right of it than you do. No, don't scowl at me, girl. It's true."

"Don't shoot the messenger," Vin said. He leaned painfully on his walking stick to pat an orange tabby cat that was rubbing his head on his homemade deerskin moccasins. This entailed ripping another ferocious fart.

Wymie sat back down.

"I don't care about that!" she stated.

"We all have to live here," Dorden said gently. "That means continuing to get on with our neighbors, best we can."

"I'll leave, then!" she half screamed. "Once I get Blinda avenged."

Vin straightened creakily. He shook his head. "The impetuosity of youth."

She glared at him. "What does that even mean?"

He beamed toothlessly at her.

"Never mind," Dorden said. "But maybe you can set things straight without making enemies here among your home folk."

Wymie kept her jaw clamped on the bile she wanted to spew on him. She knew he spoke out of genuine friendship. She also, deep down somewhere, knew he was making sound sense.

But she wasn't in the mood for sense.

"And what if you're wrong?" Dorden said softly. "You take your vengeance on the wrong people, that leaves the real murderer out there free to murder more. You don't want that, do you?"

"I know what I saw!"

"You need to help us see, too."

She frowned so fiercely it almost shut her eyes, and angled her face toward her lap.

"What'd you have in mind, Dorden?" Mance asked.

"Simple," the older man said. Wymie heard the smile in his voice. "You need to look for evidence to back your claim. You got a power of folks hereabouts willing to help. Everybody wants to see justice done for your family—and the chillin' stopped. This here's a peaceful district in a world full of strife and misery. We mean to keep it that way."

She didn't miss the warning in his words, but she had to admit he had a point.

Better people help you than stand in your path, she thought.

"And while we're out lookin' for evidence to show you're right," Mance said, with eagerness growing in his voice as he spoke, "we can also start lookin' for the outlanders. You gotta find 'em to take care of 'em, right?"

"They been triple good hidin' their tracks," Duggur said.

Garl was taking advantage of the conversational distraction to spoon the rest of the scrambled eggs directly from the serving bowl into his mouth. Yellow fragments bounced off his chins and down the massive slope of his belly.

"Nobody knows where their dig is, or their camp, should it be a different spot," Duggur said.

Wymie sucked down a deep breath, then let it out in a shuddering sigh.

"You're right." She felt tears drying on her face, leaving salt-sticky tracks down her cheeks. "That's a double-good thing I can do. And I *can* do it!"

Her cousin squeezed her shoulder. "I'm with you, Wymie!"

"We're all with you," Dorden said, "in findin' your family's killers."

"Wymie, dear," Widow Oakey called in her cracked voice from the entry to the parlor. Wymie hadn't been aware she'd left the room. "There's a crowd outside to see you. I'd let 'em in, but they'd frighten my babies."

Wymie stood up again, trying not to be too obvious about kicking away a black cat that was slithering up against her leg. She managed to shift it a ways with her boot.

"I'll come see," she said, her heart pulsing faster.

"You know, Miz Oakey," Dorden said, "not to be overly critical, but you need to clean out your cat boxes more often."

She blinked rheumy brown eyes at him. "Cat boxes?"

"FOR A LONG time we've enjoyed an island of stability in the midst of the chaos of the outside world," Conn said. "I hope it's not invadin' to stay."

His nephew, Zedd, who had tan, freckled skin and rusty, tightly curled hair, emerged through the door.

"Looks like Layna and Mord, Unk," he said.

"Ugh," Nancy said. She turned away. She was hard as nails about most things, but had a squeamish touch. Her cousin and employer, Conn, respected that in her; it made her seem more human.

"How do they look?" Conn asked, despite his cousin's visible discomfort.

Zedd showed pressed-together teeth. They were white and mostly even. Patriarch Tarley enforced hygiene in his clan with an iron hand, despite his normally easygoing ways. He had a rep for being tough when it counted.

"Like you'd expect," Nancy said, as if she were gritting her teeth to hold in puke. Evidently she was hoping to stave off further details.

If so, she hoped in vain.

"Not really," Zedd said. "Chills ain't burned so much as, well, kinda roasted. And not really all over, you know?"

Conn kept his gaze steady on the young man as his cousin loudly lost her battle against throwing her guts up. "And they don't look et so much as busted all to nuke. Like they got hacked with an ax. Heads're both busted wide-open, and don't look as if their brains swole from the heat and popped through the skulls like taters in the oven."

"That's enough details right there, Zedd," Tarley said.

The young man shrugged.

"I was only tryin'—"

"Ace. Thanks. Enough."

Nancy straightened, grunting and wiping her mouth with the back of her hand. The group shifted upwind of the fresh pool of barf in the tramped-earth yard.

"Doesn't that support Wymie's claims?" she asked, all business once again. "I mean, would the weird fanged monsters the outlanders claim to've seen have done somethin' like that? Whacked them with an ax?"

Tarley shrugged. "Why not?"

"Truth," Conn said. "We don't know what these things'd do. We don't know if they're even real. It's a matter on which I'm far from makin' up my mind."

"But what difference does it make, anyway, Mathus?"

Nancy asked. "They're strangers. Outlanders. Why are you botherin' to stick up for them?"

"Fairness?" Tarley suggested. "Justice?"

Nancy scoffed. "How many magazines do them things load?"

"More than you might think," Tarley said stolidly.

"A reputation for fairness is part of my stock in trade," Conn reminded his assistant. "And let's not forget that dealin' with these rough-lookin' outlanders has been highly profitable. We can resell the scavvy we get from them to folks who want it most at considerable markup, and everybody's happy. Or do you want to go scout out their node and then dig scavvy yourself?"

She shook her head. "I'm not the outdoor type, boss," she said. "You know that. Had folks out looking, though."

"No luck, however," Conn said.

"No. They cover their tracks triple well." She frowned. "A suspicious mind might judge that as pointin' to them, too."

"A suspicious mind judges everythin' as pointin' to those it suspects," Conn pointed out.

"Wymie's on a rampage," Tarley said thoughtfully. "She ain't in a frame of mind to listen to reason. She could cause a power of mischief, it seems to me."

"Then seriously, boss," Nancy said. "Why not just throw the strangers to Wymie like a bone to a beggin' dog? Sure, justice, profit, all those good things. But if it gets her to calm the rad-dust down, mightn't that work out more profitable in the long run?"

Conn chuckled. His cousin had a way of reminding him exactly why he'd hired her, and without any sign of intent. Just by doing…what he'd hired her to: minding the bottom line.

But this time he still thought she'd made a rare mistake in her tallying.

"She's already stirred up a mob," he said. "That kind of thing is like a shaken-up jar full of wasps. It's hard to put back once you take the lid off."

"And what if she's wrong?" Tarley asked. "Then chillin' the outlanders will leave the real murderers still loose. And murderin' more, unless I miss my guess."

"That's what I fear," Conn admitted.

He raised his voice and called to the rest of the party, "Any sign of tracks anywhere?"

"Nary a scrap, Mr. Conn," Edmun replied. "Just the prints Wymie made when she got onto the trail toward town."

Edmun was an indistinct blond man somewhere in his thirties, bland as tepid water, but with a reputation for steadiness, which made it a matter of curiosity to Conn why he had first taken up Wymie's cause—when she'd carried her dreadful burden toward Stenson's Creek—and then promptly fallen away when Conn raised the voice of reason.

Conn didn't hold that highly by his own powers of persuasion. He was a skilled bargainer, with a lifetime of experience in dealing with everyone from desperate dirt farmers to booze- and crank-fueled coldhearts one twitch away from a chilling frenzy. Yet he'd always found Edmun Cowil and his like the hardest to move, once they got set in a groove.

There was something working here. It tickled the underside of his brain like gaudy-slut fingernails along the underside of his ball sack—though that was a pleasure he had long chosen to deny himself, as it was fundamentally bad business.

But no time for that now.

"Yard's hard-packed and sun-set hard as brick," Tarley said, taking a blue handkerchief from a pocket of his overalls and dabbing at his broad mocha forehead, where sweat ran out from beneath the brim of his black hat. Conn wasn't sure what good the rag would do him at this point. It was long since soaked sopping from earlier duty. But the patriarch seemed to derive some kind of comfort from it.

"Found something, Unk," Zedd called from in between the charred and mostly roofless stone walls. He appeared in the doorway holding an ax. Its head was covered in smoke and crusted crud. Its haft showed charring on what Conn reckoned had been the uppermost surface as it lay on its side and the house burned down toward it. But it looked as if it'd be serviceable enough, once it got cleaned up.

"Wonder why Wymie would leave her grandpappy's ax," Nancy said. "She treasured that dang thing."

"Even though the haft has been replaced a dozen times and the head twice," Tarley said with a chuckle for the hoary old joke. Although truth told, it likely had more than a scrap of truth, if it wasn't the literal thing.

Conn shrugged. "Reckon she had to leave in a hurry, whether the marauders fired the place, or she set it alight to trap them.

"Reckon we'll never know what really happened here. Oh, well. World's full of stuff I'll never know. Best get back to Widow Oakey's place, now, and see what kind of mischief Wymie's gettin' up to in this bright new day."

THE "CROWD" WIDOW OAKEY had spoken of turned out to consist of about half a dozen, Sinkhole residents and people from the surrounding countryside. They included a couple who had joined her sorrowful procession the night before, like Walter John and Burny Stoops, who had followed Conn's orders to carry her sister to the coffin-maker's place.

With a shock she realized she'd still have to go talk to him, to Sam, about arrangements for Blinda, and her ma, for that matter.

Mord Pascoe could lie out to feed the wolves and coyotes, as far as she was concerned. Unless the bastard had burned too far to carbon for even the likes of them to stomach. She wished he could've felt the flames that had consumed most of all she had held dear. But a person in her circumstances had to make do…

She swayed.

"We come to see how you was, Wymie," Burny said. "And to see what you wanted to do about your, you know. Quest for vengeance."

She felt her eyes fill with hot tears yet again. But this time, they were tears of gratitude.

She smiled at them.

"Thank you. Thank you all."

It's not much, she knew. But it was a start.

She could work with this!

Chapter Five

"Wait," a voice called from the scrub oak. "Don't shoot. I'm not one of them."

Mildred saw Ryan look at Krysty, who shrugged.

The midafternoon mugginess hung heavy in the air of the little glade on the slope a few dozen yards above a gurgling brook. Red oak and hickory branches overhung the clearing, masking most of the direct sunlight. Mildred didn't want to imagine what the afternoon would feel like without that shade.

"Define 'them,'" Ryan called back.

"The coamers," the unseen man said. "The albino grave robbers. The ones you're looking for."

"Grave robbers, as young Ricky suggested," Doc stated. "That adds a new dimension to our present difficulty."

"Dark night," J.B. muttered. "It surely does."

The companions had been traveling single file along a game trail a couple miles southwest of their dig site, with Ryan in the lead and J.B. protecting their rear. They had just begun to fan out on entering the clearing when Jak's warning birdcall brought them up short. They had immediately crouched or knelt, covering the brush-screen on the far side with their blasters.

"Mebbe," Ryan said. "How do you know so much about them?"

"And how do you know what we're looking for?" Mildred asked.

"I've roamed these woods nigh onto thirty years. I seen many a thing come and go, some stranger than most. And I seen the ones the locals call 'coamers.' They come and go, too. Currently they seem to be coming."

J.B. grunted in interest.

"Come out where we can get a better look at you," Ryan commanded.

"Don't go shootin' me, now."

"If we were going to, we would've by now," J.B. said. "That brush won't stop many bullets."

The branches rustled.

What appeared from the vegetation was anything but threatening, at first glance: a man of smallish to middle size, middle-aged to old, walking tentatively on rather bowed legs left bare by ragged and dirty cargo shorts with bulging pockets. A coonskin cap covered the top of his head. Around his shoulders he wore a cape made of shaggy bark that gave the locally abundant shagbark oak its name. Beneath that was a linen shirt. His round face was fringed by a shock of black hair and a beard with brushstrokes of gray in it. His eyes suggested strong Asian ancestry, but his accent, unsurprisingly, was pure western Kentucky.

He had his hands, clothed in shabby fingerless gloves, raised over his head to signal benign intentions, which was good, because he was clearly far from helpless: the butt of a late eighteenth- or early nineteenth-century replica longblaster stuck up over his right shoulder, supported by a beadwork sling, and he wore both a Bowie knife with worn staghorn grips and a single-action, cap-

and-ball revolver on either hip in cross-draw holsters, likewise beaded in colorful geometric patterns.

"Osage Nation work," Krysty said, nodding at the beaded accessories. "Nice."

"That's right, ma'am," he said. "I'm a local boy, but I been everywhere. Abe Tomoyama is my name. Abe to my friends, so you can call me that, long as you don't chill me."

Ryan raised a hand. "Stand down, everybody," he said. "Keep eyes skinned to all sides, in case the pale shadows decide to check us out."

"Don't worry," Abe stated, "yet. Them coamers don't attack when the sun's high in the sky. They only like to come out when it gets low. Like it's fixin' to right directly. Surely you noticed that?"

"Surely we didn't," Mildred said sourly.

"It does fit observable facts," Doc said. "The few we have been able to observe."

"Reckon we need to talk," Abe said. "Let's find us a place to palaver. Say, I'm a feeling mite peckish. What do you say we go to one of my campsites and chow down while we do it."

"Won't say no," Ryan said, but he had a wary furrow to his brow as he said it.

He was wondering what was in it for the strange man they'd run into. And they all had learned a hundred times over, in the Deathlands, if you didn't know what somebody had coming out of a given interaction, that usually meant it was coming straight out of your hide.

"FOLKS'RE SCARED, HEREABOUTS," Abe said. "They don't rightly know of what—shadows dimly seen at dusk, strange cries in the dark. Rumors of people disappearin' out in the woods in the dark of the night. But I reckon I do know."

"Suppose you tell us why you think we're hunting these coamers of yours?" Ryan asked as he seated himself next to Krysty, where she hunkered down across from a small, nearly invisible dry brush fire from their peculiar host.

"I know *hunters* when I clap eyes on 'em, I reckon you'll allow," Abe said. "But you show no interest in the wildlife, other than to keep eyes skinned for ones as might be dangerous. You're huntin' man or mutie, or something close to one or the other."

Abe's camp was nestled in a bare-dirt hollow among sandstone boulders at the crest of a low rise, surrounded by brush and stunted trees. Krysty thought it a sweet spot, giving the option of surveilling the surrounding area from a height without spotlighting the fact you were there. It was already cool here, or cool for the Pennyrile, shaded at this spot from the low sun's slanting rays. The smell of a brace of ruffed grouse roasting on sticks over the little fire was tantalizing.

"So what are these coamers, anyway?" Mildred asked. "Man or mutie?"

"Ghosts," he said, and laughed at their expressions. "I don't mean the spirits of chills. I mean they appear and disappear sudden-like, and seem to leave no traces at all, as if they had no more substance than smoke. But they got substance, right enough. They eat, they bleed, they die. And they *chill*, with their long white claws and those double-big jaws of theirs, more like a dog's than a person's."

"Or a baboon's," Mildred suggested.

"That sounds consistent with the description, yes,"

Doc agreed. Mildred seemed surprised; usually the two would argue over whether the sun was coming up or going down at high noon on a cloudless day. "I have heard the term 'dog ape' in connection with the beasts."

The hermit shook his head. "Dunno nothin' about those. But I seen 'em. Just glimpses, mind, over the years. But I seen the bones they've cracked in those jaws and the carcasses of beasts they chilled for meat."

"They known to eat humans?" Ryan asked.

"Other than dead ones," Mildred added.

Abe shrugged. "Mostly I hear tell of them digging up chills and eatin' those. Prefer 'em fresh-buried. But they ain't what you'd call picky."

He sighed and dropped his gaze to the flames. His hand reached out to turn over first one, then the other plump game-bird carcass on their willow-wand spits. It looked to Krysty as if he did that by pure muscle memory, no conscious thought or intention involved.

"But like I say, there's…stories," Abe said. "Tales of folks out wanderin' the woods at night by they lonesome, who never come back, and are never heard from anymore. The Pennyrile's a big, wild place, with plenty of dense brush and caves and sinkholes. Lotta ways for a body to go missin', if you catch my drift."

"I don't," Mildred said. "Does anybody?"

"Ever hear of them attacking a camp or house?" Krysty asked.

"No. But they been getting' pretty bold this season."

"Why didn't the people in Stenson's Creek gaudy think to blame them first," Ricky began, "instead of—"

"Yeah," Ryan said, just emphatically enough to shut off the youth from blurting any more. "Never heard mention of them before now."

Ricky's dark eyes got big, and his cheeks flushed. Ryan couldn't stop him wearing his heart on his sleeve. Fortunately their host seemed too preoccupied to notice.

Ricky's close friend Jak shot him a wicked grin, half-sympathy, half-derision. Ryan had ordered the albino to sit in with them to learn whatever the woodsman had to impart. Jak had complied unwillingly, since he considered this with reason to be enemy territory, and that it was therefore even more urgent than usual that he be on patrol for danger. But he obeyed Ryan, as he generally did. Krysty suspected Jak understood the wisdom of Ryan's wishes in this case, unlikely though he was to ever admit it.

"Like I say," Abe went on, "they come and go. Like, from generation to generation. They seem to resurge every generation or two. Most of the settled folk, in the villes and such, forget about them, or think they're just made-up stuff. But the oldies, out in the hills—*they* know. They remember. And this year—well, they seem to be gettin' more aggressive than ever."

"What about you?" Krysty asked. "How do you manage to survive?"

Abe grinned with strong, surprisingly white teeth.

"I'm reckoned by some a fair shot with a blaster, hand or long." He patted the flintlock rifle he'd laid by his side on a coyote-skin cover.

Krysty shot a sidelong look to Mildred. The other woman nodded. She was clearly impressed; good shots rarely *claimed* to be, in her day or this one.

"You a hunter, too?" J.B. asked.

"Hunter. Trapper. Fisherman. Gatherer. Bit of whatever I need to be. Come from a long line of mountain men and women, I do."

"'Mountain men'?" Doc echoed. "You mean, like the solitary fur trappers and traders from earlier in my— That is, back in the early 1800s?"

Not everyone would have got a reference to such ancient history, but Abe brightened right up. He nodded.

"The very ones," he said. "I've spent time in the Rocks myself, and up in the Dark range. Used to get to rendezvous in Taos each spring, like olden times. That's where I learned my wilderness chops, from my poppa and momma."

"Reenactors," Mildred said, with a certain reflex distaste.

Abe looked at her blankly.

"Guess not," she said sheepishly. "Your ancestors— culturally, at least—*they* were reenactors. But I reckon you and your people have been the real deal for decades."

"Mebbe," Abe said, clearly not getting her meaning.

Mildred's smooth brown forehead wrinkled. "Also, how do you even know folks hereabouts are scared of these things? I thought you were a hermit."

He laughed. "Oh, I am, I am. But that doesn't mean I spend all my time alone in these woods and karst plains. Even a man like me gets tired now and then of listenin' to nothin' but the wind and the brook and the hoot-owl cries. Also I got what you might call a bit of a thirst, although I learned to keep a pretty tight rein on it, after some unfortunate happenin's at Rendezvous a few years back… Anyhoo, I head in every once in a while to Stenson's Creek gaudy, trade some pelts or gewgaws I make or trade for elsewhere, for the jack to wet my whistle. Was just in last week. I heard the stories then, mostly in whispers."

He paused to drink out of a canteen that seemed to be a corked clay pot, carried in a pouch filled with damp moss, evidently to keep it cool.

"Also, sometimes I come across isolated camps of woodcutters and hunters or other folk not too unlike myself, or of travelers. I talk to them, just like I'm talkin' to you. And they tell stories that are even scarier. And sometimes…"

He shook his head.

"I find a site in some double-lonely and isolated spot that's deserted, and shows signs of a scuffle. Tracks so blurred up even I can't identify them. Dead remains of a fire that been kicked asunder. Once or twice a spatter of dried blood on the grass or a berry-bush branch. Signs somethin' bad happened to the former occupant. Mebbe done by a bear or a painter. But mebbe not."

After a moment of uncomfortable silence, Ryan said, "So you know these woods."

"They're my home."

"You managed to catch any of these coamers? And why 'coamers,' anyway?"

"Second question first," Abe said. "Dunno. People just allus call them that, when they speak of them, which as I think I indicated, is mostly in whispers.

"As for your first question—nope. No luck there, either."

"Not track?" Jak asked. He seemed to be studying the stocky man intently. The albino tended to be dismissive of everybody else's talents in the woods, and compared to him, most humans were as clumsy and oblivious as drunken bears. Even Ryan and his strong right hand, J.B., both of whom were adept woodsmen by most mortal standards.

But the younger man's red eyes were narrowed and thoughtful. Krysty thought to see at least a glimmer of respect for the self-proclaimed mountain man. She wasn't sure what Jak was basing his judgment on; he put less stock in words than J. B. Dix, and that was saying plenty. But whatever he saw in this man, it looked genuine to him. Or so she sized it up.

"They don't leave much sign," Abe said. "Not even scat. And that looks just like a normal person's, if tendin' to be runnier than most. I don't reckon they get much roughage in their diet. But they're elusive as puffs of wind, and only rarely much easier to see."

"Ever chill one?" J.B. asked.

"Had to fire 'em up a couple times. Just in the last month. They never plagued me before, other than I suspect them of raidin' my snares for squirrels and rabbits and the like. Hit a couple, too, judgin' by the squallin' I heard and the blood I found on the leaves nearby. But I couldn't prove it. I never found a carcass. It seems they take their chills with them as well as wounded."

"To eat later?" Ricky asked in a tone of eager horror.

The mountain man shrugged. "Seems likely."

"So even you can't track them, is what you're saying?" Mildred said.

Krysty felt a moment's apprehension that her friend's usual bluntness—or tactlessness, more closely—might annoy their host, which would be a pity just as the grouse were smelling done. But the man just nodded.

"Not far, anyway. After a few steps it's like they vanish off the face of the Earth."

Krysty looked around. Her friends seemed as distressed by the revelation as she was.

"How do you reckon they do that?" Ryan asked. "I doubt they fly. Or use magic."

"Oh, no," Abe said, grinning. "They go to ground, like foxes."

"What do you mean?" Mildred asked.

"I mean when they vanish, I usually find some kind of hole in the ground nearby. No more than a coyote burrow would have for an entrance, commonly. But they're built on the slim side, and don't seem like they'd need much room to wiggle through."

Jak frowned at the revelation. Krysty guessed it was because he himself had not yet spotted the fact.

"They have dens?" Ryan asked.

"Mebbe. But remember this district is peppered with sinkholes like a plank shot with buckshot, and honeycombed by caves beneath. They could have a whole underground empire with roads and villes, for all we know."

That struck Krysty as fanciful. It surprised her in someone as practical and…earthy as Abe seemed to be. All the same, he seemed pretty sharp, and his kind of life would offer plenty of time for flights of fancy.

"Ever checked?" J.B. asked.

"Do I look like I got a death wish, friend? Also, you'll notice I'm built more for endurance than agility. If I could fit myself down one of them rabbit holes, I shudder to think what might be waitin' for me on the other side."

Krysty's mind filled with a vision of Blinda's face— or the raw red concavity where it had been—and she shuddered too.

"Anyhoo," Abe said, reaching for a spit, "looks as if our dinner's ready to serve. Now—"

His black eyes got wide, seemingly fixed right on Ryan. He slapped leather with his right hand.

At the same time, Ryan, staring right back, went for his own blaster.

As quick as a pair of diamondback rattlers, the two men drew their weapons, pointed them straight at each other and fired.

Chapter Six

"Anything?" Wymie asked.

She stopped to catch her breath and wipe sweat from her brow with a handkerchief. She was used to hard work in the hot sun, but not all this walking up and down hills, bashing brush most of the time.

Her cousin Mance, face streaming sweat from under a bandanna, shook his head. "Not yet, Wymie."

He sounded worried. She understood. She had started out with nineteen or twenty helpers. The past two days of fruitless searching had whittled them down to a round dozen.

"Should we head back to the Mother Road," asked Dorden, who to Wymie's amazement was not one of the ones who had abandoned her, "or keep searching this area?"

She shook her head helplessly. Who knew it would be this complicated, hunting for her sister's killers?

Because the outlander coldhearts only ever came to Conn's gaudy house, or rarely to Sinkhole proper by way of it, she reckoned their hideout had to lie somewhere to the west. So they'd started out following the Mother Road, which paralleled Stenson's Creek away from Sinkhole, to begin her search.

After about six or eight miles, though, the wooded hills gave way to flatter karst country, more given to grass and patches of scrub than pine or hardwood forests. Dorden had suggested it was unlikely the outlanders laired up in such open country, despite the occasional harsh limestone ridge. She'd agreed.

"We're what," she said, "mebbe a mile south of the road by now?"

They were following a game trail. It was the best thing she could think of, and not even know-it-all old Dorden had come up with better.

"That's right," Mance said.

"And nobody we came across has seen hide nor hair of them," Lou Eddars said. He was Mance's friend and their chief tracker. His freckled face streamed with sweat, though nothing it seemed could keep down his frizz of orange curly hair. He had ears that stuck out, big buck teeth and an Adam's apple that looked like a baseball lodged in his throat. But he was an accomplished hunter who knew the countryside around Sinkhole as well as any.

As well as anybody who'd chosen to throw in with Wymie and her quest, anyway.

"What about the signs of recent campsites," Mance asked his pal, "like that one we come across the last ridge back? Fire ashes were still warm, even."

Lou shook his head. "Too small," he said. "Looks like folks who camped there heard us coming, or spotted us, and lit out for the brush. We got too many weps showin' to look triple peaceful-like, which is also why we can't raise too many local folk to ask if they seen the outlanders."

Wymie sighed.

"Let's follow this trail a spell farther," she said.

"If at first you don't succeed," Vin said with a cackle, "try, try again."

It also surprised Wymie the oldie had stuck right with her throughout all the exertion and frustration. But thinking about it, she realized it shouldn't. He might look as if he could scarcely totter across a room, especially with the limp he'd had for decades, but he still spent much of his days tramping around the hills around Sinkhole. He lived for excitement, such as was to be had for a man of his great age in a peaceful, quiet backwater like the Pennyrile. She had no idea whether he actually shared her conviction as to the outlanders' guilt or not, but it made no difference, she guessed, as long as he—and his giant Peacemaker handblaster, with which he was still a dead shot—stayed by her side.

"But, Wymie," Burny whined. "There's a hundred square miles of these wooded hills around Sinkhole, and miles and miles more of these pissant deer trails crisscrossed all over 'em. Got to be. We could follow them until we all grow long gray beards and only find a sign of the coldhearts by sheer strike accident."

Fury blazed within her. "Are you doubtin' me?" she flared at him. "You lookin' to bail on me too?"

Old Vin tittered. "Oh, ye of little faith," he said.

Burny's eyes widened and he took a step back.

"No, no," he stammered. "All I's sayin' is, we need a better plan, seems to me."

"And backin' out on me's a better one?" she shouted. "Is that your plan? Turn tail and run, like your buddy Walter John?"

"But, Wymie, he *had* to. He got an ailin' wife and two kids to take care of. You know that."

"Listen to me, Burny Stoops," she said, dropping her voice low and menacing as she stepped up to him. Her anger had brought the others clustering close around. "I will keep after these outlanders, and I'll find them. Once I do, folks'll rally to me. You'll see. And then there'll be a day of reckonin'! And not just for them, but for them as sided with the child murderers by not helpin' me! Which side will you be on, Burny Stoops?"

"Yeah!" Mance echoed. "Which side, Burny?"

"You with us or against us?" demanded Angus Chen, a carpenter from Sinkhole.

"With us or against us?" the others began to chant. They closed in threateningly on Burny.

He cowered. "No, Wymie, no!" he said. "It ain't like that at all. But—people are startin' to wonder if we're ever gonna find them."

"You wonderin', you mean?" Wymie asked.

"No. I just heard— Oh, shit hell, Wymie. I'm with you. Please. You *got* to believe me."

She looked in his brown eyes and saw only fear. And submission. After leaving him to wiggle in the spike of her gaze for half a minute she nodded.

"All right," she said, turning away. "That's better. Anybody else goin' weak in the knees on me?"

She knew at least half her remaining people had spent the morning grumbling about a wild-goose chase, but now they stumbled all over one another and themselves to assure her they were in all the way.

"Right," she said. "Let's keep on this trail over the next rise. Then—we'll see.

"All we need's just a trail, even, that we're sure leads to those stoneheart bastards. And then we'll go back to town and see who's really with us, and who's with the outland baby-killers."

"Mathus Conn might not take kindly to that, Wymie,"

Dorden said, "without more evidence the outlanders are the ones who did it."

"Then coamers can eat Mathus Conn's guts!" she cried, invoking the terrible half-remembered childhood legend that for some reason sprang into her mind.

"The worms go in," Vin sang. "The worms go out…"

"Oh, put a sock in it, you wrinkled old loon!"

"FIREBLAST!" RYAN YELLED.

And indeed that happened, straight for his face from the muzzle of Abe's blaster.

Ryan felt the heat of the yellow black-powder flame-flare from their host's blaster like a dragon's breath on his face. Its glare dazzled his good eye, and he felt hot powder specks pepper his cheek right below the socket.

He wasn't aware of hearing its roaring report nor the sound of his own 9 mm SIG Sauer blasting.

An agonized scream from right behind him ripped even through the ringing in his ears.

At the same moment he saw a pale shape, indistinct among the scrub that rimmed the boulder-lined bowl, rear up behind Abe, throw hands in the air at the ends of long but manlike arms and topple backward. Though vague blue blobs floated in his monocular vision, he had gotten the impression of a third, red eye opening above the two he had glimpsed glaring at him from the brush just behind and above their host.

Krysty was on her feet, aiming her Glock handblaster at Abe with both hands. A side-glance showed her face to have gone bone-white.

"Back off the trigger!" Ryan barked. "Everybody, blasters out and eyes outward, now!"

He scrambled to his feet, his SIG held out before him.

Their host continued to kneel, his Ruger's blue-smoking barrel tipped toward low, scattered clouds, finger off the trigger and thumb on the hammer.

Everybody else jumped up. When Ryan Cawdor told them to do something in that tone of voice, they did it, even when they didn't have an apparent face-up gunfight to galvanize them.

"Muties!" Ricky yelped. He was hauling his big double-action top-break Webley revolver from its holster as he scrambled to his feet, coming perilously close to toppling into the fire as he did so. He cursed as he bumped the roasting-spit branches, toppling the grouse into the flames in an upward rain of orange sparks, already bright in the fading afternoon.

When Ryan saw their host turn around—without bothering to get up—to cover the way Ryan was looking, he followed his own order and whipped around. No targets presented themselves. He saw a thrashing in the brush about where he reckoned the old woodsman had fired. As he watched, it seemed to diminish.

Krysty's Glock snarled out a burst at full auto. Leaves and branch and bark fragments flew up from the scrub oak.

"Hold fire!" Ryan snapped. "Don't shoot unless you got a sure target!"

"What if they start throwing rocks?" he heard Ricky say from behind him.

J.B.'s dry chuckle followed. "Then you got a target, son," the Armorer said, "even if it's only to discourage that behavior."

They stood there with blasters pointed outward from the fire, straining their eyes into the screen of leafy branches surrounding the little dip in the boulder-outcrop's top. But as soon as the limb-thrashing died away completely, they saw nothing more.

"The sun is setting," Doc said. He had his rapier in his right hand, and his gigantic LeMat handblaster in the left. "Is that not when Mr. Tomoyama says they begin to attack in earnest?"

"It was," Abe answered. "And no 'mister' stuff, please. Makes me sound like my daddy."

"Why do they even do that?" Mildred asked. "They've thrown crap at us while the sun was shining. Why not kill then, too?"

"Are you seriously asking any of us what does or does not motivate a bunch of blood-crazed cannie killers, Mildred?" Ryan asked, gently, he thought, under the circumstances.

"Um—no. I guess I'm not."

"Ace," Ryan said. "While we're asking questions we'll never know the rad-blasted answers to, why in the name of glowing night shit do they bother hassling us by chucking trash at us? If they mean to chill, why don't they just come at us?"

"Our situation must be precarious indeed," Doc said, "if our taciturn leader finds himself reduced to asking rhetorical questions."

"Mebbe not that rhetorical, Doc," J.B. said. "If we know more about why they do what they do, that might give us a leg up on reckoning what they're *going* to do."

Abe made a rumbling sound low in this throat. "I must be getting senile," he said. "Shoulda put out some telltales before we sat down to palaver."

"'Telltales'?" Ricky and Mildred echoed.

"Means alarms, I reckon," J.B. said. "Little something to let him know when something—or somebody— is creepy-crawling around his camp."

"That's it exactly, Mr. Dix!"

"Abe, I'm not my daddy, either."

The old woodsman laughed. "Ace on the line, J.B. Yeah, I set string lines of little bells and bits of jingly stuff like old bent-outta-shape nails and shards of glass along the brush around my site. Makes it harder for anythin' or anyone to sneak up on me. It's one of the reasons I managed to keep from starin' up at the stars long before this."

He sighed. "Best I go out and set that straight before it gets any darker. Y'all just sit tight, make yourselves to home. I won't be a minute."

"Look for chills?" Jak asked Ryan.

"You won't find any, most likely," Abe said.

But Ryan knew the young albino was furious—at himself for not detecting the attacks earlier and at Ryan for shackling him and his stealth skills and senses by making him join the others by the fire to hear Abe's lecture, rather than letting him roam around them like a watchdog.

"Go," Ryan said.

Abe frowned dubiously after Jak as the young man vanished into the scrub without so much as shaking a twig.

Krysty smiled. "Don't worry, Abe," she said. "He wouldn't be likely to trip your alarm system even if he didn't know you were putting it out."

"One of those, eh?"

Mildred sniffed loudly. "I smell something burning."

"¡Nuestra Señora!" Ricky yelped. "I knocked them into the fire, I'm afraid. Sorry, Mr.—Abe—for ruining your supper."

"Pshaw." The stocky mountain man bent and deftly fished the half-charred spits from the flames. He straightened, holding the two grouse aloft like miniature torches.

He blew out the flames that were feeding on the fat that oozed out of the birds.

"It's just added flavor," he said.

SOMETHING BRUSHED WYMIE'S right cheek.

At first she thought it was an early hawk moth, trying to get a jump on its kin sucking sweet, sweet nectar from night-blooming forest flowers. Then she heard a thump and a curse from behind her.

She spun. Angus Chen was looking outraged and rubbing his cheek as if he'd been stung.

"Somethin' hit me!" he declared.

Something else blurred through Wymie's peripheral vision. She turned to her left to see a stick with green leaves on it bounce off the short grass to the right of the track they'd been following through a patch of berry bushes.

"Movement up ahead," called Lou Eddars, who was a bit out in front of the rest of Wymie and her party, scouting for signs of their quarry.

"What the nuke is— Shit! Somebody threw a rock at me," Mance said from right behind Wymie. Several other voices cried out that they'd been hit too.

"Oh, my God, it's the night chillers!" The voice was so shrilled and distorted from fear that Wymie couldn't recognize it, and she had known every man in her search party since she was a little girl younger than poor Blinda had been.

"Dark dusted!" Mance cried. He was holding it together better, but only just. "They're all around us!"

Blasterfire erupted from the entire raggedy column. The noise momentarily deafened Wymie. As if by magic, she found herself enveloped by a fog bank of swirling gray smoke. She crouched in her tracks, disoriented and unsure of what to do.

Yellow flashes stabbed through the sulfurous clouds of powder smoke. Concussions beat her eardrums like fists. She suddenly heard a ripple of blasterfire that, though quickly ended, made her think of what a machine gun had to sound like. She'd heard of them, but had never seen one herself, nor heard one fired.

The burst of shots ended in a scream, of what Wymie thought to be surprise and fear, like one of Widow Oakey's cats whose tail she had stepped on hard, and mebbe not entirely by accident.

Most of the group's firearms were single-shot, whether muzzle-loaders or breech. As quick as it had started, the storm of shooting died away.

Wymie's ears were ringing. She was trembling. She wasn't accustomed to blasterfire at all. Her father had a shotgun, which he used to hunt meat for the pot, but he hadn't used it close by the house very often. And Mord had hocked it to buy booze from Conn's gaudy.

This much fire and smoke and shattering noise, happening all around her, all at once the way it did, had come close to overwhelming her. Just for a moment. But she instantly hated herself for weakness, and made herself stand upright despite the quivering of her legs and the looseness of her knees. She threw back her shoulders and held her head high.

Through the ringing that filled her ears she heard a strange rhythmic sound. It took a moment for her to recognize it as laughter. An oldie's cracked voice, cawing like a mirth-filled crow.

"Them as don't know what they're shootin' at," Vin declared, "might as well be pissin' bullets away."

That wasn't one of his dark-dusted old saws, at least not one she recognized as such. But even when he wasn't speaking in overused phrases, he managed to make it *sound* as if he was.

"Nuke you, you wrinkled old bastard," shouted Mance, who was trying to stuff two hand-loaded shells of brown waxed paper on brass bases into his cracked-open double-barrel shotgun. "They was there, I tell you. I saw the bushes move."

Wymie found her voice. "Who's hurt?" she asked. "What was all that squallin' I heard?"

"That was just Burny," Dorden reported. "All the chambers in his Colt 1860 went off at once. Sprained his wrist and scared him somethin' fierce."

The dense, stinking smoke-clouds were beginning to thin, though the smell seemed to coat her sinuses and tongue in the heavy, humid afternoon air.

"Anybody else?"

"I—I'm bleedin'," Angus said, staring in horror at the blood gleaming red on the fingertips he held before his face.

"You got a cut on your cheek," Mance said. "You'll live, likely."

"Anybody else?" Wymie asked.

A couple of the others reported they had had sticks or rocks bounced off them. Nobody else seemed to be bleeding, though, inside or out.

"Well, we must have chilled *some* of the coldhearts, with all that shootin'," Wymie declared.

She stood with arms crossed waiting while Lou and several of the others, including Mance, roved the bushes around them in the deepening gloom. Every second that passed without reported result stoked the embers of her smoldering rage.

"Sorry, Wymie." Mance emerged from a service-berry brush to report apologetically and more than half-nervously. "Nothin'."

"Not even any blood?"

"No blood."

"Any tracks?"

Mance shook his head.

"I didn't think there was any way all of us could miss," he said.

"Might as well have just been shootin' the breeze." Vin cackled. "Can't miss fast enough to catch up."

"Anybody see the white-haired mutie?" Mance asked. He seemed eager to placate his increasingly furious cousin, and acted as if he hoped to be able to throw at least some kind of bone.

"Albino," Dorden muttered under his breath.

"I did," Lou sang out.

"Me too!" Edmun called.

"But you were tail-end Charlie, Edmun," Dorden said. "Lou was walking point."

"What are you trying to say?" Wymie shrieked. "Are you doubtin'? Are you?"

The middle-aged man shrugged. "Just sayin' he'd have to be triple fast, is all."

"They won this round," Vin said. "Tomorrow is another day."

For a moment Wymie almost felt calm. "That almost made sense," she said.

"What were they doin, Wymie?" Dorden asked. "They weren't rightly attackin' us. Even after we started blastin' 'em."

"They were afraid to, once we started blastin'," Mance declared heatedly.

"But couldn't they see we had blasters?" Burny asked. "Don't take me wrong, Wymie, I ain't doubtin'. They was out there—I saw 'em movin' too, though I never got a good look at the taints through the berry bushes. But why'd they try us on in the first place, even? Couldn't they see we have blasters? Don't nobody want to get shot."

That caused the rage to come boiling up her throat in a scalding-hot column.

"Nuke it!" Wymie yelled in frustration. "They're tauntin' us, is what they're doin'! Those stonehearts think they can just—just play with us."

She raised her strong hands before the others and clenched them into fists.

"That does it! Mathus Conn can't catfish on us anymore. After what they did today, he'll have to own up that I was right, and he was wrong!"

"*Dead* wrong," Vin said, then cackled wildly.

Chapter Seven

A chalk-white face, with bloodred eyes beneath lank white hair, appeared out of the brush ahead.

"Found."

Walking second in line behind Ryan, Krysty recoiled slightly, then she felt shame. Her hand came away from the square butt and extended magazine of her Glock, holstered by her right hip.

But it was true what that unfortunate young black-haired woman said: he *did* look like the strange creatures who flitted around like pale shadows, the ones Abe Tomoyama said once were called coamers, but who apparently had been largely forgotten by the locals, at least here in the western Pennyrile near Sinkhole.

They and Abe had parted ways a few hours earlier.

"Found what?" Mildred said grumpily. She was footsore and tired of tramping around the hills and flats, on a search for what, no one could even rightly say. Now they were back in a region of limestone ridges clad with more scrub than forest, as the hot, damp day wore on. "When will you start using nouns? You spend words like drops of freaking blood."

Jak showed his white teeth in a quick grin. It wasn't as if he wasn't fully aware his clipped pattern of speech frequently aggravated his companions, Krysty knew, and sometimes baffled them.

"Come see," he said, then vanished.

Ryan glanced back at Krysty. His craggy features looked as impassive as they usually did—if you weren't his life-mate and longtime companion. Krysty knew the minute furrowing of his brow meant he was more than a little annoyed at Jak's uninformative ways, himself.

She grinned.

He grinned back, then shook his head ruefully.

"It's not like he doesn't tell us what we need to know when we really need it," he said, which was true.

"I guess he didn't spot an ambush, then?" Ricky called out. He was walking last but for his idol and mentor, J.B., who as usual liked to pull tail-end security for the party. They switched off sometimes, of course. Everybody could do every job in a pinch; Ryan insisted on that. They even sometimes substituted Ryan, J.B., or Krysty for Jak as scout, much as he chafed when that happened.

But when things were tense they tended to keep to the roles they fit best in.

"Smart-ass," Mildred grumbled.

They followed the vanished scout. When Krysty passed through the clump of brush he'd called to them from, she found herself at the end of the ridge they'd been following. It fell away to what looked like a creek running through a stretch of flats about a hundred feet wide that wound among the ridges. He was hunkered down in plain sight next to what looked like a random jumble of small boulders sprouting weeds and scraggly brush like hairs from a mole on an oldie's face. He had his head up, watching them, though it scanned from side to side. Always on guard.

They joined him. When Krysty saw Ryan draw his

SIG handblaster, she did the same. She knew from Jak's posture and manner there was no immediate threat, but something was making the short hairs rise on his nape, as well as making the longer strands of sentient red hair on her head start to curl up on themselves.

"What have you got?" J.B. asked. He had unslung his Smith & Wesson M-4000 shotgun and held it in his left hand. He and Ryan came up flanking the scout to either side. The others followed, spreading out in a cautious semicircle.

Jak pointed two fingers at the ground. There was a gap among the boulders on the side closer to the stream. It was mostly hidden by the tall grass, but there was a bare patch of pale soil to one side of it.

In that bare soil was an impression. It wasn't clear, at least not to Krysty's eye. But she could make out an unmistakable partial footprint, ball and the dot-marks left by some toes, in dirt still pliable from one of the frequent showers.

"Human or mutie?" Ryan asked.

Jak shrugged. "Looks human," he said, in a sidelong way that indicated he wasn't staking his life on that particular identification.

"It's not as if every mutie's got clawed feet and sucker fingers like a stickie," the Armorer stated.

"So what is it?" Ricky asked eagerly. He was dancing around the rear of the group holding his DeLisle longblaster in both hands. He was dying to see but didn't want to jostle his friends to get a closer look. And he was also, even in his convulsion of curiosity, swiveling his head constantly on his neck, looking out for danger. He took his duties no less seriously than Jak or J.B. did, which was one of the reasons why Ryan had allowed him to become one of his companions, despite his sometime puppy-dog fumbling.

That and the fact he was a good shot, either with the silenced carbine or his Webley handblaster. And when it came to protecting his friends—the only family he had, since stonehearts had slaughtered his own back in Puerto Rico and stolen away his adored older sister, Yamile, to sell to mainland slavers—he could be as cold-blooded as J.B. ever was.

"Burrow," Ryan said. "Or bolt-hole."

He looked at Jak, who shook his head. "Not know."

"So, there's no telling if this leads to the den, or a network of tunnels," J.B. observed.

He tipped his battered hat farther up his retreating hairline to scratch beneath where the sweatband had been riding.

"The way these bastards pop up like prairie dogs, and disappear as if they dropped off the surface of the Earth, leads me to suspect the latter," the Armorer continued.

"Been reckoning that myself," Ryan said.

"So," Ricky said, "are we going in?"

They all turned to look at him.

"You first, kid," Mildred said.

Ricky blushed.

"Whether it's a den or it leads to a whole underground city," Ryan stated, "it's certain-sure that if these cannies do live down there, they know it a lot better than we do, and know how to fight triple better than us down there."

"This whole district is underlain by a substantial network of caverns, I do believe," Doc told them.

"Yeah," Ryan said. "And if that really is where these things live, I for one am not eager to go in after them."

"It would appear suicidal on the face of it," Doc agreed.

"What are we going to do, then?" Krysty asked.

Ryan briefly clenched his jaw. She knew he sometimes did that when he didn't much like the taste of the words he was about to say.

"Keep looking," he said. "Keep on hunting for something we can take back and clear our names with before that crazy girl brings the whole nuking Pennyrile down on our necks. And we know one thing, sure."

He pointed at the footprint.

"No matter how good these nuke-suckers are at hiding out and covering their tracks, they do screw up. Sometimes."

"They're only human," Ricky said.

Everybody gave him another look.

"That still seems largely conjectural, young man," Doc said mildly.

"Well, I meant like—not ghosts or anything."

"Ghosts don't chuck sticks and stones at people."

"People still sometimes talk about poltergeists," Mildred pointed out. "They used to, at least. I never used to believe in the supernatural, but then some of my perspectives have shifted a touch, you know, these past few years."

"I heard about them, too," Ricky said. "Back home on the island."

Ryan stood up.

"Ghosts don't bite kids' faces off," he said. "All right. Enough talk. Time to get back to it. We're bleeding daylight here, people."

"NO MORE EXCUSES, Mathus Conn," Wymie hollered as she walked through the door. A passel of her followers jostled one another trying to crowd in behind her. "You got to quit standin' up for these outlander baby-chillers and help us *now*!"

Conn looked up from behind the bar, where he was polishing a mug and trying to calculate whether the rim was chipped badly enough it might gash a patron's lip. While many of his customers spent much of their time in Stenson's Creek gaudy in no condition to notice whether they'd nicked their mouths or not, he generally made it a policy that people not leave his establishment with blood on their faces. It was bad for business.

"Good to see you, too, Wymie," he said. "Why don't you and your friends sit down and take a load off?"

Tarley Gaines was chewing the fat with his old friend Conn, while a pair of younger members of the clan sat in respectful silence. A couple of other idlers from Sinkhole were all the rest of the gaudy occupants. It was a slow start to a night, but Conn reckoned it'd pick up.

He hadn't reckoned on *this*, though.

Wymie wasn't to be deflected so easily, much less mollified, as he'd expected. But as his granny always told him, you didn't hit what you didn't aim at.

"What happened?" Conn asked resignedly.

"They attacked us!" Wymie declared.

"The outlanders?"

"Who else would it have been?"

"Did any of you actually see any of them?"

"I did!" Lou said and Edmun chimed in, "Me, too!" a beat later.

Nancy had come in from the kitchen when she heard the fuss. She stood with her plain face set in a look of determined skepticism.

"Were you two together?" she asked.

"Nope," Lou said. "I was walkin' point. Edmun was pullin' drag."

"How could you both have seen the same person, then?"

"We went through this!" Wymie yelled. Nancy's frown deepened.

Conn was grimly amused. His cousin and chief aide was the one who had taken him to task for not going along with Wymie's somewhat crazy agenda from the first moment, for the sake of peace with neighbors and customers. Now her own reflex practicality had led her afoul of the young woman's overamped sense of vengeance.

The furrowed-brow look Nancy shot Conn indicated she wasn't really buying they both had seen the same man at more or less the same time, though Conn didn't judge Nancy to be passionate enough about truth in the abstract to kick up a fuss about it. She just didn't suffer fools gladly, was all. Nor foolishness.

"Not here, we didn't," Conn said, pitching his voice to carry without overtly raising it. It was a knack he'd developed years ago. It turned out to be useful to a gaudy owner. Folks around here tended to be laid-back and peaceful, of course. He just intended to keep them that way when alcohol began loosening their tongues and the dampers on their emotions.

"How many casualties?" That should be a safe diversion from what was plainly an explosive subject, though he wondered the same as his cousin had.

"Burny like to got his hand blowed off!" Lou said. Burny held up a hand crudely bandaged in a handkerchief that looked as if it hadn't started the day particularly clean to begin with. No blood had seeped through.

Vin, who had crowded in with a dozen or so others, cackled wildly. "Triple-stupe bastard was too lazy to stuff the ends of his chambers with lard, once he loaded 'em up," he declared, with the obvious pleasure known only to a man who was able to say *I told you so.* "The grasshopper spends the summer dancing, and when winter comes must beg the ant for a crumb to eat."

Several people, including Wymie, stared at him, stupefied. Conn, who'd been listening to the old man's platitudes his whole life, merely smiled.

"Leavin' the chamber mouths open means when you fire one, the flash can spread to all the others," Vin explained. He was always readier to lecture on blasters than he was to try to explain his frequently indecipherable pronouncements. It was one of the few things that made him tolerable, or at least his company. "It's called a gang-fire. As you reap, so you sow."

"Sure," Conn said. "So Burny blew his own hand off."

"It ain't that badly hurt," Lou said. "Just mostly scorched, and sprained to the wrist and trigger finger."

Burny clutched his forearm above his bandaged wrist and looked reproachful at his comment.

"So was anybody hurt by the actual attackers?" Conn went on, only a bit more pointedly.

"Angus got his face laid open," she said, pointing to a small cut on the carpenter's cheek. It had clearly long since stopped bleeding on its own, and been cleaned up. Or *off,* since it had likely been done with somebody's spit.

Conn was something of a student of ancient history, and so he knew that those among humanity who were most susceptible to disease or infection had died off in the plagues that followed the Big Nuke, and the decades of skydark that followed before the sun came back. But you could still press your luck and end up dying of infection or gangrene. It was why he insisted on hygiene inside his establishment, and did what he could—with at least some success—to encourage its use among his neighbors and patrons outside his establishment.

He reluctantly refrained from pointing out what a poor idea a spit-cleanse was for a face wound. He had long since also learned to pick his battles.

"How'd that happen?" he asked.

"Coldheart threw a rock."

"A rock." He looked at her and drummed his fingers on the bar. "A rock? Does that strike you as somethin' baby-killin' coldhearts would do? Throw rocks?"

"Coulda chilled me!" Angus said plaintively.

"Sure."

"But don't you see?" Wymie cried. She held out her hands to the sides and turned about, clearly playing to the idlers, in hopes of enlisting their sympathy and support, and she certainly had their undivided attention.

Conn judged that had mostly to do with the amount of imposing white bosom revealed by her red plaid shirt, which she'd left unbuttoned almost to the breastbone against the heat of the day and her exertions.

"This settles it? Doesn't it? They know we're gettin' close, and they're tryin' to scare us off!"

"Why'd they bother?" Tarley asked, blowing foam from a stoneware mug of Conn's famous house brew. "They got modern blasters. Plenty firepower to chill you and your friends. Or enough to make the rest lose interest in anythin' but runnin'. Why would they screw around throwin' trash at you?"

"Mebbe they're short on ammo," Vin suggested.

Tarley raised his eyebrows and nodded. "Good point. But that doesn't answer my question. Not really. They could bushwhack you a lot more convincin'ly than that without shootin' at you. Especially if they're such masters of stealth that you never catch a glimpse of any of them, except flashes of the albino one. It doesn't make sense."

"Why would anyone throw rocks at us, if they were chillers?" Dorden asked. "Not that I'm doubtin' you, Wymie. It's hard to see why anybody'd do that."

"I don't pretend to know how baby-chillers think," Conn said evenly.

"Nor I," Tarley said. "But I got to tell you plain, Wymie, that I ain't buyin' it. You always been a good girl, hard worker, with a good head on your shoulders. And I understand you're hurt and angry, surely I do. I'd feel the same if that horrible thing happened to any of my kin. But I'm not about to go on any blood-hunts without knowin' for a fact I'm huntin' the right prey."

Conn saw Wymie set her jaw and grind it. Her big, strong hands were clenched into fists at her sides. Her big breasts rose and fell in an eye-catching way as she sucked in deep breaths and blew them out.

"Tarley Gaines," she said, "just you watch yourself! Time has passed for sittin' on a fence. You're either with us or against us."

Tarley shook his head and set down his mug with a deliberate thump.

"You need to back off the trigger of that blaster

straightaway, Wymea Berdone," he said. He rose, and his junior clansfolk rose with him. "We're headed back to Gaines Hill, and there I reckon we'll stay until this fuss blows over. As a man who means you nothin' but goodwill, I tell you steer clear of there, or you'll find out just what it means to step to the Gaines clan."

He tossed a handful of jack on the table.

"Obliged to you, Mathus," he said. "Best take care."

Conn nodded. "I always do."

The three left.

Wymie turned a glare on Conn that, if he judged the intent right, should have reduced him instantly to a pile of smoldering ash.

"What about you?"

Conn flicked his gaze aside at Nancy. His cousin was frowning at him. He suspected she was back to her position of go along to get along, despite her earlier common-sense-based outburst.

He reckoned life had been too easy too long there in the western Pennyrile, but he meant to hold on to what he could. He sighed.

"I'm not against you, Wymie," Conn said evenly, "however you may think. But I mean to see the peace kept. Bring me evidence—actual evidence, not just rock-throwin' phantoms that don't sound like anything at all, much less these outlanders you're so stuck on—and I'll do everything in my power to back you. Short of that, I have my responsibilities."

She glared at him even hotter, if that was possible. Chad and Tony had come out of their dorm rooms to take up their duties for the evening, and now stood quietly with burly arms crossed over broad chests. Wymie's posse stood behind her—outside the baleful sweep of her vision—shifting uncomfortably and passing around uncertain glances.

But in the end it seemed Tarley Gaines's quiet yet deadly-confident defiance had shaken her out of the mood for more threats.

"Could be you'll live to regret your choice, Mathus Conn," she said, her voice lethal-low as a copperhead sliding through autumn leaves.

"Could be," he agreed. "It wouldn't be the first time, and it likely won't be the last."

Wymie spun and walked toward the door. She didn't even seem to acknowledge the ragtag mob of a dozen or so followers who had trailed her inside. Wordlessly, they made way for her. Then, shuffling their feet without a backward glance at Conn or his people, they went out into the early night as well.

Nancy blew out a long breath.

"You may have stepped in it this time, Math."

"Mebbe so. But this time my gut agrees with my brain."

"These're your neighbors," Nancy said. "Our neighbors. Your customers. And people hereabouts are scared. Somethin' was spookin' them even before what happened to Wymie's poor sister. Somethin' needs to be done."

He allowed a hint of his irritation to show on his face.

"I'd expect you of all people to know, Nance," he said, "that somethin' done for the primary reason that 'somethin'' has to be, is only going to help by accident, and is more likely to do harm than good."

"Is doin' nothin' helpin'?" she asked.

"Yes," he said. "At least, helping more than joining a random lynch mob.

"That's like an old-time nuke. Once you let the mushroom cloud loose, it's triple hard to stuff it back in its shiny metal shell. And you never really know in advance which way the fallout will blow."

Chapter Eight

"Found somethin'," Lou said. Wymie thought he looked a bit green.

"What?" she said, starting forward.

He held up a hand. "Wait, Wymie. Uh, mebbe not you?"

She scowled at him, as much out of puzzlement as annoyance.

Dorden pushed past her in the grassy clearing, in a hollow that led down to karst flats. "Let me check it out," he said. "You just bide here a moment."

She didn't care for taking orders, least of all at the head of her own search party. But Vin Bertolli followed the stocky gunpowder-maker, looking unaccustomedly grim. Mance laid a hand on her shoulder, briefly, and followed.

She stood waiting. There was no overhead cover between her and the afternoon sun. She wished she had a hat. Flies buzzed lazily around. A sluggish breeze stirred the grass around the ankles of her jeans.

Her posse murmured uneasily to themselves, fondling their weapons and eyeing the trees around them. They didn't seem to include her—seemed at pains not to, which was fine by her. Even Wymie's helpers, it seemed, had a tendency to dilute her purpose.

She would not permit that. *Could* not. Vengeance for

Blinda wasn't just her mission. It was now her life, and she had consecrated herself to that vengeance in blood.

She realized a pair of turkey vultures were circling in a cloudless sky. Not quite overhead, but orbiting a point that looked mebbe fifty yards farther down the gentle slope, possibly out on the flats themselves.

Wish I had a wep, she thought. For the first time since her crusade began. Once she'd left her daddy's ax behind in the burning inferno of the home she'd been born into and grown up in, that had seemed superfluous. Her fury and hatred seemed weps themselves, and the group she had gathered around her—currently swollen to nineteen or twenty, seemingly by news of her group's latest encounter and her subsequent confrontation with Conn and Gaines—sufficient to make her passions real.

But now she felt helpless.

And even with so many followers, she didn't feel secure, waiting on the unknown but indubitably horrible like this and all. Mebbe I should get me a shotgun, she thought.

A few of her party drifted down the trail to disappear into head-high grass, spring green already starting to yellow as the heat turned into summer, where Dorden, Mance and the others had gone before. She made a growling sound deep in her throat and wiped sweat from her eyes. She was getting impatient.

Mance and Dorden came tramping back. Mance's face was as green as Lou's had been. The older man had a thunderous expression.

"I reckon you best come with us after all," Dorden said gruffly. "It's against my better judgment, frankly. But Mance here and the others insist you need to see."

She nodded and followed as they turned about and walked back.

Sure enough, the track led into tall grass sprouting on the flat land itself. She was warned by a sudden thickening in the buzz around her, and what she first thought were bees buzzing before her eyes. Then she realized they were bluebottle flies, fat and gleaming with carapaces like blue metal.

Then the smell hit her. She knew the smell of death; you didn't come up a country girl as she had, even in the peaceful backwater of the Pennyrile hill district, without getting to know that on an intimate basis. So she also knew too well how fast meat turned to reeking carrion in the humid heat of late spring. It was a constant problem in staying fed, how fast game spoiled.

But this death stink had an added edge of sweetness. She hadn't smelled it before, and somehow it made her guts turn over the way no half-rotted deer or rabbit carcass ever had.

Between that odd, never-known but familiar smell and the way the men in her party were acting, she knew roughly what she'd see before she stepped out into a wide spot in what had turned into a game trail through the grass and found herself confronting horror.

She almost stumbled on the first chill. It lay on its belly as if crawling toward the trail, right arm outstretched as if to plead for help. The bearded face, untouched except for smeared-on mud apparently from a brief midnight shower, was upturned. The gaping mouth and eyes showed unspeakable horror, agony and what Wymie had a crawling sensation was *disbelief*.

The back of the man's plain linen shirt had been torn

open. So had his back, so that blood soaked the fabric so completely its original color was impossible to guess at. Ribs had apparently been wrenched from his torso from behind, and half-chewed chunks of organ were scattered around the body, masked by writhing skins of flies.

The body ended at about the waist. A tail of two or three vertebrae, blood-dyed crimson, stuck out. A single purple-gray strand of intestine trailed over the ground for eight feet, to connect to the hips and what remained of the legs. The severed legs were, horrifically, front-upward. The canvas trousers had been clawed open, and the muscles torn to shreds and ripped out in chunks, presumably mouthfuls, exposing still red bone.

"Got another one over here," called Burny, who along with most of the rest of the search party had followed Wymie forward. "It was a woman. I…think."

"The two of them had a campfire here," Dorden called. Various items—torn-up bedrolls, a cast-iron cooking pot—lay strewed about. Whether by the brutal slaughter or from vandalism Wymie couldn't tell. "If there *were* just two of them."

He looked meaningfully at Lou. The scout-tracker shrugged.

"It's hard to say," he admitted. "There's mostly grass underfoot, springy enough not to take good tracks. And the bare dirt's been scuffed over by a power of feet. Some of 'em bare, that's as much as I can tell."

"It happened last night, to judge by the…state of decay," Dorden said.

Wymie nodded. Had the chills been there longer, the rotting process would have progressed further than it had.

So, last night, she thought. While I was urging Conn to act, and while he and that fat ass Tarley Gaines were refusing to face the truth that was as plain as the noses on their triple-stupe faces! A fuse lit inside her, and it was a fast one.

Mance gently took her arm. "You sure you're up to this, Wymie?"

She shook him off. "They're not my people," she said.

And then the fuse burned down. Rage blazed out of her, as hot as a fired kiln.

"Nuke take them!" she screamed.

Everybody jumped, weapons raised.

"The cannies?" Mance asked. "The—the outlanders, I mean?"

"Conn and his nuke-sucking wafflers! While they shilly-shallied around, those outland coldhearts were doing this. Eatin' people!"

"Any idea who the chills were?" Angus asked.

Lou shook his head. "Man don't look familiar. The woman—well, her own kin'd likely not recognize her."

"So were they outlanders, too?"

"They were innocent victims!" Wymie shouted. Why couldn't anybody see the plain truth? It made her want to explode.

"Sure, Wymie, sure," Mance said. "So, what do you want us to do?"

"Best bury these poor devils," Dorden said. "Don't want *other* animals buildin' up a taste for human flesh."

"We need to do whatever it takes to track these coldhearts down," she said icily. It wasn't that the fury was gone, exactly. It was more like it was suddenly channeled. "We need the manpower to do it with."

She looked around her search party. Her eye lit on Lem Sharkey, one of the new recruits to her searchers. He was skinny, restless, shorter than she was, with a stand-up shock of sandy hair and a bony face that was always clenched like a fist ready to hit. He had a reputation as a hothead, and was always ready for action. Especially when he had his younger brother, Ike, or one of his bigger cronies to back his play. Just the sort Wymie needed to rouse more of the local folk off their complacent fannies.

"Lem, take Ike and Gator with you and back to Sink-hole," she said, naming one of those cronies, Gator Mal-loan, who had come along with him on the search party. "Round us up some more warm bodies to hunt down these nuke-suckers. We can't let this happen again!"

"What about Conn?" Burny asked. "He won't like it one bit."

She felt her lips peel back from her teeth.

"Remind him what I said—that if he ain't with us, he's against us," she said. "Let him know double hard!"

"This isn't working," J.B. said. "It's not getting us anything but blisters on our feet, and worn to a nub."

Though the pale green sky still held light, the sun had set. The gloom already filled the spaces between the trees, so thick even J.B., not given to poetical flights, would swear he could almost touch it. But it should have been prime time for the task at hand.

Which was hunting cannie. They hadn't had a scrap of success since Jak had turned up the bolt-hole the day before.

Around them early crickets sawed away at the thick, dark air. They were in a patch of forest where the canopy of leaves was evidently thick enough to discourage much undergrowth from filling in the gaps between tree boles. Now it was only letting in the odd spike or sprinkle of the light from the full moon overhead.

"You're right," Ryan said.

He stood thirty feet ahead of J.B., holding his Steyr Scout Tactical longblaster angled muzzle-down in front of his hips. By habit on entering the relatively open area, they had spread into a loose V formation, with Ryan taking point, Krysty and Mildred on either side behind him, Doc and Ricky after them, and J.B. pulling drag. Ryan whistled softly.

After a moment Jak seemed to materialize out of the leaf and acorn duff almost at Ryan's right shoulder. Not even Ricky, whose eyes if not double strong were definitely skilled at watching, spotted him approach.

"Been following," Jak said. "Not now."

"Thought not," Ryan replied. "Crickets don't chirp when they're around."

"Why have they not attacked us?" Doc asked. "Abe Tomoyama told us that they launch serious attacks only after sundown."

"Why did they only make a serious play on us when we were at the dig site, anyway?" Ricky asked. He swatted at the back of his neck where a mosquito had likely targeted him for dinner. "That's what I want to know."

"What's the point of even talking about it?" Mildred asked.

"They're cannibals. If they're the people who killed that angry girl's sister. I know it wasn't us who bit her freaking face off, so the weird baboon-snouted white humanoid things seem like the best suspects."

"Which means they're bat-shit crazy. So why even try to figure out what makes them do what they do? Or don't do? What is even the point?"

"Wait," Krysty said, her brow furrowed in thought. "I think he's got something."

"I hope it's not catching," Mildred said. Jak laughed, once, briefly. J.B. knew he was best friends with the Armorer's young apprentice—they were by far the closest in age to each other. But that never seemed to stop the albino from enjoying the occasional joke at his buddy's expense.

"You're right, Krysty," Ryan said. "The one time they came after us with what seemed like serious intent was a couple days back, at the dig."

"So?" Mildred asked. She was hot, she was tired and she was grumpy.

"So mebbe," Krysty said patiently, "we need to be looking for them there."

"I admit to perplexity, dear lady," Doc said. "If we cannot find our quarry by hunting for them accurately, how might we find them by waiting passively at one point?"

"We'd get more digging done, anyway," Mildred said. "We're just getting down to where the good scavvy likely waits. We might as well go for that, instead of wearing ourselves out tramping up and down these bastard hills all day and night while the cannies laugh at us."

"Not just waiting," Ryan said. "Baiting."

Everybody looked at him, except Krysty, who was nodding with a slight smile. Even Ricky was coming up blank.

After a moment J.B. chuckled. "Dark night!" he said. "That might be our best trick, at that."

"So enlighten the slow section of the class," Mildred said.

"Out here roaming the woods—'tramping up and down the bastard hills,' and I quote—they either ignore us or shadow us for a spell and then go off to wherever it is they go," Ryan said.

J.B. knew that Jak was frustrated at not having been able to turn up a hint as to where that was, although *underground* seemed the most likely bet. Unless they took to the trees.

"The once place we know they came after us hard was the dig. So let's spend a day or two there and see if we can lure one close enough to grab us a chill after we blast them."

"While that might well work," Mildred admitted, "I'm not really keen on us just putting ourselves dead in the X-ring as targets for these white-haired freaks. Uh, no offense, Jak."

"Not mutie," Jak said. "Not cannie, neither."

"Point taken," Mildred said.

"I'm not in love with that part, either," Ryan said. "You got a better idea, Mildred? The night is young, so there's a lot of darkness left if you love walking up and down hills so nuking much."

"You know what?" Mildred asked. "I love this plan. Let's go back and sit in the dig pit and paint big red targets on our foreheads."

"Don't reckon we need to go that far, Mildred," J.B. said.

She looked at him intently.

"What?" he asked.

MATHUS CONN HAD just awakened from a sound sleep when he heard shouting from the taproom.

His room lay to the east of the bar, on the right as a person came in the door. That wing was the shorter, with the slut cribs and guest rooms to the west, and the kitchens and storage rooms on the north side. The only other occupants of the short hallway were his chief aide and cousin, Nancy, and his bouncers, currently Tony and Chad.

It was male voices doing the hollering. He didn't recognize them right away. From the light seeping in through drawn scavvied venetian blinds, it had to be late afternoon.

Time I was getting up and getting to work anyway, he thought. Normally he'd leave the matter to Nancy and the bouncers. It was their job; and loudly irate customers weren't exactly rare in Stenson's Creek. He rose, pulled on his clothes and shoes, and padded out the door.

He was yawning as he turned into the short corridor, shutting the door behind him and locking it with his key.

The shouting continued and got louder as he approached the open entryway to the central room. He recognized the main shouter, and scowled.

"Lem Sharkey," he said, striding through the entry, "I thought I told you you weren't welcome here anymore."

Then he stopped.

The tableau in his barroom burned itself indelibly into his mind, and flooded his gut like acid. On his right, Nancy and his two bouncers stood in front of the bar with their hands held up by their shoulders, palms forward. Arranged facing them from ten feet away in a rough semicircle were Lem, his younger, stockier brother, Ike, and his rad-scum pals Tupa and Gator. Ike carried an ax handle. Gator held an actual ax. Tupa stood, turning a big beer stein he'd picked up off a table over and over in hands that made it seem teacup-sized as if he'd never seen one before.

Lem was holding a double-barrel black-powder shotgun by his hip, the hammers pulled pack and the muzzles pointing toward Conn's people.

Chapter Nine

"Yeah," Lem said, sneering. "Don't sound so nukin' high and mighty now, do you, Mr. Conn? Don't try no shit with me, or I let 'em have it!"

"What do you actually want?" Conn asked. Despite the circumstances, he made no effort to keep his annoyance out of his voice. He knew the wiry, wound-tight youngster could be volatile—that was why he'd been banned in the first place. But Conn suspected *submission* would have the same effect on him as a jolt on a jolt-walker.

"Wymie sent us to take care of you," Gator said, showing some of his too-many, too-jagged teeth in a smirk.

"'Take care' of us?" Conn demanded. "What in the name of glowin' nuke shit is that supposed to mean?"

"You been shelterin' them murderin' coldheart outlanders," Lem said. "We're here to stop that. One way or another."

"What does that mean?" Nancy asked.

Conn's jaw tightened. She didn't suffer fools gladly, and apparently the fact one had a scattergun pointed at her vitals only made her less inclined to suffer him.

"Time to get with the program," Gator said. "Stop gettin' in our way."

"I'm not in your way," Conn stated, in as patient and calm a tone as he could muster. He didn't try sidling toward the front door, not edging back the way he'd come, even though he had a Winchester carbine loaded and waiting in his room, for serious emergencies. Lem gripped that blaster so hard it quivered like a leaf in a hailstorm. The slightest extra pressure would set it off for sure.

"Not in Wymie's way, either. I just haven't agreed to go along with her."

He noticed Tupa was screwing up his enormous face in a funny way. Tough guy though he was—lead rival to Potar Baggart, both as ville bully and at the limestone quarry where both of them worked—he was prone to allergies. And in a place like Sinkhole and its environs, this time of year something was always blooming. Under the circumstances it registered on Conn as nothing more than a minor, passing detail.

"She said, you're with us or against us!" Lem barked. "You don't join up, you're standin' in our way!"

"Here, now," Conn said, "that's no-how reasonable. How does it matter a whit whether I—"

Tupa sneezed.

Lem jumped and jerked. His reflex action yanked the twin barrels of his blaster up and to his left. At the same time his finger tightened convulsively on the trigger. The scattergun went off with a head-shattering roar, blasting both its charges into Conn's ceiling.

Lem fell right straight on his skinny rear end.

Nancy started to dive behind the bar. Conn knew at once she was going for the 10-gauge scattergun, likewise double-barrel, Conn kept there.

"Nancy, no!" he shouted. His own reflex was—now that Lem's once triple-lethal blaster was no more than a not very effective club—to try to defuse the situation.

Talk everyone down and ease these bad boys out of here with nothing more getting broken.

Apparently Ike realized what she was doing, as well. He lunged for Conn's assistant, grabbed the back of her shirt and flung her back bodily toward the center of the room. At the same time Gator swung his ax in a whistling horizontal arc, stopping both Chad and Tony, who'd started to make their own moves, dead in their tracks.

Flailing her arms for balance, Nancy teetered in a half circle. It brought her almost face-to-face with the looming Tupa.

He was rubbing his nose with the back of his left hand. With his right he backhanded the woman across the face with the stoneware stein, almost casually.

Her head whipped around with unnatural speed. She fell straight to the floor in a loose-limbed, random heap.

For a moment everybody froze in place: Lem, still clutching his empty blaster, halfway through scrambling back to his feet; Gator and the two bouncers he was menacing with his ax; Ike standing big-eyed by the bar with his ax handle in his hand. And most of all, Tupa staring blankly down at the body sprawled by his booted feet.

Mathus Conn didn't know why it had happened, but he knew what had happened.

"You fat coldheart bastard!" he shouted. "You chilled her!" And just like that, abandoning years of carefully maintained level-headed self-control, he launched himself at the big quarryman.

Still clearly stunned by the results of his blow, Tupa just managed to get his hands up to fend off Conn. The gaudy owner had been a brawler of sorts in his time, and a noted wrestler in friendly contests, and some not-so-friendly ones. But it had been years since he had practiced any of those skills. He found a calm manner and polite yet businesslike speech, combined with a willingness to pay fair value for what he got, tended to get him anything he really wanted with much less wear and tear than *fighting* did.

But now he had lost control. He flailed his arms. A forearm caught Tupa across the nose. Conn felt it break, just as he was starting to come out of his fury-fugue.

Roaring, Tupa slammed his cannonball dome forward and head butted his attacker. Conn's skull filled with sudden swirling darkness, shot through with lightning. He dropped, stunned.

Through eyes that had gone blurry except for a circle of clarity in the center of his vision, he saw Chad and Tony spring forward at the four invaders. Through the roaring in his ears, he heard one of the bouncers bellowing anger.

As if it were happening to someone else, somewhere in the middle distance, Conn saw Gator slam his ax down into the front of blond Chad's chest, just to the right of his neck. The burly bouncer sank to his knees with a groan. Blood fountained, splashing across Gator's shirt and lumpy face.

Tony got close enough to Tupa to rock his head back with an overhand right. Tupa lashed out with the mug with which he'd inadvertently chilled Nancy. Ike landed on Tony's back. He tried to grapple with the black bouncer, hampered by the ax handle he was still holding in one hand. He seemed as if he'd forgotten all about it.

Tupa brought his ham-hock-sized left hand up in an uppercut into Tony's downturned face. The bouncer's knees bucked. He toppled backward onto his ass on the floor. Ike scrambled to jump free.

Off to one side, Conn became aware of Lem Sharkey sitting up with his shotgun cracked open. He was muttering to himself as he fumbled in his pockets, apparently for fresh shells to load into the wep.

Tupa, his brown eyes bloodshot, wagged his head from side to side like a bull cornered by a pack of wolves. He noticed Conn lying almost at his feet, still dazed. He reached down, grabbed a handful of the front of Conn's shirt, and hauled him up bodily back to his feet as if he weighed no more than a rag doll.

"Wait," Conn tried to say, "can't we talk about it?" But a fist like a dark moon eclipsed his vision and slammed into his face. It struck just a glancing blow, but it was enough to send fresh sparks shooting behind Conn's eyes, and his stomach sloshing to a fresh wave of nausea.

Suddenly an arm like a pale tree trunk coiled around Tupa's enormous neck from behind. The huge fist cocked back for a second try at caving in Conn's face instead grabbed for the forearm. The other let go of Conn's shirt and dropped him back to the floor.

The sharp crack on his tailbone roused Conn from his fog. A second hand, no smaller than Tupa's own, appeared around the round head from the other side, grasped the man's jaw and yanked it hard to the left.

The bull neck snapped with the sound of a dry hickory branch broken over someone's knee.

The smell of fresh, wet shit hit Conn like another, invisible fist as the huge man's bowels voided. The arm released his neck. He slumped into an oddly shapeless heap.

"That'll teach you, you taint," Potar Baggart snarled. "Where you get off, laying hands on Mr. Conn?"

Mathus Conn was more astonished than relieved, but

as his scattered wits pulled themselves back together, he realized Lem Sharkey was crawling, open-breeched blaster in hand, across the floor toward a pair of brown waxed-paper/black-powder shotgun shells that had rolled away from him.

Urgency filled the gaudy owner. He rolled onto his own hands and knees. As he did, his vision swept the sprawled body of his assistant.

Her blue eyes were open, and staring right into his. *Nancy…*

Through his mind flashed an image of them standing by a stream—Stenson's Creek—when she was eight and he was mebbe ten, watching her swing back and forth on a sling made from a length of scrap deer hide from her father's tannery, watching her long blond hair stream out behind her as she flew against the clear sky, to splash down into the brown-green water. How the droplets turned into a spray of tiny rainbows…

Then he saw Chad, still on his knees, with the ax embedded in his shoulder, clutching at it with his right hand. His square-jawed jock face slumped forward, eyes wide and blanked with pain. The skin had grayed and hung on his face like an old man's.

No blood on his mouth, the cooler part of Conn's mind said. No froth from his nostrils. Lung isn't hit. Likely he'll live.

But he didn't indulge himself wallowing in that thought, either. He scrambled toward the gap past the end of the hickory bar that led to the doors to the kitchen annex out back—and to the back of the bar. As he moved, he willed himself to push up off the floor. His brain was still spinning, his stomach seethed with nausea, and his limbs seemed made of lead and connected loosely with wet bar rags.

But though he was no man of action, Conn had dedicated his whole life to doing what needed to be done. And now, despite the unlikely and timely intervention of Conn's near-nemesis, Potar Baggart, in taking down the monstrous attacker, the odds were nowhere near even yet. He knew they were fixing to get worse once that little snake Lem got his scattergun recharged.

As he ran, more or less, in a bent-over wobbling rush, he saw Ike Sharkey straddling a supine Tony, pummeling his face, while Gator whacked at his arms and legs with his ax handle. The second Sharkey brother was clearly looking for a shot at the bouncer's head. Conn knew such a hit from a hardened hickory club like that could prove just as lethal as a blow from the head of a full-on ax. But Gator's flying if inexpertly targeted fists were getting in his way.

Like a granite boulder falling from its ancient perch and starting to roll downhill, Potar moved forward. Like the boulder he resembled, he gathered momentum as he went. Conn saw him as he caught himself, just on the verge of pitching back onto his face, on the end of the bar.

As he thrust himself upright, biting down hard against a columnar rush of sour vomit, and turned around behind the long counter, Conn saw Potar catch the younger Sharkey with a mighty booted running kick in the small of the back. Bones snapped. With a wail of agony, surprise and what sounded like frustration, Ike was flung right off Tony and hurled against the bar.

Conn was a man on a mission. On the barroom floor Lem clapped his hand over the rolling double O shotshells. Trapping them with his palm and triumphantly scooping them up, he reared up on his haunches and stuffed them right into the yawning breeches of his piece.

Gator swung his ax handle frantically at the charging Potar's red-moon face. The enraged man raised a forearm like a senior branch of the tree the ax handle had been cut from, and like a thick oak branch, it snapped the hard, seasoned wood right across it.

Gator screamed as if it had been his own ulna and radius Potar had snapped.

"Gotcha!" Lem howled. He closed the barrels of his blaster with a snap, then raised his head to target Potar's vast back. The shotgun's sawed-off barrels came up.

Conn's double-barrel shotgun was full-length, which made it harder to wield, but also made it marginally less likely to blast bystanding customers with incidental .33-caliber pellets. It was bad for business to put holes in hides that *didn't* deserve it.

His target did. He snugged the steel buttplate against his right shoulder and squeezed the double triggers hard.

The flames that erupted from the 10-gauge tubes were yellow and dazzling in the gloom of the gaudy house, deepened by the greenish cloud of smoke from Lem's earlier, missed shots, settling back down from the rafters as they cooled. A fresh billow of smoke gouted out with the fire.

But neither flash, nor smoke, nor the recoil that kicked the big blaster upward despite its heavy barrel prevented Conn from seeing the double column of shot hit Lem full in the middle of his skinny face.

The heavy spherical double O pellets pulverized the young man's cheekbones and blasted through into the brainpan beyond. Conn actually saw Lem's look of gloat-ing triumph turning to horrified surprise, his features collapsing in on themselves like water down a drain with the plug fresh-pulled. His whole head expanded and distorted like an elk bladder inflating on a blacksmith's bellows.

Lem's blaster dropped from suddenly lifeless fingers, unfired. As the powerful recoil from the double discharge kicked Conn's barrel toward the ceiling, the gaudy owner saw the young man simply fold back over his lower legs where he knelt on them.

Potar had grabbed Gator by the front of the shirt, shaken him like a terrier with a big brown rat, and now was slamming his body again and again against the floorboards, roaring in word-defying rage as he did so.

Conn slumped forward onto his bar. He felt suddenly drained. The nausea in his stomach and weakness in his knees was subsiding, but now he felt a pounding headache coming on.

None of that stopped him from cracking open the breech of his shotgun barrels and fumbling out a pair of fresh shells from the cubby under the counter to reload the weapon. Business was business, after all, and there was nothing more businesslike than a blaster reloaded and ready for action.

"I think you can stop now, Potar," he said to the angry man, who was still whaling on Conn's floor with Gator's totally limp body. "I'm pretty sure he's chilled now."

Potar had such a head of steam worked up that he pounded the young man against the planking three more times before he stopped, straightened and looked down at what he was holding in his hand. Gator lay completely sprawled downward from his massive grip: head, hands, legs. Even his body hung in a backward bow as if some of the key structural bones were busted all to nuke.

"Huh," he said, panting a bit but in a normal tone. "I guess he is."

He dropped him. The body thumped, flopped, lay still. Conn saw the dark eyes rolled up in their sockets.

Leaving the reloaded and relocked blaster on the bar, he forced himself up. It took all his strength of will as well as body. He wanted nothing on this Earth so much as to just slump down to the floor, curl up in a ball and sleep.

But now was not the time for that. There was business to attend to.

Though both his eyes were blacked, the bruises already purple against his dark skin, and his right cheek was puffing out all swollen, Tony knelt beside Chad. He murmured, "You're gonna be all right, man. You're gonna be all right."

Walking like a reanimated chill, and feeling about as poorly, Conn teetered out around the bar. Even though Tony looked none too steady, he put a hand to the bouncer's rock-solid shoulder to help him hunker down next to him.

"Right," he said. He cupped Chad's chin with his hand and raised his head.

"Sorry...boss..." the bouncer said.

"No problem, son." He braced on Tony and pushed himself back up. It was hard going.

Potar stepped up, gripped him by the arm with surprising gentleness and hoisted him back to his feet as if he were ten years old again.

"Thanks," he said. "For everythin'. Tony, I need you to run into town and round up some help. Tell I'm payin'."

"But Chad—"

"Is beyond our helpin', I calculate. Fetch Granny Weatherwax. She's the best healer in the western Penny-rile. She can set a bone with the best of them, too—even a collarbone. Along with all her herb-lore and such. Make sure she brings her special moss to pack the wound."

For a moment Tony just stared at his boss. His face was ashen where it wasn't bluish-purple—and now starting to show the yellow and green of serious bad bruising.

"Pupils the same size," Conn remarked. "Likely not concussed. You up to it?"

After a moment Tony nodded, then stood up.

Conn looked at Potar. The big man had let his arm go, but still stood close by, poised to grab the gaudy owner if he toppled.

"It's lucky you happened by," Conn said. It turned into a croak. His throat was suddenly dry. "When you did and all."

Potar nodded. Then he looked Conn, a strange gleam in his eyes.

Almost as if he, too, were calculating.

"Reckon you owe me now, boss," he said with a grin.

Conn stared back at him a minute, just long enough to see doubt appear in his blue boar-hog eyes.

Then he nodded. "Reckon I do," he said, deliberately. "And you're a smarter man than ever I reckoned. I can use that."

"Meanin'?"

"Take it…out," Chad suddenly said. "Please?" He clutched the handle of the ax right above the head with both hands, as if he cherished it and didn't want to let it go. "It hurts."

"Shouldn't we take it out?" Tony asked.

"No." Conn shook his head. "Leave it. We'll bind it up first."

"You sure that's the right thing?"

"No. I'm not the healer. But I do know he's not bleedin' out as double fast as he was, and I suspect if we yank that thing free, he'll start right in again."

A scream came from the door. Tony and Conn jerked. Potar turned his massive head with equally massive deliberation.

Mrs. Haymuss stood just inside the front door, with a couple of kitchen helpers also coming on shift with her, and her hands pressed to her plump cheeks.

"¡Dios mío!" she exclaimed. "What has happened? Senorita Nancy!"

"Dead," Conn said grimly. "These bastards murdered her."

He staggered around the bar, bracing himself with his hands.

His foot nudged something soft right in front of it. It stirred and moaned.

"Help…me," Ike muttered.

Conn picked up the shotgun by the long twin barrels. They had cooled down enough to touch now. Without even glancing at the man, he slammed the buttplate down, hard.

He felt and heard the satisfying crunch of cartilage as Ike's Adam's apple imploded. He commenced to thrash and make strangling sounds.

Still not looking down, Conn replaced the blaster on the bar. His eye fell on his cousin's huddled form.

That one's for you, Nance, he thought. I'll do my grieving later. Right now there's much to be done.

"Tell you what," Conn said. "Carlos, you run and fetch

Granny Weatherwax the healer. You run faster than Tony at the best of times, and he's none too steady on his pins right now."

He filled in the same instructions he'd given the battered bouncer. The slightly taller and darker of Mrs. Haymuss's helpers nodded and dashed out the door.

"Mrs. Haymuss, you and Marky help Tony bind that ax where it is so poor Chad doesn't have to hold it in his own chest until help gets here, if you please. Then have a look at Tony. He's not exactly doing well himself."

"Of course, Mr. Conn," the sturdy woman said. She waded right in. She was as businesslike as he was, in her own way, and since she did the hog-butchering and other such chores as needed, she wasn't one to let squeamishness get in her way.

"What about me, Mr. Conn?" Potar asked.

"You're hired, if you want on."

"I do!"

"Ace."

"What do you want me to do, then?"

Conn looked over his two bouncers. "Gonna need some more muscle," he said.

And an upgrade, he added mentally. He didn't say it out loud. No need to be unkind to his help, especially one who'd taken an ax in the collarbone, and another who'd been beaten lopsided with an ax handle, leaping to his defense. He'd see Tony and Chad done right by no matter what. That was his way.

But his mind, always planning, always reckoning, had shifted into overdrive.

"What now?" Potar asked.

Conn sighed.

"Get this mess cleaned up," he said. "Get Coffin-

Maker Sam rounded up and taking care of poor Nancy. This other trash, too, I suppose, if their kin want to pay for them. Far as I'm concerned, they can go to the ville dump.

"And then, I think, we need to hunt up Wymie Berdone and have a little talk with her."

Potar smiled. It wasn't a pleasant sight. Except to Mathus Conn, under the circumstances, it sort of was. He was starting to see the form their...working relationship was likely to take.

"You gonna settle with her?" the huge man asked.

"Not exactly. I'm goin' to join up with her. On my terms."

"Wait, boss," Chad croaked. Mrs. Haymuss had made him lie back down on the floor while she and her assistant tied the ax in place with some kitchen rags. It wasn't the most sanitary arrangement, and Chad was making some noise at the necessary way they had to lift and shift him to get the thing bound in place to await the healer. But it was all going to have to do.

"You can't mean that! Not after she sent these fu— Sent these coldhearts after us!"

"I don't rightly think she did, Tony. I think young Mr. Sharkey, here—"

He glanced at the former ringleader, who still lay folded back where he was. His face looked like a punched-in and half-deflated predark soccer ball that somebody had splashed with about a bucket of red paint.

"I think he kind of took the bit in his teeth. He was always looking to start trouble, preferably the sort where he got to hurt people. I think she gave him some instructions that he interpreted in accordance with his desires."

Tony blinked at him. The bouncer was not normally a

feeb—brighter than poor Chad, in any event. But *events* had clouded his wits, somewhat, for which Conn couldn't rightly blame him.

"Events have happened that we've got to deal with. I prefer to do what I can to see that minimum damage is done to you, to Sinkhole and to me. And if I stay in opposition to Wymie—triple crazy as I think she and her scheme are—I'm not going to be in a position to do any of that."

"But you don't mean to take orders from her," Potar said. It wasn't a question.

Conn smiled and patted the younger man's muscle- and fat-packed cheek.

"I knew you were smart, Potar."

Chapter Ten

From the bushes that fringed the top of the dig-site pit came the tweeting call of an eastern whip-poor-will. Ryan knew it was Jak.

The crickets had stopped, and so had the tree frogs. Only the rustle of breeze in the branches broke the dead-heavy stillness. And that piping cry again.

"Here we go," J.B. murmured.

"Eyes skinned, everybody," Ryan said out of the side of his mouth. He kept digging beside the entry hole to the buried facility. "Blasters down, but grab them when I say."

It was past dark. The six of them labored on—or pretended to—by the pungent, resinous, black-thready smoke and yellow flickering glow of pinewood torches.

Ryan had chosen to size up their unknown foe as being essentially like stickies: sometimes they acted as if they were no more than clever animals. Sometimes they acted people-smart. In the case of the rubbery-skinned muties, it seemed to vary according to tribe. With these white-haired cannies, they just didn't have enough hard facts to judge. So he assumed the worst—full human intelligence—without getting welded to the notion.

But now they had come, and Jak had spotted them.

Now if only they don't spot him, Ryan thought.

As he pitched a shovelful of yellow earth from one

place to another, Ryan kept his lone eye in soft focus, to maximize the acuity of his peripheral vision. After a moment, he saw a branch twitch up to his right.

"Wait for it," he said, barely moving his lips as he tossed away another scoop of dirt.

"I didn't think they'd come after us so quick," Mildred said beneath her voice from somewhere behind him. "First night we try—"

"Shut it," Ryan said quietly, but not whispering. He knew that a whisper carried better than soft words— and also generated a hint of *suspicion*. He didn't know whether the coamers—might as well call them that if anything—knew human speech, or if they did, if it was even English, but he was assuming worst-case scenario here.

He stuck the shovel into loose dirt to one side, turned toward a rude table they'd made with a scavvied door and a couple chunks of concrete, picked up a canteen with his left hand and drank. His longblaster, like Ricky's carbine and J.B.'s scattergun, were propped against it. The Armorer's Uzi lay on the table.

They all wore their sidearms, and if close work suddenly became necessary, Ryan had his panga, too, in its holster offsetting his SIG. He reckoned he could do some good work with the shovel, if it came to that.

Around him the others acted as if they were knocking off for a quick break themselves. Straightening, they wiped their faces, looking as if they hadn't a care in the world.

From somewhere above them came a strange scream, an inhuman ululation, rising, falling, like a hand-cranked siren.

Working hard not to show it, Ryan braced for the inevitable hailstorm of rocks and branches.

Instead, what burst from the top of the pit all around them was a wave of screaming, white, red-eyed bodies.

WATCHING HIS BROTHER-COUSIN Vurl smear grits and mashed peas in his thinning hair, Buffort Sumz remembered what he really loved about family dinner at home: he wasn't the dumb one at the table.

Poor triple-stupe Vurl was older than him by all thirteen fingers on Vurl's hands.

"This possum sure is good," Yoostas Sumz said, sucking the meat off a boiled foot.

"Well, it's been gettin' fat off eatin' our slops and garbage," said Paw-Paw, who was named that to be funny in the family because he was his own stepdad. "So we's just gettin' our own back, is why it tastes so good!"

Buffort laughed until tears ran down his cheeks and pounded his fist on the table until Sister-Maw told him to knock it off on account of he was rattling the tableware and threatening to spill everybody's homemade Towse lightning. But it was triple funny! Even Vurl laughed, after looking around blankly with a sprig of boiled collard green trailing down his bulging forehead for a full minute.

He was comfortable with the smells of home: wood smoke, familial sweat, food boiling on the stove. And the pigs, dogs and chickens that jostled and brawled and squalled between the legs of the diners at the big central table, and by the various other tables dotted around the big common room of the sprawled main house, hunting for discarded bones and such. But not many scraps, because very little escaped the voracious appetites of Buffort's family, of which there were many more than he could count.

Of course, Yoostas liked to point out that didn't take a double-large family. Buffort loved his brother, but sometimes he hated that the smaller man was so fast and shifty, and could use those traits to elude the head-thumpings he earned from Buffort. Most of the time.

"Betty Jo," Paw-Paw said, ladling up some boiled possum into a wooden bowl, "give Grammaw Allis her share."

A pudgy pigtailed black-haired girl nodded and carried the steaming food to the shriveled old woman who sat bent all over in a corner by herself, singing an endless song without words or notable tune.

"That constant noise drives me crazy," said Buffort's Aunt-Sis Sallee. "We should feed her to the hogs and be done with it."

"Here, now, Sallee," Paw-Paw said indulgently. "She's family, and one of the better lays I've ever had, in her day. We should at least wait until she gets sick or breaks somethin'. That'd be the charitable thing."

"Gertie-May!" Sister-Maw exclaimed, turning back from the stove where she was stirring a kettle of grits with a long wooden spoon. She was a sturdy woman wearing a dress that seemed sewed together entirely of patches, and a grimy apron on which squiggles had been hand-embroidered, years before. Yoostas, who could read some, said they spelled out "Worldz Best Cuk." Buffort didn't know whether the little weasel was funning him or not.

"You stop diddlin' your brother underneath the dinin' table! What will the neighbors say?"

Bobby-Joan, who was a ragged-haired blonde girl,

hooted laughter. "Black dust, Aunt Momma, they all know she'll do anythin' with any boy from miles 'round!"

"Nevertheless." Sister-Maw turned back to the hot stove shaking her heavy, gray-bunned head. "Folks'll think we're no better than muties."

"What's that?"

It was Johnny-Blue, one of Buffort's more distant cousin-brothers, not much younger than him or Yoostas but a half-pint even compared to the redheaded wiseass. He was skinny and had a shock of jet-black hair that fell over big black eyes. He had an eerie touch to him, and no lie. But he also had the keenest senses in the whole extended clan. That mebbe came from his mother, Buffort thought, an outland woman from the flats clear over to the hollow. She had sadly not been smart in the ways of the wood, and got killed by a bear before Buffort could even get a crack at her.

"Don't you go rilin' up your brother and sister cousins with none of your nonsense," Sister-Maw said.

But Yoostas had stiffened with his spoon halfway to his mouth. Laying it back on his tin plate, he sat up straight in his chair. "Crickets stopped," he said. "Is that what you heard?"

"Part," the black-haired boy replied.

Somebody screamed. It came from outside the big house, clearly.

A couple of the diners jumped to their feet. Paw-Paw reacted more deliberately, taking off the greasy napkin he had tucked under his multiple chins like a bib. It wasn't as if it did him much good, anyway. As much grub wound up on the front of his shirt or in his lap as on the napkin anyhow.

"Easy, now," he said. "It's probably nothin'. If there was trouble about, them hound dogs'd start barkin' up a storm."

The hound dogs, penned over by the barn for their supper, commenced to barking up a storm.

"Well, now," Paw-Paw said, pushing back from the table. "Ain't that a thing?"

As quick as it had begun, the barking stopped. A lone dog voice rose in a sudden shrill series of yips, then it cut off.

Paw-Paw stood up ponderously. Bits of food cascaded off his swinging gut. Chickens crowded around his feet and began pecking furiously at them.

"Somethin' on the roof," Yoostas said.

Buffort heard it too, a shuffling *thump, thump, thump*, with a sort of scratching to back it up.

"It's nothin'," Aunt-Sis Sallee scoffed. "Just a big old 'coon up on the roof."

Johnny-Blue sat staring straight ahead, his scrawny face set in concentration. "Double big for a 'coon," he said. "Too big."

It sounded then to Buffort as if a second set of feet had joined the first, climbing uninvited onto the roof. Paw-Paw turned and picked up the old muzzle-loader shotgun he kept leaning by the back door.

"Time to go see what's what," he said. "Mebbe we'll have more meat for the pot soon, huh?"

A rain of small dust particles began to fall on the table.

Buffort looked up. Larger flakes of crud started coming down from between the greasy, smoke-stained rafters. One landed in his left eye. He cussed out loud, looked downward and commenced to try to get it out.

"Don't go rubbin' at your triple-stupe eye, Buffort," Sister-Maw scolded.

Then the ceiling fell in.

FOR JUST THE thinnest-shaved sliver of an instant, Ryan froze.

Naked bodies erupted from the scrub all around the rim of the dig site.

He recovered fast though. "Fire them up!" he shouted, drawing his SIG Sauer P226 as the white bodies slid down the sides of the pit, raising wakes of earth from their bare feet.

Ryan flung out his arm to full extension, the front sight lined up on a naked sternum. He squeezed the trigger. The handblaster bucked and boomed.

The figure fell to the ground, its feet flying up in the air, and skidded several feet down.

So many, so fast, Ryan thought. He hadn't expected the pale shadows to attack in such numbers.

"Thin them out!" J.B. called. He grabbed his Uzi from the table and, holding the machine pistol in one fist, swung it left to right, pumping the trigger to rip the closing circle of white cannie bodies with short pulses of full-metal-jacket slugs.

Ryan saw cannies go down, blood spraying from sudden holes. Behind him, he heard the snarl of Krysty's Glock 18C handblaster firing on full auto in the other direction from J.B.

At least three had fallen in Ryan's limited field of vision, perhaps four, squalling and thrashing and tripping the others. But the full-auto blasterfire didn't break the white-skinned charge.

It did slow it up a step, though, enough so that the unexpected coamer-wave attack didn't simply swamp the companions grouped by the entrance to the scavvy site.

Instantly, anyway.

Ryan blasted another mutie between small but flat and flopping breasts—a woman, if such a term was applicable. She screeched and gurgled and fell on her back, dirty claw-toed feet kicking air not four feet from Ryan.

He yanked out his panga with his left hand and thrust it straight out in front of him. Its broad tip rammed through the sternum of another cannie, this one male, with a sound like rotting floorboards giving way underfoot.

Even as Ryan committed himself to the thrust, another coamer darted howling between him and J.B., who was in the process of letting his Uzi, its magazine exhausted, fall to the end of its sling so that he could grab up the shotgun leaned against the table. There was nothing between the creature and Krysty's unprotected back.

And there was nothing that Ryan could do about it.

Chapter Eleven

In times of stress a human tended to do that to which he or she was most accustomed.

During her predark life, Mildred had spent hundreds of hours practicing to acquire the skill necessary to become a member of the U.S. Olympic shooting team. That included turning her right side toward her target, placing her left hand on her hip, extending her pistol to arm's full length, taking deliberate aim and carefully squeezing the trigger.

But sometimes the stress was so great you just had to say to hell with that.

With monsters with chalk-white skins, yellow fangs protruding from wide-open, shockingly doglike jaws, and eyes the color of fresh blood racing balls-out toward her and her friends, she didn't have the inclination to engage in the niceties of the Olympic firing line. She took her usual two-handed grip on her Czech-made ZKR 551 target revolver, but she took aim fast, and squeezed off shots as quickly as she could the millisecond the blocky front sight post lined up something paper white.

Mildred got off six shots in a handful of seconds. She was sure she hit at least three of the devils, possibly four, but she could only be sure she saw two go down. There was no time to confirm any of it, no attention to spare. The way the albino chillers leaped and skidded and cavorted down the loose-dirt slope meant she knew for a fact she'd dropped the hammer with only empty air in front of the blaster's muzzle at least twice.

The cylinder empty, she tipped the barrel up while releasing the catch that allowed the cylinder to fall out to the side. Spent .38 Special cases cascaded out, smudged with powder burns and stinking with the salty odor of burned propellant. To her right Krysty had emptied her own extended magazine, and dropped the empty out of the well of her handblaster even as her left hand snagged a fresh mag from a back pocket of her faded jeans.

Naturally Mildred was already reaching to her own pocket for a speed-loader containing six nice, new cartridges. Or at least unfired ones. But then she realized something that made her blood run cold.

The damned things were on them *right now*. If she tried to reload, fast and expert as she was, the cannies would be clawing at her with their long hooked fingernails or biting her face off the way they had that poor child's.

As the horrified thought flashed through her mind in the fraction of a second, she made a decision that ran contrary to all of Ryan and J.B.'s preaching as well as her own well-schooled habit. She rolled her wrist clockwise, causing the cylinder to fall closed and snap back into place, and then shoved her blaster hurriedly back into her holster without trying to reload it.

The hand that would have been fishing out the reloads, the left, was already reaching blindly for the table behind her. As she holstered her revolver, she turned to look where she was grabbing—and saw one of the cannies, buck naked, hair flying and cock and balls just swinging wildly between skinny pallid thighs, elude both J.B. and Ryan and race right for Krysty's back.

Mildred's hand found what it was reaching for: the handle of a pick propped against the makeshift table on this side of the entrance to the dig. She yanked up the heavy tool with fear-crazed strength, cocked it back over her shoulder and only when she launched it in a blurring arc got her other hand onto the hardwood haft.

She didn't have much experience swinging a pickax against a moving target. She wasn't sure *anybody* did, even these days when murder was the number-one sport.

But with fiendish satisfaction she saw the heavy, downward-curved tine of the pick stab through the matted hair right above the charging cannie's forehead. The creature's hands, raised to grab and rend, flailed wildly as random electrochemical impulses blasted through its brain.

Momentum carried it forward. Its convulsing put it onto the ground right beside Mildred's left boot. Unwilling to let go of the haft, Mildred found her arms cruelly wound around into an unnatural position.

As she tried frantically to turn the right way to untangle herself, she saw a pair of cannies closing in fast on Krysty, with a third behind. The redhead was still going for the reload. She wasn't going to get it done in time to keep the horrors from closing in on her.

"Krysty, *shovel*!" Mildred cried.

Without hesitation, Krysty stuffed the magazine into the well, thumb-clicked to let the heavy steel slide drive home, jamming a fresh cartridge into the breech—and then stuck the blaster into her waistband and front-kicked the cannie that was almost on top of her.

The creature squawked and staggered back into the

arms of the one behind it. The other cannie dodged around the pair. With balletic grace Krysty pivoted and picked up the shovel she had stuck in the dirt when the creatures attacked. She spun back the other way, swinging the implement two-handed at waist level.

The cannie that was almost on top of her somehow managed to dance back out of the way of the whistling stroke. Krysty stepped into it and pistoned the end of the shovel handle into its sternum. It uttered a croaking sound and fell onto the pair behind it even as they untangled themselves.

Meanwhile, with a heave of frantic effort, Mildred jerked the pick free of the cannie's skull. It was still twitching unnervingly against her calf, but she reckoned she could count it out of the fight. Choking up on the ax handle with her right hand, she thrust its head into the wide-open, yellow-fawned mouth of a cannie.

Teeth splintered loudly. Too much blood erupted then for Mildred to make out any more details of the damage done, but since the thing went down holding its face and gurgling and choking on its own blood, she liked the result.

Her triumph was short-lived.

They were all around her.

SWUNG SIDEWAYS, HELD so that it presented a sort of wooden blade, the stock of Ricky's DeLisle carbine made a most satisfactory sound as it crunched in the left side of a loping cannie's skull. He felt blood droplets hot against his cheek, chin and lower lip.

It grossed him out less than the saliva that had been projected there moments before by the thing's panting breath.

He barely remembered scrambling up here to the tricky, loose-earth slope above the hole to the buried office, or whatever it was they'd been excavating. That was the obvious weak point to their defenses, since they couldn't guard it without breaking routine. But Ryan didn't want himself nor any of his people to end up staring at the stars because they'd underestimated the strange albino creatures' intelligence.

In his peripheral vision he caught another white blur rushing him from behind his left shoulder. Fortunately the cannies were slipping, sliding and getting bogged down in the loose dirt. Otherwise he'd have been chilled in a hurry.

As fast as he could, Ricky wheeled clockwise. By reflex he bent his elbows and tucked them in tight to his rib cage.

He felt the jar through the steel sleeve that shrouded his carbine's pierced barrel. His buttstock had struck the right forearm the creature was extending to grab or rake him with long black nails. It lacked the force to break the bone, but deflected the attack. Ricky swatted the cannie in the face with the butt. It also wasn't strong enough to do damage, but it either surprised or disoriented the cannie enough that it fell back with a croak of dismay, partially lost its balance in the treacherous, shifting soil and started to fall backward.

It got a hand down to prevent it from falling on its butt, though that opened it to an angry thrust with the steel buttstock right into its throat.

It fell back, clutching its neck, kicking and gagging. Or she did, Ricky thought. It's a woman. Or a girl, or whatever. Even though the small bare breasts weren't badly shaped, they didn't attract him. She was trying to kill and eat him. Or maybe just skip straight to the eating part and let his dying take care of itself; he doubted the cannies were picky that way. So he reckoned the naked breasts didn't count even before he punched in her windpipe.

An apt pupil of his río Benito, as well as of J. B. Dix, Ricky was not thrilled to use his finely tuned blaster as a bludgeon. But as he had helped his uncle build the weapon with his own hands, he knew that the Ishapore-built Enfield military longblaster they had made it from was justly renowned for the strength of its action. And, as a military long arm, it was *designed* to be used for hand-to-hand combat at need. The changes he and his uncle and mentor had made—rebarreling the piece, re-chambering it for .45 caliber, modifying the magazine well to accept magazines made for the ubiquitous Model 1911 semiautomatic handblaster—hadn't weakened it in the slightest. His uncle Benito believed in building to last, and had passed that belief on to Ricky.

But even the best-made weapon couldn't give him eyes in the back of his head.

Arms enfolded Ricky from behind. He gagged on foul carrion breath that gusted over his left shoulder. Taloned hands clasped each other before his sternum.

He imagined doglike jaws opened wide to bite into the back of his skull. The frightful dished red void that had been young Blinda's face when her grief-crazed sister deposited her on Mathus Conn's gaudy-house floor filled his mind.

Before curving yellow fangs had a chance to do likewise, Ricky swung his head backward, hard. A tooth gashed the crown of his skull, then he actually felt the tooth snap, as his head continued back to smash into the cannie's upper jaw.

I'm gonna get infected! The thought flashed through his mind. He understood that disease was far less rampant in the world he lived in than it had been before nuke day. Those who were susceptible to disease didn't live to see the other side, along with hundreds of millions of others. But he also reckoned there couldn't be a worse way to push your luck than getting bitten by a cannibal.

An *unwashed* cannibal. That was clear now, too. From getting up close to the white creatures, he wasn't sure their breath smelled worse than the rest of them.

To get infected he'd have to live, a lot longer than he seemed likely to. Even as he threw himself forward, twisting his body to break the weakened grasp, more hands were seizing him, pinching him cruelly, raking him with their claws.

Screaming, he struck and kicked and struggled for all he was worth. But treacherous footing or not, there were too many of the reeking white bodies for him to fight off. Individually they didn't seem strong—not even as strong as Ricky was. But in a mob they were formidable.

As he battled merely to keep hold of his blaster and delay the inevitable tearing of yellow fangs into his vulnerable flesh, Ricky saw that his friends were likewise all about to die.

Chapter Twelve

With all her strength, Krysty wielded her shovel with authority.

She was keeping the swarming white bodies back. For the moment.

But even as she watched, Doc, who had impaled a cannie on his rapier, vanished under a sudden onslaught of white bodies. The old man continued to flail at them valiantly with his emptied LeMat, but his efforts were clearly doomed.

She swung the shovel again, screaming, not with fear—or not *primarily* fear—but with falcon fury. But she was looking not at her own foes, but at Ryan's.

She saw Ryan Cawdor, her life-mate and love, intercept a cannie leaping from upslope over his head by slamming a palm to his bare sternum midair, his panga cocked back to deliver the skull-splitting chill-stroke. He already stood on top of a blood-slick, writhing mound of fallen foes. But still they came for him, shrieking and wailing, claws outstretched and toothy jaws wide.

As she swung the shovel in whistling arcs, holding the vile beasts at bay, she looked around, blinking sweat from her eyes. She saw J.B. ram the muzzle of his shotgun into the solar plexus of a cannie, then raise the blaster and bring it down with piston precision to snap its neck with the steel buttplate. Then another creature landed on the Armorer's back, knocking his hat off, jaws straining to tear away the flesh of his face.

J.B. jabbed a stiffened thumb back for its eye. It turned its own weirdly protracted face aside to take the strike on a chalky cheek.

"No!" Mildred screamed. She slogged forward, boots sinking deep in the loose dirt, raising her pickax high over her head.

"Mildred, don't!" Krysty yelled. Her friend was so freaked out by the threat to J.B. that she was about to risk driving the tine of the pick straight through both the cannie's body and his.

The redhead was so distracted that she allowed another cannie to launch itself beneath the howling arc of her gore-spattering shovel and grab her by the legs. She yelped as sharp fangs sank into her calf.

Quickly she spun the shovel and stabbed the creature's head down into the back of its neck. Blood sprayed as the broad blade glanced off the vertebrae and sliced through the right side of the neck, severing the carotid artery as well as the jugular vein on the side. The cannie slumped to the soil as its brain was abruptly short on blood-supplied oxygen. But a half dozen of the horrors converged on her, grabbing her arms and the shovel handle, snapping at her face as she kicked out powerfully.

Another cannie flew away, but there were too many. For her, for everybody.

About to call on Gaia to give her strength for what she knew would be the last time, she heard a scream.

Despite her own peril, Krysty looked toward the sound: up, over the heads of her short, scrawny, but wiry foes at the top of the slope. Another coamer had burst from the scrub, but this one had another white-faced, white-haired figure on its back.

It was Jak Lauren. He had his right elbow locked around the cannie's neck and a trench knife gripped in the fist. His ruby eyes glowed with demon glee as he yanked one of his butterfly knives out of the creature's back with his left, then immediately plunged it back into its kidneys.

Its shriek was that of a human in intolerable agony.

The attacks on Krysty had ceased. The cannies about to swarm her and bring her down were all staring at the same grisly spectacle she was.

The cannibal's knees buckled. Jak let his black sneakers hit the loose-dirt slope, released his hold on its neck and allowed the creature to fall free. As it convulsed and screeched in agony on the ground, he stepped to one side.

As slick as a conjurer, he made the small blade in his left hand disappear. He drew his big Python and fired a blast into the small of the back of another cannie who was sliding down the slope a few feet ahead and to his left. Its own howl of pain could be heard even after the ear-shatteringly sharp report of the .357 Magnum handblaster.

Krysty realized her own attackers had lost all interest in her. They were too shocked by this sudden attack from behind—and the agonized cries of their comrades.

She smiled.

FOR A LONG moment Buffort Sumz and his family sat frozen in silent surprise, staring in shock at the bizarre and terrible creature crouched on top of their dining table and the ruins of their supper, with chunks of busted roofing lying around it.

It was like nothing Buffort had ever seen outside a nightmare. It looked like a person, if a triple-scrawny one. Mostly. But it had that awful dead-white skin and lanky white hair hanging to the sides of its face, and it was the face that had all the horror; it was mostly human, too, except for being all drawn out in the mouth so that it looked as if the creature was half wolf.

Buffort was not smart. He knew that, and was content to leave the figuring to Yoostas, who was clever enough for both of them and more. But the thing's resemblance to the face Wymie Berdone had glimpsed out the window where her sister was chilled was unmistakable.

It was obvious even to him that he was staring into the wild, wide, bloodred eyes of the being that had bitten off a little girl's face at a snap, or one of its kin.

The thing's pale dick was swinging right through what had been a piled-up platter of mashed potatoes.

It launched itself straight at Betty Jo. Its impossibly long jaws snapped shut on the black-pigtailed girl's plump face with a sound like Paw-Paw biting into a big slice of watermelon. Except instead of pink the juice that squirted out was deep, glistening red.

The monster that was clinging to the front of Betty Jo, who still sat upright at the big table, turned its head.

It was crunching face bones loudly in its jaws, a scrap of skin hanging out the side of its lower jaw. It tossed its head up and the flap disappeared as its gullet worked.

Betty Jo's face was gone—the whole thing, just as if it had been scooped out by the monster's inhuman jaws. Just like little Blinda's.

That broke the spell that had been holding the Sumz

clan motionless and silent. Women screamed; men screamed.

Suddenly the white things were falling from the caved-in ceiling like dislodged rats, snarling, leaping and snapping. Screaming, "Betty Jo!" in pain and horror, Sister-Maw made as if to move to her daughter's aid. But another creature dropped between them, rearing up with black-nailed hands raised to rake at her big boobs.

She seized the searing-hot handles of a cast-iron kettle of stew simmering on the stove and hurled its contents right into the cannie's face. It shrilled in agony and clapped already blistering hands to its steam-gushing face. As it fell writhing to the floorboards hidden under a thick, spongy layer of fallen food and other trash, a creature swung from the rafters briefly, then landed on Sister-Maw's back and sank its fangs into her stout neck.

Buffort sat as if his rear end had grown roots to his chair. His mind could not absorb what his eyeballs tried to show it. Most of the other Sumz family members were bolting and fleeing from the table, screaming in panic. Buffort saw four cannies with Eddie, who was pretty much the runt of his litter, held by his arms and legs spread-out between them. As Buffort watched, still not really understanding, one of them wrenched the boy's left arm clean out of the socket and commenced to gnaw on it like a roasted turkey leg.

But Yoostas knew what was happening. Little red-headed banty cock that he was, he didn't run or scream. After only a heartbeat or two of frozen shock he jumped right up, picked up the three-legged stool he'd been sitting on and commenced to bash a cannie's face with it.

Seeing his littler brother take the fight to the invading monsters moved Buffort to action. They kept dropping in, right onto the tabletop, scattering bowls and plates of perfectly good food, which they ignored, every last one of them, in favor of munching on live and howling Sumzes. With a roar, Buffort stood up, too. He put his slab hands on the underside of the table as he did so.

It was a great big table, about twenty feet long and a good four wide, braced by all kinds of slantwise struts from the legs beneath. It weighed hundreds of pounds, but no one ever accused Buffort Sumz of being weak in his *body*.

Up went the table, spilling squalling naked cannies. Shifting his grip to both sides of his end of the huge table, his natural strength driven by a sudden surge of fear and fury that made his face flush with heat like a triple-bad sunburn, he raised the entire table up by one end. Then he turned, just a bit, grunting like a boar sexing a sow, and smashed it right down again.

Four of the cannies got caught clean beneath it. They were squashed, with a satisfactory cracking of bones like a big old sap-rich bonfire, and big splashes of blood shooting out to either side. Another got its lower half pinned beneath. Its upper part lay facedown, snapping its jaws at the floor and clawing futilely with its hand.

Yoostas swung the stool with extra force, right to left. It practically exploded against the side of a cannie's face. So did the cannie's head.

A half dozen cannies converged on Yoostas, one falling on him from the gaping hole in the ceiling. He jabbed one of the stool legs he was left holding in either hand over his shoulder into that one's face. It fell off him, mewling and clutching an eye that streamed fluid.

The others grabbed Yoostas's arms and held him. He kicked one away. Another grabbed him by the ankle and held that. As he screamed in sheer outrage and struggled furiously to break free, another jumped on his back. This one grabbed his face and twisted it viciously to one side.

Buffort heard his brother's neck snap. The little man folded to the floor like an empty grain sack.

"Yoostas!" Buffort shouted. He had to drop the table, whose weight had overpowered even his rage-boosted strength. But he got his mountainous mass moving toward his fallen brother, who had disappeared under a seething mass of bare white buttocks and reddened muzzles, hoping against hope there'd still be something he could do for his brother. Already it seemed the rest of his family members were down. He slipped on a floor made slippery by inch-deep blood, torn-out organs and ripped-off limbs.

The creatures looked at him with their strange red eyes. Then they began to leap at him.

Bellowing, he batted at them. He felt bones break as he slammed a creature with one of his tree-trunk forearms, heard a monster squall most satisfactorily. Another, and another. He caught one's head in a ham-like hand, lifted it off the floor, grabbed its skinny shoulders and unscrewed its head a full turn.

Suddenly a heavy weight descended on his head. He felt claw-like nails digging beneath his bone-shelf brows for his eyes. He cried out shrilly, slapping at the horror. It stank even in his nostrils. He felt its breath hot as an open oven on his cheek.

Sharp pain shot through his left eye socket. He squealed, frozen momentarily by intolerable agony.

His vision crazed. He seemed to be looking down at his own capacious belly, straining against the front of his homespun shirt, *and* gazing in horror across the room as two of the cannies played Keep Away with Bobby-Joan's blond head. He always hated that game—he always lost…

His right palm connected with the creature on his back. He slapped it, hard. Then he smushed it against himself with that hand while his left grabbed hold of its greasy hair. Shifting his grip, he managed to catch its head in both hands and fling it across the room.

He plucked the others off himself and flung them away, hard, but they just kept coming, grabbing at him, biting him. He felt claws rake his arm and sharp fangs sink into the bulge of his belly.

He slammed a hammer fist down on the side of the face of the one who was biting his gut. It crunched and dropped away.

Buffort broke. He didn't like to fight. Never had. He hated pain, and never had much interest in causing it to others. He just wanted to hang with his kin and laugh and fuck whatever woman or girl felt like having him, the way Sumzes had done since time in a memorial, as Paw-Paw said and Buffort never could understand. And he couldn't see right.

He started crying and lumbered into a run. His boots slogged through deep, squishing gunk. He couldn't see for shit, what with one eye looking ahead and the other showing the front of his overalls and beneath, the seething red mess of the floor like the world's grossest stew.

He managed to bat away the things that jumped for him, chittering and snapping. Around him he heard the sounds of ripping and chewing, and the moans and screams of the sadly not-yet-dead. His family. His loved ones. Who just moments before had been enjoying a peaceful family supper, the way they had a thousand time before.

He got to the front door of the house and yanked it open. Outside was a hell-scape like the one inside, except more spread-out and lit by torches and the flames of a burning outhouse. There were white things everywhere, and the numerous members of his clan who hadn't been at dinner were fighting a losing battle against the creatures.

Or were just being eaten.

He cast around with his one eye that pointed where he wanted for something to use as a weapon. Then suddenly there was another of the horrible things, clinging to his belly and grinning right up into his other eye.

He squalled and tried to swat it away, but others suddenly fell down from the roof, grabbing his arms and weighing them down.

The cannie that was clinging to his belly began to dig. Buffort struggled mightily, smashing the creature hanging on to his left arm against the cabin wall, but others came, landing on his head, grabbing on to his legs, his arms…

Others joined the one clinging to the front of his overalls. He watched in horror as they tore the tough fabric open—and then his belly. Hooting with what sounded like demon laughter, they began to yank out greasy wet coils of his own guts as unimaginable pain shocked through him.

Chapter Thirteen

A coamer had wrapped its arms around Ryan's chest, effectively pinning his left hand to his side. To get a hand-on wristlock behind Ryan's powerful torso, the monster had to turn its muzzle aside and press its cheek against the man's chest, unable to try to bite with its doglike jaws.

As favors went, it was a small one. At least two others had hold of Ryan's right arm—the one he was using to swing his heavy panga to such deadly effect against them.

Feeling the grips on his arm slacken, Ryan wrenched it free with a grunt of effort. He brought the pommel of the panga's hilt down hard, busting a skull.

Jak fired again. The bullet punched through the shoulder blade of another cannie racing to join the two dozen or so already in the deadly scrum by the entrance to the dig, erupting through the creature's chest in a shower of gore.

Ryan sensed the intent of his own attackers waver. He could almost smell their fear, over the stink of their never-washed bodies and rotting-meat breaths, and the stringent smell of already burned blaster powder and lubricant.

To perceive was to act. He sheathed the panga to draw his SIG handblaster from the waistband of his jeans, where he'd thrust it after the slide locked back in battery position over an empty magazine. He clicked the release to drop the spent mag. His left hand deftly fished a full magazine from a pocket of his coat and slammed it home in the well. Then he pushed the slide release with his thumb. The heavy steel slide slammed home, stripping a shiny cartridge off and powering it into the breech of his handblaster.

Jak added his own chilling wolf howl to the screams of his wounded victims. Ryan felt the cannies shift away from him. The sudden onslaught and howling unnerved them.

He stuck his SIG's muzzle almost into the reeking tangle of hair on the back of a cannie's head. Perhaps sensing its imminent doom, the creature started to look around.

Instead of the back of the skull Ryan triggered the blaster a finger's breadth from the horror's left temple. He smelled burned human flesh as the white skin sizzled in the muzzle-flash. A fountain of brain chunks and blood, black in the lamplight, blew out the far side of the thing's head.

"Rip into them with all you've got!" Ryan shouted, his voice hoarse. "Take it to the bastards hard!"

He swung his panga into the back of a cannie clambering up pyramid of its vile kin to get at Krysty, who was immobilized by a mob of the creatures but was still fending them away from her face and head and chest by jabbing with the handle of her shovel, which she now held with hands far apart for maximum leverage and control. The heavy blade bit deep with a wood-cutting sound. The coamer squealed in pain and bent backward with shocking flexibility, trying to claw the pain from its back with long-nailed hands. Ryan ripped the big knife free as Krysty stuck the monster in the throat. It fell off its fellows, choking to death on its own crushed larynx.

The others were already starting to lose interest in the statuesque and violent redhead. As Krysty kicked one off her, Ryan shifted his attention elsewhere. His lover could take care of herself from here on.

He saw a cannie fly up into the air propelled by a long, stork-like leg. A moment later Doc seemed to lever himself off the ground. He smashed the butt of his LeMat into the face of a nearby attacker and thrust another, who seemed unsure of himself, through the neck.

J.B. managed to crawl from beneath a seething pile of bodies. He had his Uzi slung over the back of his battered leather jacket, which now had a few more scuffs in it, his M-4000 shotgun in his right hand and his fedora on his left. Pausing to settle the hat firmly on his head again and straighten his wire-rimmed glasses on his nose, he stood, swapping blasters and replacing a spent mag in his Uzi with a fresh one.

The cannies noticed at once they were basically all wrestling with one another. The Armorer pivoted neatly and sprayed the pile with expert short bursts of 9 mm death. Blood and gobbets of flesh flew everywhere. Cannies screamed. Those that could, bolted.

The shattering blasterfire and the flight of their comrades unsettled another struggling mass of coamers. Two of their matted-hair heads suddenly slammed together. Mildred rose from among them like a goddess of wrath.

"You bastards have got to take a nuking *bath* once in a while," she yelled, punching furiously in all directions.

The coamers routed. They steamed back up the sloping sides of the cave-in on all fours, like the baboons their muzzles made them resemble. Even Jak stopped shooting or even cutting them to spur them on their way with hearty boots to the backside.

"Well, that was nasty," Mildred muttered. "Never smelled anything so bad since we had to crawl through thirty yards of fermented feral-dog shit."

With no one left to fight, Jak joined the others. "What took you so long?" J.B. asked half-humorously. But only half.

Jak grinned his white-wolf grin. "Busy," he said.

"Everybody fit to fight?" Ryan asked. The words rasped his throat. He put away his weapons, took out his canteen, unscrewed the top and took a sip of water to rinse out the dust and less mentionable substances that had gotten in there when he was fighting for his life. He spit it out and took a hefty swallow.

"If you want to call it that," Mildred said.

The others concurred. Jak and J.B. actually sounded chipper. Adult though he was, Jak was still a bloodthirsty wild child at heart. And bone practical though he was, J.B. loved nothing better than a good scrap.

Especially when his side won.

"So why now?" Ricky asked, slogging down from his position above the entry to the sunken office complex.

Like all of them, the youth was covered head to boots in a mess of gore, caked dirt and ropy cannibal slobber. Ryan realized that included him, too. Nonsqueamish though he was, that didn't make him happy.

"Was that not the point of the exercise, after all?" Doc asked. He dusted off his coat sleeves and shot his cuffs. It didn't help his woeful appearance any, but Ryan understood the gesture.

"To get swarmed like that?' he asked, coming down to join them. Clearly hoping his friends wouldn't notice, he more collapsed against than leaned on the one makeshift table that hadn't been knocked down, ignoring the naked, blood-twined pair of coamer chills lying on top of it.

"I thought they'd, like, throw stuff at us the way they have before, maybe give us a chance to pick one off in a position where we could get to the chill before his buddies did. Or her buddies, I guess," Ricky said.

Most of the dead cannies were male, but a few were clearly female.

"It was a straight-up human-wave attack," Mildred said, nodding around at the pale-skinned chills and the few moaning wounded, a good two dozen of them, strewed around the dig site. "If you can call them that."

"What do you mean, Mildred?" Krysty asked. She propped her shapely butt against the table right next to Ricky.

"I mean, are these ugly bastards even human, with dog faces like that? Are they mutants? Animals? Or are they something else?"

"Animals," Jak stated vehemently.

"I think he's right," Ricky said.

"I find myself unsure," Doc added. "They clearly display—not what we would consider overabundant intelligence, perhaps, but a clear, and clearly nonbestial, sense of purpose."

"He's right," J.B. said. "Take them one at a time, they don't act that bright. But just like there's some reason they haven't hassled us much before, and mostly here, I reckon there was a reason they decided to swarm us tonight."

And night it was. The sky overhead was clotted with ugly, bruised-looking clouds, mostly visible only because of the yellow lightning threading through the ones to the south.

"Hive mind?" Mildred asked.

Ryan shrugged. "Details don't reload any blasters," he said. "Human or mutie or animal, they attacked us now in a way they never did before. And yeah. I'm thinking there was a reason beyond instinct, or they just got all triple peckish at once and needed a good feed. That's worth knowing."

"'It is said that if you know your enemies and know yourself, you will not be imperiled in a hundred battles,'" J.B. said.

"Is that something else Trader said?" Mildred asked.

"Sun Tzu," Doc said. *The Art of War.*"

"But the Trader liked to quote it," Ryan said, allowing himself a faint smile. "Don't let J.B. snow you."

"What now, lover?" Krysty asked.

"Get these fire-blasted chills cleared out of here before they start to stink, but pick out the best-looking one, so to speak, to take into Sinkhole as proof of who's behind the attack on those people."

"Shall we carry it to Mr. Conn's gaudy tonight?" Doc asked. He was already sounding vague. Like all of them, he felt a deep letdown in the aftermath of a hard fight. It made him more likely than usual to lose focus and wander off among his memories.

Ryan looked up at the sky again. As if on cue, a single raindrop hit him in the patch that covered the emptiness where his left eye had been and exploded.

"Storm's coming," he said. "Sooner rather than later. We'd best fort ourselves up here, underground, and wait for morning. We don't want to risk hitting the trail in the dark, anyway, in case the coamers decide to come back for a rematch."

"It's not going to matter anyway," Ricky said cheerfully. "Even that crazy *chica* will have to admit we're innocent of killing her sister now!"

"THIS IS BAD, WYMIE," Mance said. "Triple bad."

The black-haired young woman could only nod. Nausea and rage warred in her belly.

Triple bad didn't begin to do it justice. Not all the lives in the world could ever mean as much to her as her murdered baby sister, and she had never had much use for the Sumz family and their frankly degenerate ways.

But if the slaughter of the unknown couple back at their camp had been an outrage, this was beyond a nightmare.

She was grateful that the curdled-milk dawn light seeping through and spilling over the pines to the east turned all the blood and gore and ripped-out organs to shades of gray. Even by lamplight, the blood of her mother and stepdad splashed all around the inside of their well-built house of stone had been bright, so shockingly bright red…

Morse Hoskin was a neighbor of the Sumz clan, who'd made the trip to their homestead in the predawn hours. Just what errand took him there at such an hour he'd been remarkably evasive about. Wymie suspected it was to visit one of the notoriously loose Sumz womenfolk. For a passel of proud and deliberate inbreds, some of them sure liked to spread it around.

What he had seen there had sent him skittering for Wymie's posse as fast as his spindly shanks could carry him. Mance had awakened her in her makeshift tent to bring her the dreadful news.

But nothing could have prepared her for the impact of the sight. Or the smells. It was like the aftermath of an explosion in a slaughterhouse. Or an outhouse. Not even the pervasive stink of the turpentine distillery could mask the reek of death.

Even the structures had suffered in the attack. The big house had its roof caved in, with busted beam-ends sticking out at crazy angles. A couple of their shanty-style outbuildings had been largely knocked in on themselves.

Wymie couldn't tell if that was because of the battle, or the outlanders' sheer joy in destruction for its own sake. She wouldn't put anything past Blinda's murderers.

Dorden approached, looking even graver than usual.

"A terrible thing," he said. "So much devastation. The whole clan appears to have been wiped out—at least two dozen souls."

He stopped and mopped his forehead with a handkerchief. It was already a muggy day, and the air was still in the hollow were the Sumzes had built their home.

"Hard to believe the outlanders could have done all this," he said.

"They must've had help," Wymie said. Her anger was bubbling. "Some traitors from among us."

"Like Conn?" Mance asked.

She shook her head in irritation. "He's just a feeb," she said. "I don't see him as a traitor. We'll find out who is, though, and root out that corruption."

She frowned. "I wonder what happened to Lem and Gator and the help they were supposed to bring back. It'd come in handy right about now."

Somebody made a crack about trying to recruit the gaudy sluts at Stenson's Creek. Wymie glared at them.

Then someone called her name.

It was Angus Chen. "Come look at this," he said. He looked as if he were about to puke.

Wymie followed the carpenter, picking her way over and around debris she didn't want to look at too closely or think about at all. Up ahead, a couple of her followers were staring down at the ground.

At first she wondered why the cannie outlanders would leave a string of sausages lying out in the yard with just the end chewed off. Mebbe they got full? They'd done a power of eating, from the evidence of gnawed-up limbs and chewed-off faces, which lent credence to her theory they now had helpers.

Then she realized she wasn't looking at sausages. She was looking at guts. Human guts.

They had been pulled out like thread off a spool, and left to lie in their own blood splashes in the dirt. It made her own innards roil to think about what that had to have felt like.

The trail led into a wood shed that had half fallen in on itself. Moaning came from the darkness within.

"Somebody's alive in there," Edmun said. "Poor bastard."

From inside the shed came the strained voice of ace tracker Lou Eddars. "It's Buffort! He's goin' fast."

Resolution didn't settle her queasy stomach, but it kept it and the remnants of whatever congealed and half-heated leftovers she had gulped down for breakfast where they belonged. She scrambled bent over into the opening, and winced as she felt a link of intestine squelch beneath her boot.

She didn't even know if a person's guts could feel anything, once they got yanked out of the body. But the man they belonged to was clearly past caring. Even in the gray dawn light filtering in through the doorway,

Buffort Sumz's face was bloodless, and knotted with suffering she couldn't begin to imagine.

His right eye dangled on its stem clear down his slab of a cheek. The skin was drenched in half-dried blood and fresh tears.

"What happened here, Buffort?" she asked. She realized what a triple-stupe question that was even as it was leaving her lips, so she hurried on. "Who did this to you?"

"They come—through the roof," he groaned. "Tore poor little Eddie apart like an ol' chicken."

"Who did?"

"Yoostas fought 'em. Fought 'em hard. But they got him. I tried to fight, but they—hurt me."

She knelt on top of the split hardwood chunks, barely noticing how they gouged her knees through her jeans. She cradled his huge blood- and tearstained face in her hands.

"Buffort, who? Who hurt you?"

"White," he groaned. "White face, white hair. Red... eyes!"

He sat up, causing unpleasant squelching sounds to come from his big ripped-open belly. He screamed, his breath stinking in Wymie's face. Then his good eye rolled up in his head and she felt him die.

She let him go and jumped up, banging her head on the caved-in roof as he flopped back like a dead fish.

Without even knowing how she found herself in the yard outside, hands on knees, panting for breath like a hound that had just helped tree a 'coon. Even the smells of turpentine, outhouses whose contents had long since got the better of the lime poured into them, and the guts and gore splashed everywhere smelled pure and fresh after what was inside.

"Wymie?" Mance asked. "Are you all right?"

"That's a stupe question, son." It was Dorden. She made herself straighten as the portly man approached.

"This is terrible," he said. "We have to do somethin' now."

"Now we got 'em," she said, her triumph rising above even nausea and anger. She looked around at Angus, Lou, Mance and the half-dozen others who had crowded around the shed entrance when she went inside. "You all heard him—he saw the albino!"

They exchanged uneasy glances. Then Mance piped up, "You betcha, Wymie! We heard, all right."

She gazed around at the rest of her posse, who had given up whatever they were doing to converge on her outside the shed of death.

"Time to end this," she said. "Mebbe the Sumzes wasn't the most popular folks in the Pennyrile, but they didn't deserve this."

"Wymie?"

It was Burny's voice, even more tentative than usual, from the back of the crowd. He had a wild-eyed girl with him, gawky and just a few years younger than Wymie herself. Wymie knew her. Her name was Aggie Coal. Her people lived north of here, right on the Mother Road that ran through the region from east to west.

"Aggie says she may know where the outlanders are," Burny said. "At least in a general sort of way."

Chapter Fourteen

"On three," Ryan said. "One, two—three!"

He and J.B. straightened simultaneously. The rope harness they'd rigged around their shoulders cut into Ryan's.

In between the cannie lay, wrapped in a blanket too old and smelly for even them to continue to use any longer. Plus it was starting to be more hole than cloth. Wrapped around the chill a couple times, though, it would be strong enough to hold.

It wasn't that long a trip to Stenson's Creek, anyway, and they could use the Mother Road most of the way.

"Ready, partner?" Ryan asked. He and the Armorer had decided that, as first and second in command, they should lead by being first to tote the dead cannie, which was in pretty good shape, considering, having been taken out by two rounds from Ryan's 9 mm blaster right through the breastbone and the cold, black heart beneath. They might not even need to hand off the macabre burden, although neither of them would hesitate to do so if he felt the need. Being tough was one thing; tiring themselves out enough to slow their reflexes if it came to a fight was begging to join the supposed "coamer" in death.

J.B. nodded. Jak did too. He turned and started up the loose-dirt slope of the cave-in.

"Does Jak even need to scout ahead?" Mildred asked. "The cannies don't do much by daylight, and if any of that crazy chick's mob of peasants with pitchforks find us, the dude there should show them we're not who they're looking for."

"How were you planning on stopping him, Mildred?" J.B. asked mildly.

"Cannies didn't attack us outright, either," Ryan said, grunting as he adjusted his grip on the load. It wasn't heavy—the cannies weren't big, though they were wiry. "Until they did. When did we start taking our safety for granted, Mildred?"

He sighed and shook his head. "Truth to tell, I did, last night. I reckoned they'd only do the usual, snipe at us with rocks and sticks, and mebbe give us a chance to chill one and claim the body. And so when they hit us for real they near as rad death overran us. If it wasn't for Jak making a big show of attacking them from behind, we'd be on the last train west right now. Or inside their bellies, more like."

Krysty placed a hand on his arm. "That's in the past, lover," she said. "We need to do what we always do— walk on."

"Literally," he said with a grin. "Right. Time to shake the dust of this place off our heels and go clear our names!"

"It was last night, 'long about sunset," Aggie Coal said. She had a mop of tangled brown hair that currently had a bunch of grass and leaves stuck in it from sneaking through the brambles. "Just as it started to come down dark for real. Donny saw a light, off to east of us. Pa came out and we heard blasterfire."

Wymie had led the group a couple hundred yards up the road that led from the Sumz location to join with the Mother Road, a mile or so away. The girl had been visibly upset by being surrounded by all that blood and death, and Wymie made a mental note to yell at Burny later for bringing her smack into the middle of it. Wymie wasn't double comfortable in that mess, either, truth to tell.

"Did you go and investigate, child?" Dorden asked gently.

Aggie shook her head vigorously. "No, sir! We been seein'…things in the twilight. Flittin' about the house and spookin' the animals and all. Sometimes the dogs been barkin' and the horses get to neighin' and tossin' their heads in the black of night, same as they did earlier when were seein' the shadows move about. Weren't nobody going out by night without more reason than curiosity."

"Curiosity killed the cat," Vin said, and cackled as if that were the funniest thing ever.

Wymie tamped down her flash of irritation hard. She had a feeling in her gut they were going to be sorely needing the oldie's talents with a handblaster, and sooner rather than later. She could almost taste how close they were to *real* action—and vengeance.

"So you don't know for sure what happened?" Wymie asked.

"No, ma'am. But we reckoned 'twarn't none of it good."

"You really think it was the outlanders?" Dorden asked Wymie.

"Who else could it be? You saw how many blasters they were flashin' around Conn's."

"No sign of any blasters used at the Sumz place," Angus said. "Except one or two by the Sumzes themselves. And one of those had the barrel blown up and peeled back like a steel flower."

"Are you sure, Wymie?" Mance asked. "I mean, from what we found at the Sumz main house, the outlanders hit 'em 'round about suppertime. Could they also have been in a firefight a couple miles to the northeast and then got here while the Sumzes were still eatin'?"

"Whose side are you on, Mance Kobelin?" Wymie flared, letting him have the full burst of her sense of righteous betrayal.

"Them Sumzes could do a power of eatin'," Angus said. "Might have been about it awhile."

"See?" she said.

Mance went pale. He dropped his eyes from hers.

"What do you want to do, Wymie?" Dorden asked with gentle firmness.

"Go find them," she said with venomous conviction. "Find them and chill them."

"How're we gonna do that, Wymie?" Angus asked.

"Search the woods and the hills!" she yelled. "Didn't you just listen? We know where they are!"

"We couldn't make out for sure," Aggie said. Then she sidled behind Mance as if afraid of Wymie's reaction.

Dorden pursed his lips and blew out a long breath as he shook his head.

"Don't take this wrong, Wymie," he said. "We're with you—we're all with you. Especially after what we just saw. You'll have the whole county with you, sure. But that is a power of country to search. Could take some time, yet."

She sighed. "You're right," she said, her shoulders sagging. She felt tired. Though her purpose—and her rage—never faltered, she was suddenly filled with a sense of the hopelessness of it all.

"But what else can we do but search?"

"You set up base camp at the road, that's what you do," old Vin said. Though still cracked, his voice and blue eyes were unusually clear. "Send out your searchers from there, but keep the road blocked. They'll come that way, sooner or later!"

"He's right," Dorden said. He looked at the oldie in something like amazement, and something like admiration. "They'll want to trade their latest scavvy at Stenson's Creek. To be honest, I didn't think you had it in you, Vin."

"Even a blind squirrel finds a nut sometimes!" Vin exclaimed. He seemed fully the senile old wrinklie again.

"Wymie!"

The shout came from up the side road to the main thoroughfare. Everybody looked that way. Edmun jogged toward them with a couple kids from Sinkhole in tow, his usual dishwater-dull manner replaced by swaggering self-importance. He got that way, sometimes, on those rare occasions when he thought he might be doing something grand.

"What is it?" she called back. She felt annoyed at him strutting in like this, right on the cusp of her own triumph. "We're busy here."

"Not too busy for this. You know how you sent Gator, Lem Sharkey and his brother, Ike, into the ville last night to round up reinforcements?"

"I do. I wondered what became of him. Until we found…what we did at the Sumz place."

"Well, what he did was find one of his pals, Tupa Mafolo."

Dorden shook his head disapprovingly. "He's nothing but trouble, that one. Heck, Lem and his crowd are trouble."

"Not anymore!" Edmun declared, practically bursting with significance. "Four of 'em went to put the hard arm on old Mathus Conn. Leaned so hard they chilled his cousin Nancy flat dead, messed up one of his bodyguards pretty bad. Then who should come strollin' in behind them but that big, fat Potar Baggart his own bad self. He and Mathus chilled the four, between the two of them."

"That's a lie!" Mance shouted.

Edmun smirked and shook his head. "Carlos, Marky here and Missus Haymuss were arrivin' to start their workday and saw it all. It's true. It's all over the whole entire ville now."

Dorden grunted unhappily. "I believe it," he said carefully. "Lem's always been triple eager to shed blood when he thought he could get away with it, and Ike Sharkey would follow his brother into a live blast furnace."

Wymie moistened her lips. "You're right," she said. "It was my fault for trustin' Lem with somethin' he might've took for power. But we got no time for this now. We got work to do. We're finally in sight of avengin' poor Blinda!"

"What about Conn?" Mance asked.

"If he wants to take his vengeance for his own kin on me," Wymie said, "I won't resist. Otherwise, it's the same as it always was.

"Whether you're Mathus Conn or anybody else, if they're not with us on this, they're with the baby-killing cannies!"

JAK WAS SLIPPING through brush—noiselessly as the pale ghosts who so unnervingly resembled him—when he smelled them.

Not coamers. Not the distinctive reek of cannies—

whose man-eating ways manifested not just through their rotting-meat carnivore breath, but through the very pores of their skins in the form of sweat and body oils—but the locals, rural laborers and ville-rats alike.

They didn't smell any sweeter to Jak's well-tuned nostrils, but were at least unmistakably different.

He froze. The breeze was light, but enough to carry the smells to him from the west. They were in the woods and the scrub on the south side of the major road that transversed the area locals knew as the Pennyrile. The same side he was on.

He held his breath for a moment. Sure enough, he heard them: rattling brush, crushing fallen vegetation beneath their boots, even a gut rumbling, presumably longing for a missed breakfast.

They were soft sounds. The sounds of people who were trying to be sneaky, but weren't particularly good at it.

Through a screen of bayberry branches just beginning to fruit out, he dared a glance west along the road, to where the Stenson's Creek gaudy house lay, and beyond it the ville of Sinkhole. Sure enough, nobody was there.

They were hiding. He couldn't know for sure why. But then again, when somebody lay in wait hidden by a well-traveled path, when did they ever mean someone good?

He grinned a feral wolf grin. Not when *he* did it, that was for sure.

His grin widened. He smelled the sharp stink of tobacco burning. Somebody was actually smoking a cigarette, and to go along with that, the hiss of whispering.

There was no question now: he'd just blown an ambush, and the ambushers were making every stupe mistake in the book.

Now to get back to report to the others. Ryan would know best how to handle it. Somehow Jak had the unmistakable crawling sensation in the pit of his lean belly that the people to be ambushed were him and his friends. He had no evidence of that, but he had learned to heed his gut—and so had Ryan and the rest.

As he started to turn back, he heard someone whisper from not twenty feet farther along the way he'd been headed. "Nuke this. I need to piss right now or I'm gonna burst."

Before Jak could slip deeper into the scrub, a man appeared through a screen of brush. The only thing between them was some lower bushes. Jak was as plainly visible to him as he would have been on a predark pool table in a high-price gaudy house.

The man stopped. He was obviously a local, a ville dweller by his scavvied pants and jacket, which most of the local farmers and other country types might have reserved for special occasions. He also had a longblaster in hand, which he whipped up to aim at Jak. Even with his wiry catamount strength and reflexes to match, Jak knew he didn't have time to whip a throwing knife from his sleeve and drill the local with the blade before the man raised the alarm. Most likely Jak would run right into the full blast of whatever was stuffed in the weapon's lone, long barrel. Instead he dived out of the line of fire, drawing his Magnum revolver as the longlaster barked.

The .357 Magnum discharged its head-shattering roar and puked yellow fire, the barrel riding up. Because he was no quick-shot artist like Ryan or J.B., Jak triggered off a second round the instant he acquired the falling target.

Even though the big revolver promptly kicked up

again, Jak saw the upper right—his left—corner of the man's head fly right off, accompanied by a spurt of pink. The man was already folding to the ground, suggesting Jak had already chilled him or the guy had croaked on his own of a heart attack.

Cries erupted farther up the road, from both sides. "There they are! We got 'em now, boys!"

Crouching in the brush with his handblaster at the ready, Jak yelled, "Ambush!"

He realized his friends knew that already. He just wanted them to know he was fit to fight.

Chapter Fifteen

By the time she heard Jak yell, "Ambush!" even Mildred—who didn't fancy herself the keenest tactical mind in the bunch—knew already that's what was happening. The gunshots and cries of what she reckoned were going to turn out to be premature triumph had told her as much.

"Ditch the chill and take cover," Ryan yelled. "Defensive positions—cover the road."

Obediently, Mildred shrugged out of the front end of the rope harness and dropped the dead cannie in its blanket shroud on the rutted roadway. She had been cursing herself for her eagerness to show that she could pull her own weight, which led her to volunteer to take over for Ryan when they were barely out of sight of the dig.

Ricky, who had volunteered to help her, continued to stand there, bent forward under the not-enormous weight of the corpse pulling on his own shoulders.

"But what if it gets lost?" he asked plaintively. "How will we prove our innocence?"

The yells from ahead were getting closer fast.

"Son," J.B. said, "from the way they're all screaming 'chill the baby-chillers,' don't you kind of reckon we're past that point?"

AT THE SHOTS, Wymie straightened behind her clump of scrub oak. As usual, she wasn't carrying any weapons herself. It just seemed unnecessary, surrounded as she was by dudes with blasters and an evident hankering to use them.

As the second shot still reverberated through the woods, Dorden and Mance both looked at her.

"Well?" she demanded furiously. "What are you waitin' for?"

The two looked at each other, then back to her.

"The ambush, Wymie," her cousin said. "Isn't it, well, kinda blown?"

"We got to strike while the iron is hot," Vin said.

"For once I agree with the crazy old coot," Wymie said. "We finally got my sister's coldheart killers where we want them!"

She stood upright, waved her hands, and at the top of her lungs, screamed, "Let's get 'em, everybody! Chill the baby-chillers!"

With a cheer her whole posse, its numbers swelled to at least fifty from new volunteers streaming in as word of the Sumz horror filtered through Sinkhole and the surrounding countryside, roared to their feet and out of cover to attack straight down the road at their enemies.

I CAN'T BELIEVE IT, Ryan thought. They're running right down the road at us.

He had gotten his people into the best available hasty defensive positions on both sides of the dirt road. One thing he knew for sure: they were smart and seasoned enough not to cross fire each other. It was one of the edges they had over most opponents.

Then he started wondering what was taking the ambushers so long to attack. From all their hollering it was pretty clear they weren't planning on bailing and trying their luck at a different time and place.

Yet here they came: a mob dozens strong, waving weapons from a Mini-14 blaster to a leaf rake, running toward them in the open around a bend. All of them were screaming for blood at the top of their triple-simp lungs.

He didn't need to tell his companions to hold their fire until he gave the word. They knew to do that, too, just as they stood ready to open fire on their own if it proved needful to defend themselves, or one another.

Ryan, like Jak on the far side of the road, was lurking a ways off the right-of-way, handblaster in hand, to ward off attempts by the ambush party to flank them. He had made sure to put himself in a position where he still could see pretty much what the others could, through a light screen of brush.

One young man with a pale face and wild black hair led the charge, waving a double-barrel shotgun over his head and hollering. Ryan drew a quick bead on him with his SIG Sauer P226 and fired a hammer into the middle of his chest, followed by allowing the handblaster to fall back into line with his eye again and firing the millisecond it came to bear, without acquiring a second sight picture.

The young man was a moving target, but happened to be moving almost directly at Ryan at that moment. The one-eyed man couldn't actually see where his rounds hit, but was confident at least one struck near the sternum. The kid dropped, flopped and was trampled by the person right behind before half a dozen more stumbled over him and one another and hid him from view.

With Ryan's shot for a signal, his companions opened fire as well, in a shattering torrent of sound. Ryan had cut it fine, taking a big risk by letting the mob get within about twenty yards of his concealed friends before cutting loose. But they were never going to shoot them all. He wanted to maximize the moral effect, the shock of a close-up volley by powerful, smokeless magazine firearms.

He wanted the enemy to run, and preferably not stop until he and his companions had escaped from the Pennyrile.

He saw J.B. coolly step into the road and fire a medium burst from his Uzi with the folding stock extended and snugged to his right shoulder. A man to Ryan's left of the one he'd shot, a surprisingly portly middle-aged man with a high forehead and a Ruger Old Army blackpowder revolver in his hand, screamed and clutched his paunch as a line of red dots was suddenly stitched across it. He fell howling and kicking his boots at the ground.

Ricky, crouched next to Ryan, raised his Webley handblaster to aim at the wounded man. Ryan leaned forward to grab his arm.

The youth turned and stared at him in shock. "Move on to someone else, kid," Ryan told him. "That bastard's down and out of the play. Let him howl and discourage the rest."

Ricky nodded his understanding. When Ryan let go of his arm he shifted targets and fired. Another man fell.

The chill joined at least a dozen others fallen in the roadway. Some were flopping around like beached fish. Others lay still, doing nothing and not looking likely to ever move again. The others were faltering.

At the rear of the mob, which had lost momentum and begun to mill about, Ryan saw a lone figure, just visible before the bend. It was a tall woman—the only reason he could spot her at all—with raven-black hair and creamy skin. She looked shocked, and her eyes were wide.

It was Wymie, the woman responsible for all their problems—including the fact they were now fighting for their lives against what seemed like half the population of the ville.

"Fireblast," he said, and lowered his aim to shoot a young man trying to point some kind of flintlock at them right beneath his grimy red bandanna.

"Why didn't you chill her, lover?" Krysty called from the cover of the nettles across the road.

She had glimpsed his initial aim—and seen him change it. Somehow. He didn't know sometimes whether she could read his mind, as part of her mutie powers, or just knew him that well.

"She's the leader," he called back. "She's beat. She'll spread it to the rest, once we chill or drive off the hardcore."

Even as he said that, he saw it start to happen. The initial volley of blasterfire from his team, crouched in cover to either side of the thoroughfare, had dropped so many of the attackers they formed a living roadblock. Those behind, mad-eyed and baying for blood a heartbeat before, now faltered, seemingly as unwilling to trample their friends and kinfolk—some of whom were still kicking and screaming, none as loudly or enthusiastically as the man whose guts J.B. had pulped with his Uzi—as they were to continue to run into the flashing blaster-muzzles of their intended prey.

Long ago—back when he was a baron's third son in Front Royal—Ryan had heard the phrase "he who hesitates is lost." To that the ever-canny Trader had added: *nobody wants to get shot.* It took unthinking fury to run into the face of heavy blasterfire. And this mob had clearly let self-preservation reassert itself in the face of their waning bloodlust.

They were done. It was all over but the fleeing.

None of the group, not even Ryan, could match the hunting-tiger sharpness of Jak's senses. But in turn none of them, including Jak, came close to Ryan's keenly honed sense of danger, the unconscious ability to flash sort through even the tiniest fugitive sensory inputs to identify the pattern that added up to *threat*.

That sense screamed a warning now. From the corner of his lone eye, Ryan saw a skinny old man, standing by the side of the road, leveling a single-action Peacemaker at Ryan's head.

But just as Ryan's sense of danger had its limitations, so did even his striking-rattler reflexes. He already knew he was nuked, even as his brain sent his body the impulse to dive aside.

The ancient blaster and its ancient shooter alike vanished in a giant yellow muzzle-flash. It instantly echoed in a blinding red flash inside Ryan's skull.

Then blackness. Then nothing.

Chapter Sixteen

"They're running!" Krysty heard Ricky shout.

His gleeful cry wasn't needed. The locals' resolve had withered in the face of the companions' blasterfire. The front rank—the survivors, who hadn't tripped or fallen over the dozen or so wounded or dead who had been the mob's front—had turned and were pushing back into the faces of their fellow locals behind. But the rout fever had already taken root among them, and the men and a few women at the rear had already started running back out of sight around the bend in the road.

And at the rear of it all stood Wymie Berdone, head down, shoulders slumped in dejection. The fleeing crowd, growing larger by the heartbeat, split to flow around her to either side. Krysty wondered whether it was lucky that they failed to trample her—or if she'd be luckier if they had.

Ryan was right, she thought, pausing to swap magazines in her Glock. After an initial full-auto burst, just to get their enemies' attention, she'd been firing single rounds.

No matter how hot the fire of vengeance-lust burned inside her, the black-haired woman's days as a successful mob leader were through. Leaving her alive to spread defeat to her followers was the worst blow Ryan could strike against her.

The shooting from their side died away as it became clear the mob posed no further threat. As far as Krysty could tell, the attackers had fired no shots at them, though she had the impression a couple locals had discharged their blasters into the air, by accident or from overenthusiasm.

And then she saw an oldie, standing in weeds by the side of the road letting his panicked fellows flow past, drawing bead with an enormous blaster held steady in both wrinkled hands.

Before she—or Jak, or J.B., or even Ryan himself—could react, the blaster went off with a roar that seemed to consume Krysty's world. She saw blood fly from her lover's head, and he flopped bonelessly in the weeds.

Screaming with wordless rage, Krysty leveled her Glock and emptied the entire magazine into the oldie in a single, shuddering burst. The old man did a jittering death-dance as 9 mm copper-jacketed hardball slugs sleeted through his shriveled frame. It was as if Krysty's stream of blasterfire was all that was holding him upright. Only when the slide locked back on her blocky handgun did she give him permission to lie down and die.

It wasn't enough. It could never be enough. She couldn't kill him enough for what he had done to her lover.

Ever-alert and rapid to act, J.B. had sprung to Ryan's side where he lay invisible in brush and grass across the road from Krysty. "He's alive," he called. "Bullet just clipped his head. Out cold, though."

"Not good," Mildred said grimly. "He's concussed at the least."

Krysty actually shrugged at that. "He's alive," she

said. "And one thing we know about my Ryan is, he's ace at staying that way!"

Mildred had to smile. "He is that."

The last of the crowd of locals disappeared around the bend, except for a few walking wounded, limping or helping each other along. A pair of husky farm lads grabbed Wymie by the arms and dragged her along with them out of sight. She wasn't resisting. She just wasn't doing anything on her own.

The nonwalking wounded scattered among all the chills in and by the road moaned. Except for the middle-aged balding man. He was screaming fit to make the woods ring.

Krysty dropped the heavy steel slide on a fresh magazine of 9 mm rounds. She straightened her arm, grasped her blaster hand with her left and pulled on it for stability, lined up the fat white dot of the front sight and squeezed the rather heavy trigger.

The blaster bucked to a single shot. The wounded man's balding dome of a head jerked.

His screaming stopped. So did his thrashing around.

"Why did you do that, Krysty?" Ricky asked. By his tone the youth clearly wasn't reproaching her, but genuinely wanted to know.

"Fight's over, boy," said J.B., as he dragged Ryan out of the brush by the armpits. "No need for him to go on carrying on like that."

DESPITE HIS RESOLVE, Mathus Conn's heart lurched when he saw the firelight from what he'd been told was Wymie Berdone's base camp through the trees ahead.

But what if I'm wrong? he thought.

He laughed, silently so the looming shadowy figure

of Potar Baggart, standing behind him on the forest path, wouldn't ask what was funny. He didn't feel like having to explain that, no, indeed, they didn't call it the Death-lands for nothing. And that applied inside the Pennyrile as well as out. He suspected it always had.

And not just in the Pennyrile. Nor North America, either, for that matter. Old-days people sure weren't im-mortal, to judge by the fact they called it the *Megacull*.

The fact was, Mathus Conn was a man who asked probing questions and thought things through. That had been the case long before his cousin Nancy had come to work for him, and would continue now that she was star-ing up at the unlit ceiling of Coffin-Maker Sam's chill cellar. And after he'd failed to find Wymie the previous night, when he'd gone looking for her, he'd had a power of time to consider his course of action.

Which was pretty much what he'd started out intend-ing to do, even before poor Nancy and her murderers got cold.

I'm right, he told himself. And if I'm not—well, no one leaves this world alive.

He raised his head, threw back his shoulders and strode forward as importantly as he could.

He could see maybe a dozen of them in the clearing, huddled around a dispirited-looking bonfire. A few pine-wood torches burned around the perimeter. The yellow light made their sagging faces look jaundiced.

By survivors' accounts, Wymie had had at least half a hundred eager mob members when she set them on the outlanders that morning.

In the midst of her sad remnant, Wymie knelt next to the bonfire, stroking the upturned face of Mance Kobelin. From the waxiness of his pallid complexion, so like her own—not to mention the dancing gleam of firelight on unblinking eyeballs—he would have been able to tell at a glance the young man was dead. Even if he hadn't heard enough reports of Mance's demise to believe them.

When the first survivors straggled back to Sinkhole, stopping by way of Stenson's Creek to wet their parched throats and restore their failed courage, he had learned what happened. And decided to let Wymie stew in her own juices for a spell.

Just that single glimpse told him all he needed to know about the current state of Wymie's enterprise.

She had stewed more than enough.

He compressed his lips. He *had* made sure to send Coffin-Maker Sam on ahead. He had a job of work ahead of him. He wasn't pleased to see poor dead Mance still here. A body commenced to stink mighty fast in these parts.

Mebbe Sam only had so much room in that old hay-wagon he uses, he thought. He doesn't usually get so much custom all at one go. And Wymie no doubt had been reluctant to let go of her cousin.

If only I could be sure that this madness had ended, he thought. But the thing that caused it is getting worse, not better.

They all noticed him, or more likely his shadow Potar, at the same time. A dark-haired kid leaped up from where he'd been squatting on his skinny shanks near Wymie and raced at him.

"You bastard!" the kid hollered.

Conn recognized him as a boy from the ville named Danny. He was the sort who seemed to just drift, as if mebbe looking for a purpose to his life.

And now, from the fury that twisted the dark, lean and none-too-clean features beneath his hank of black hair, he seemed to have found one, despite the day's earlier disaster. His very fury reinforced Conn's resolve.

"This is all your fault! You—"

He broke off when Potar took a thick-legged stride past Conn to piston his palm heel into the charging boy's breastbone. Danny went flying back with his feet kicking up higher than his head. He landed on his rump and skidded two more feet.

"Show more respect to Mr. Conn, you little bagworm," Potar growled. He glared pugnaciously about at the rest of them. "Anybody else tries a stupe trick like that, I'll twist his head around like he was a chicken!"

There were still plenty weapons in evidence, and not just farm tools and axes, but blasters. But nobody made a move for any of them. Maybe it was because the fight was already out of the rest of them—for the moment. But Conn reckoned his new self-appointed bodyguard was just that intimidating.

"Stand easy, everyone," Wymie said. She stood up and walked forward, slowly, but without signs of hesitation. She did, however, keep her eyes on the ground before her feet.

"Reckon I know what you come for, Mathus Conn," she said. "I never intended the wrong that got done to you and yours. I never intended to get a mess of people chilled, either. If you're here to get your revenge, you can take my life and I won't kick none."

"No," he said, "I know you didn't tell that little coldheart Lem to do what he did."

He looked around at the others then, and made his

voice ring without yelling, a useful skill for a gaudy-keeper to have.

"I'm here because I see now you were right."

That got them. Before they'd been watching him blearily or not at all, slouched, listless. Now they all snapped to attention, and the eyes turned toward him were bright in their suddenly less-slack faces.

"I went to the Sumz location this morning," he said, "after you were there. I saw the horrors these monsters committed, and I knew I had to face the fact—there is an evil abroad in our district that needs to be hunted down and destroyed, root and branch.

"I look at you, and know that it's growin'. It's not just these outlanders who shot you up so badly. They've got help."

He looked at Wymie.

"So I'm here to help you. However I can."

She spread her hands. She left her head hanging, though, and would not look at him.

"I thank you kindly," she said. "But what can you do? What can I do? I got a power of my people killed today. And most of those who survived have given up and gone back home."

"They'll realize soon enough the danger they're in," Conn said. "As for what you can do—keep carryin' the torch. People will come to you. New ones, as these terrible things keep happenin' to their friends and neighbors and loved ones. And even the ones who have abandoned you, most of them will come back, if you just keep the faith. You'll see."

She raised her face and looked at him. Tears gleamed yellow and orange on her cheeks in the fire glow.

"As for what I can do," he continued, "I can help make

sure your voice is heard across the width and breadth of the Pennyrile. It's time everybody woke up to the threat we're all livin' under, and started bandin' together to put an end to evil.

"Now is the time we stand together—or fall apart."

Chapter Seventeen

Ryan opened his eye to darkness.

His first thought was that he was blind, and he had to fight down panic. How could he help his friends, his lover Krysty, stay alive and make their way in this cold-heart world without even one good eye?

But he beat down the panic almost at once, even before he noticed a slight glow creeping in at one edge of his vision, and heard the murmur of voices from nearby.

Ryan made himself sit up. His hips felt like a rusty hinge. Dizziness rushed him. He swayed.

He forced himself to stand. He swayed again. He started to put out a hand to steady himself, but the light was too faint to give him an accurate picture of his surroundings.

Whatever's wrong with me, it wouldn't help to bust my arm flailing around in the dark like a feeb, he thought.

Somehow he managed to stay upright. After a moment the dizziness passed, mostly. He began to walk toward the light, tottering at first, and then growing more steady with every step. The floor was tilted at a funny angle beneath his feet, but not enough he couldn't handle it.

It also told him where he was: stashed inside one of the outer rooms of the swallowed-up office complex they had been excavating the past couple weeks. Before everything went south.

Or, mebbe, returned to normal.

"Well, look at that," he heard Mildred say as the sunlight, weak though it was, dazzled his eye. "The dead walk!"

"Mildred!" Krysty said sharply.

"Sorry," Mildred said. "But it's not like we haven't known he was alive the whole time."

The sun was just beginning to rise above the eastern lip of the cave-in, breaking into sharp spears among the branches of a berry bush.

"Why're we here?"

"You mean, 'Thanks for saving my life and bringing me to a safe place, and why are we here?' right?" Mildred asked sweetly. She was squatting by a fire turning what looked to be squirrel carcasses on a spit.

Ryan waved a hand at her. "Yeah, yeah. I was getting to that. Now answer the fire-blasted question."

Krysty gave him a big smile. "You already provided a pretty good synopsis yourself as to 'why,' lover," she said.

She turned away from chopping up some kind of herbs on one of their sorting tables, by the smell that came to him, and tilted her face to kiss his cheek.

"This place is way more defensible than our old campsite," Ricky said. He and Doc were squatting by a second fire set on the other side of the entry to the sunken facility in which Ryan had awakened. So, to Ryan's mild surprise, was Jak, pouring himself a blue steel mug full of something aromatic from the coffeepot that had been suspended over the low fire. From the smell it was that awful chicory they made do with around here, and pretended to like.

Suddenly, Ryan realized he was ravenously hungry.

I must be, if that stuff smells good, he thought over the sudden rumbling of his stomach.

"What're you doing here, Jak?" he asked. "Did Krysty drag you down here by the ear again to make you eat something?"

The albino grinned. "J.B. spelling," he said, which made sense; Jak only really trusted the Armorer and Ryan himself to keep watch on the group in place of him, and then not overly much. He sometimes forgot to do basic stuff like eat and sleep in his protective zeal.

"Okay, ace," Ryan said, accepting a mug of steaming coffee sub from a grinning Krysty. "So it made sense you brought me here. Now how the nuke long was I out?"

Krysty and Mildred exchanged glances. "Two days," Krysty said.

"Two *days*? Fireblast! And what are we still doing here, with the whole district no doubt up in arms and looking for us now?"

"No better sanctuary seemed to offer itself," Doc said.

"We weren't going to drag your dead-to-the-world ass clear out of the Pennyrile," Mildred stated. Her usually smooth forehead was creased in a frown.

"She was really worried about you," Krysty said. "Didn't like that a blow to the head put you under for so long. I told her you were too mean to die of something that didn't chill you straight off."

Mildred let out a long sigh. "Finally I figured it out," she said. "Your body kept you under that long because you needed rest. Even after a comparatively quiet spell, we're all running on empty."

He sipped the chicory. Nuke, but it tasted good. That showed how deprived his body was.

"Why didn't you just leave me?" he demanded.

Krysty looked shocked. Mildred eyed him narrowly. "Are you still concussed? Beause you're raving."

"You'd have done the same for us!" Ricky chirped. Ryan knew the boy was trying to be helpful, but he was so cheery this morning Ryan kind of wanted to strangle him.

More than usual, even.

"What? Left you behind?" Doc emitted a bark of uncharacteristic laughter. "Come now, Ryan!" he said. "After you have saved all our lives a hundredfold? You expect us to believe you would abandon one of us, if we were temporarily incapacitated?"

"Keep telling yourself that," Ryan grumbled.

He heard the cry of a red-tailed hawk. The big bastards were everywhere, and they, like most birds of prey, had almost comically thin, piping voices.

But there was no wide-winged shape visible circling against the low-hanging clouds. He'd known there wouldn't be.

"Nuke shit," he said, but softly. "Where's my blasters?"

The others had gone tense as well and were all staring up and around at the brushy lip of the cave-in.

"Inside the first room, to the right," Mildred said without looking at him.

Jak flung his coffee on the ground with a curse and stuck the mug in a pocket of his jacket.

With scarcely a rustle of vegetation, J.B. appeared and began sliding down the loose-earth slope toward his friends. One hand held his shotgun, the other clamped his fedora to his head.

"Armed men," he said, "a lot of them. And they're all around us!"

I'M SORRY, MY FRIENDS, Mathus Conn thought. But as poor, demented Wymie says, after all, in the end you're only outlanders. Sometimes sacrifices must be made. For the greater good, of course.

And better you than any of us. Though, realistically, he already knew how inevitably it would come to that. But he would hold out as long as he could. Just as he was going to stay the course, whatever it cost, and do whatever it took. Because it was much too late to back out and have a hope of continuing to breathe.

Around him the camp of his nascent army was already fully alive before the sun was doing more than silhouetting the boles of the trees on a ridge to the east with precursor light. The scouts he'd sent to the area around where Wymie's informants had seen the lights and heard the blasterfire had reported back with their quarry's location. It wasn't even a mile from Conn's current bivouac, off to the southeast. Now the forces were mustering to move out.

Putting his hands on his overall-covered thighs, Conn stood up from the folding camp stool in his tent. I've let myself get fat, soft and old, he thought. Going on campaign like this should go a ways toward fixing at least two of those things.

He did not anticipate the effort to purge the Pennyrile of ruthless cannie coldheart killers would be short, even as his army, with at least a hundred fifty armed men and women and growing almost by the hour, closed in for the kill of the seven outlanders.

Because, of course, he knew they weren't guilty.

Outside the tent, a bull throat cleared itself loudly.

"Mr. Conn," he heard Potar Baggart call. "It's time."

"I'm comin'," he said.

He picked up his hat and went to the tent entrance. He carried no weapons. Wymie hadn't since launching her crusade, and didn't. He thought that was a useful example: allowing the willing to bear arms on his behalf, while keeping his hands clean.

It had served her, initially—until her apparent lack of a clue had gotten a dozen locals killed in a massacre almost of the scale of the destruction of the Sumz clan.

"Boss," Potar said respectfully as he stepped outside.

Conn nodded at him. The morning air was rich with the smell of a stand of loblolly pines. They set off toward the enemy camp. The bulk of his force had moved out already, leaving a contingent of Potar's sec men behind to stand guard on the camp.

"Any more trouble?" Conn asked.

Potar smiled and made *hur-hur* noises deep in his thick throat. "Oh, yeah," he said with relish.

Conn had moved quickly since Wymie ceded control of her mob to him. As promised, he'd sent out emissaries the length and breadth of the Pennyrile, spreading alarm—and the warning, if you're not with us, you're against us.

Plenty of people laughed off the threats—both of them—especially farther away, such as away in the hollow to the east. But that was ace with Conn, for now. Plenty had responded to his call, and more kept coming in.

And of course, even some close to hand were reluctant to see the light. Some, like Tarley Gaines and his clan, were too powerful to mess with for the foreseeable future. Others—well, Potar and the crew of like-minded bullies he had gathered around him as sec men had already proved their worth several times over. They hadn't even had to chill anybody—that Conn was aware of.

Excited scouts met them when they were still a hundred yards of brush interspersed with stands of hardwood trees from their goal. "Mr. Conn! Come lookit what we found!"

"Show me what you've found, Sairey," Conn said to the young woman who had spoken. She was a skinny little ferret with brown hair sticking straight above her sharp face. Conn wondered how she could see with the camo bandanna she wore tied around her forehead seemingly half covering her dark brown eyes, but the Maccum Corners teen was acknowledged as the best scout and tracker in these parts, even by local Lou Eddars.

Lou himself was standing by a patch of open ground, still muddy-tacky from some overnight rain. He was standing stock-still, but his whole manner bespoke quivering alertness, like a hound that had just fetched the fresh trail of a bear. A handful of other scouts clustered around, squatting and standing, pointing to the ground and jabbering in soft voices among themselves.

"Quietly," Conn said softly. "We don't want to tip the coldhearts off now, do we?"

They shut up instantly. From the gleams of still-faint dawn light on their eyeballs, it seemed they were looking more at the mobile mountain of Potar Baggart behind him than at him.

"Tell me what you have."

"Check these out," Sairey said. She squatted and pointed.

Putting his hands on his thighs, Conn leaned over and peered at the ground. For a moment he wondered if he was missing what he was supposed to see in the poor light.

"What other than bare feet?" he asked.

"That's it!" Sairey said excitedly. "Them outlanders all wear shoes."

"And there's a power of prints around here," Lou added.

Conn straightened and scratched at his beard thoughtfully.

"Coamers," he heard someone say in hushed tones.

"Ain't no such thing," Wymie said from behind Conn. She at least had the sense to keep her own voice low, crazy girl or not.

Conn turned. She was walking up the same path he and the rest had taken, with only a couple of her hangers-on for company.

"That's just an old myth, the coamers," she went on. "Just a boogeyman story made to scare kids who ain't actin' right."

"Stories say they eat people, too," Sairey said thoughtfully.

Wymie rounded on her, black hair flying and sapphire eyes blazing. "I saw what I saw!" she hissed. "It was them outlanders!"

"Easy," Conn said, with as much urgency as he could muster and still keep his own voice low. "We don't want to spook the outlanders, now, do we? Not after you went through so much work and heartache to track them down and bring them to justice, Wymie."

"It's just some barefoot hillbillies, turned to help them," she insisted. "Bad sort of people. Like—"

For a moment Conn was sure she was going to blurt out, "Mord Pascoe, my stepdad!" Instead she turned and walked away, her retinue of two casting uneasy glances back over their shoulders as they followed.

"How fresh are the tracks?" Conn asked his scouts.

"Not very," Sairey replied. "Made around midnight latest, mebbe."

Conn nodded. "Right. Well, thanks. We'll follow this up later. Right now—you all don't want to miss out on the fun, do you?"

Despite the butchery of Wymie's crew by their intended targets just a few days before, the scouts grinned like hunting dogs and set off for the objective, which Conn had been told was a spot where a sinkhole had caved in.

He hung back and watched them go. Potar stayed with him. He seemed to sense the *real* action was always going to be at Conn's side.

"Want me to do somethin' about her, boss?" the big man rumbled.

Conn knew he wasn't talking about Sairey. "No."

He shook his head and reached to the waistband of his pants for a flare gun.

"Not yet. But mebbe later—for the greater good."

From the cave-in came a muffled shout, followed by cries of triumph and rage.

He touched the big man on the arm. It was like touching a tree trunk.

"Time to go. We have the advantage of complete surprise. Our bunch should be able to overwhelm them easily. Let's go watch the kill. I think we've earned it."

He drew the flare gun and shot the round in a high arc over the hole.

Chapter Eighteen

Krysty's heart sank as she watched the pink comet of a flare rise up into the low-hanging clouds.

In answer to the question Krysty suspected was yammering in everybody else's mind along with hers, J.B. was as word-stingy as Jak at his best.

"Blasters!" he hollered.

He stopped where the slope leveled out into a shallow bowl at the bottom. He turned, bringing up the Uzi with both hands. Then he started pulsing short, loud bursts into the bushes at the top of the cave-in, turning as he did so. He carefully broke off fire and elevated the short barrel as he came to each of his companions.

"Everybody get in farther!" Ryan yelled.

Blue-tinged gray smoke billowed from the brush surrounding the pit. Half an eyeblink later the noise of a black-powder blaster, duller than the crack of the modern cartridges the companions fired, hit Krysty in the ears.

She hesitated. Other smoke puffs blossomed despite the recent raking of the vegetation by J.B.'s full-auto fire. Slow-moving bullets—relative to their own—went past her with *weet* sounds, to splat off the exposed masonry of the mostly sunken structure, or toss up pinches of yellow dirt.

Long habit took over. Ryan had barked a command. When he did that, those with him obeyed instantly, without question. Not because they were subordinates, but because he was right, far more often than not.

Krysty, not a follower by nature, had those thoughts flash through her mind as she whirled. She felt her long red hair contracting toward her scalp even as it spun about like a flag being twirled above her shoulders. Ryan's companions chose him to lead them because, even though he was human and fallible, his survival knowledge and instinct was unmatched. And his will was as hard and durable as the vanadium-steel walls of a pre-dark redoubt, cutting through the perils and hardships of the Deathlands like a blade.

J.B. fired the last of his magazine toward the bush where the first shot had come from, eliciting a cry of pain audible even over the rattling of old-time blaster-fire. Krysty heard Ricky cry out and saw him stumble as he started to go through a crazily tilted door of the excavated office structure, clutching the back of his right buttock. He lost his balance and slammed his head against the steel frame, then slumped.

Mildred, who'd gotten in a step ahead of him, and his buddy Jak, right on his heels, grabbed the stunned and wounded youth by either arm and bundled him bodily into darkness.

THE BURLY 12-GAUGE boom of J.B.'s Smith & Wesson M-4000 shotgun sounded oddly muffled, and echoed strangely in Ricky's ears, away down here in the deepest, darkest point they'd excavated in the sunken office complex.

The complex, to call it that, wasn't large, though what they had discovered of it so far was surprisingly big, given the top of the hole it had mostly vanished into was twenty or twenty-five yards across maximum. It had apparently consisted of an indeterminate number of modular steel structures, connected by corridors made, obviously on-site, of metal-roofed wood frame. J.B. had opined that it had grown over whatever period of months or years it had seen use.

Doc, in his turn, had pronounced that whatever had caused the earth to swallow it had not been a natural event. Or at least not a normal one. Though the Pennyrile was a veritable Land of the Sinkholes, this clearly wasn't one. Or at least not in his judgment, which while not as rock-solid as Ryan's tactical insight, nor the Armorer on blasters, was generally reliable and in any event greater than anyone else's.

The sound of Jak's big Python going off from the entrance still carried enough of the characteristic nasty hypersonic harmonics of a .357 Magnum handblaster going off to set Ricky's teeth ever so slightly on edge.

The shot that had struck Ricky had likely been a ball to begin with—a true old-fashioned soft-lead sphere, not an extended slug like the so-called Minié ball, much less the modern jacketed military hand or longblaster bullet that was also inexplicably called *ball.* And it had ricocheted off something before hitting him, soaking off most of its kinetic killing energy. It had not even penetrated the tough denim of his jeans, nor busted his femur beneath, which was fortunate.

It still left a bruise that had already been turning a mottled rainbow of dull colors when he, red-faced, had to skin down his pants for a quick exam by Mildred by the light of a stinking turpentine-oil lamp. And he was still going to have to endure the ribbing of Jak and the others about having gotten himself shot in the butt—at least until the next big catastrophic turn in everybody's lives took their minds away from him and his embarrassing plight, or until they were all staring sightlessly up at the office's canted ceiling, which was how they'd end up and in a hurry if the mob of attackers had their way. From the conversations of his comrades as they fended off the occasional probe, it seemed as if the whole Pennyrile was up in arms and hungering for their blood.

Feeling morose, Ricky sat with his back to the cool jumble of dirt and rock at the end of the corridor where they'd packed him off to recuperate. Desperate as their straits were, they didn't actually need him. The threat was not immediate. And as Ryan had shown a pair of locals who had been brave but unlucky enough to try to force entry by dropping in from above, a single determined fighter with a good edged blade—in this case, the one-eyed man and his panga—could hold the narrow door indefinitely by himself, without even wasting a cartridge.

Fact was, Ricky would get in the way. The rest were mostly occupied with either hunkering down waiting for the call to action if—when—the mob nerved itself to try a mass concerted rush, or rummaging through the hitherto-unsorted scavvy and checking the opened chambers for supplies to stuff into their packs. Because it was plenty clear that, if by some miracle they escaped, they'd need to travel far and fast to have a chance of staying in their skins.

Fortunately, they still had a good supply of ammo.

Ricky heard J.B. exclaim from the top of the complex, "Dark night, they're throwing burning green-brush bundles!"

A moment later he heard his friends coughing as

thick, choking smoke crowded into the entry. A cloud-burst of blasterfire broke out. From the higher pitch, it was all outgoing. Ryan and his companions holding the entrance were blindly unleashing as much high-velocity death as they could through what Ricky could imagine with horrifying clarity were big, blinding clouds of smoke, in hopes of discouraging the angry locals from following up the tactical advantage their unexpected cleverness had won them.

No matter how much ammunition they had to burn, he knew with sick certainty their only chances of keeping their determined foes out were slim and none. And *slim* was looking sickly…

It took Ricky a moment to realize that the small voice that had been murmuring, unheeded, at the back of his skull for several minutes was starting to yammer at him. He realized that he was feeling cool air, smelling cool earth and stone, not the combined smells of smoke and the sweat and grime of his friends' bodies and clothes.

To realize was to act. Only in dealing with other people did Ricky tend to dither before making a move. And at that, those delays were only in face-to-face interactions. When he faced somebody over the sights of a blaster, things were so much more clean-cut…

He was turned around on his knees and digging at the obstruction at the end of the corridor before he knew it. At first with his hands, then—with a pang at using the weapon for a not-exactly-intended purpose—the steel-shod butt of his carbine.

As the half-furious, half-triumphant blood-lusting cries of locals charging the sunken building echoed down to him, he screamed over his shoulder, "Come on! I found us our miracle!"

"OH, MY," DOC said, holding the lantern high above his head. "What have we here?"

"I don't have your advanced degrees in science or anything, Doc," Mildred said, "but it looks to me as if we've blundered into a big old cave."

"Rather, a vast and expansive cavern system," Doc said, trying not to feel smug. These were his companions, after all. And when it came to the brutal realities of the world he was marooned in—and truly, they no less than he, especially the likewise chronologically displaced Mildred—it was he who was the veritable babe in the woods, and they the knowledgeable adults.

Still, he enjoyed demonstrating his worth when he got a chance to. He waved a hand around the tall, high-ceilinged chamber of color-stranded stone.

"Behold the entrances to myriads other caves and passageways! Verily, I say, I believe we have stumbled into the enormous extended system of caverns said to underlie the entire erstwhile state of Kentucky, if not much of the rest of the Southeast United States! When they were, ahem, united."

"And states," Mildred added.

"So where do we go from here, lover?" Krysty asked Ryan.

The one-eyed man looked at Doc. "You're the science expert," he said. "Got any suggestions?"

Doc blinked at him. "What exactly is our objective, again? Aside from escaping imminent doom at the hands of a ravening mob?"

"That's a start," Ryan admitted. "But we've done that—for the moment. We can't sit around too long, though, because sooner or later, probably sooner, they're going to nerve themselves up enough to come down into the dark after us. So how do we find a way out of here that doesn't involve going back up the way we came down—smack in the middle of an enemy army? I reckon if we pop up somewhere else, behind their backs, even if it's not far we've got a chance to get clear without them having so much as a clue that we've surfaced again."

"Then what?" Mildred asked. "It seems like a pretty comprehensive job we got ahead of us, as it is. But the next step after that seems to be to get the hell out of the Pennyrile before anybody's onto us."

"What about the scavvy?" Ricky asked. Doc thought to notice tears glistening in the boy's dark eyes by lantern light. "There's so much cool mechanical stuff and machine parts we hadn't even got to!"

"Whoever's in charge of that fandango up there," J.B. said with his usual grim humor, "you can bet a bent empty cartridge case that he's got as much of their would-be mob as they can corral busy looting the stuff for him right now. Or her. Though I doubt that."

"And just why is that?" Mildred asked, in a dangerous tone. "You developing a problem with women all of a sudden, John?"

"You saw how easily we dealt with the mob when Wymie was in charge," Krysty said. "However motivated or even smart she was, she had no clue how to control them, and probably didn't even have a plan worked out beyond 'revenge.'"

"Right," Ryan said with a smile for his lover. "Somebody who's used to organizing stuff and getting it done has taken charge somewhere along the line. The name that comes to my mind is Mathus Conn. And while that cousin of his who's the assistant may be handling the planning, she seems content to follow his lead. So, yeah. For him."

Ryan looked back at Doc. "And to get back to the little matter of getting out of this with our guts still on the inside—Doc?"

Sadly, Doc shook his head. "While I have some solid grounding in the study of natural history, little of use suggests itself right now. Except to stay as close as we can to the surface, and look for a sinkhole."

"Not going any deeper into scary caves that for all we know are teeming with insane cannies?" Mildred asked. "I can handle that."

"Sounds like a plan," Ryan said. "So let's shake the dust off—"

Before he could finish the sentence, it was as if the sweating limestone walls began to give birth to the white-haired cannies, like bees being born from a honeycomb in a giant, mutie hive or maggots, scared out of a chill.

Hundreds of them, all screaming for blood.

Chapter Nineteen

Even tinged by the orange light of the fire in Conn's headquarters camp near the sinkhole where the outlanders had holed up, Sairey Furnace's sharp features were clearly drained of color.

"None of 'em came out," she said, shaking her head. "Not a one."

Mathus Conn was glad he'd had Potar's sec men and sec women—to call them what they were—ring the fire by his command tent to keep the rest of his young army at bay, although doubtless they already knew what had happened. Word spread like wildfire through the district anyway, and even Potar's huge hammer hands weren't enough to stop rumors exploding double fast through the assembly of several hundred souls.

They *definitely* did not have a need to know the presumably gory details. To whatever extent they didn't already.

"That's the third party we've sent down," murmured Frank Ramakrishnan, his sharp chin sunk to his collarbone where he stood, gaunt as a scarecrow and tall as Potar, next to where Conn sat in his folding chair. Conn's new chief adviser to replace his murdered cousin Nancy, the middle-aged Frank, was scion of Sinkhole's leading family of cloth-makers and merchants, who spun pretty fair-quality textiles out of linen, cotton and hemp grown in the region. He was in the habit of thinking out loud, as opposed to blandly stating the obvious.

"Fifteen good men and women," Sairey said, nodding. Her eyes were fever-bright in the firelight. "Armed to the teeth. Gone now, and I don't reckon they're comin' back."

Her eyes pleaded with him not to send her in to bring them back, or their corpses, doubtlessly well chewed and much dismembered.

Conn glanced away toward the cave-in, a quarter-mile or so distant. It was immediately apparent by the glow of dozens of pinewood-splint torches, which sent up a hemisphere of yellow light like a small ville. The only sounds evident were those made by the work parties, relieved of their other duties to recover and sort the surprisingly abundant scavvy the outlanders hadn't gotten to yet, who worked by the light of those torches. The booty would be disposed of by Conn.

For the greater good, of course.

"Did you hear blasterfire?" he asked the girl.

"Along with the screams? Nuke, yeah. All ours. None of that high-powered stuff like the strangers was shootin' at us. Smoke poles."

Conn rubbed his bearded chin and grunted.

"So it was unlikely to be the outlanders who attacked them," Frank said.

Okay, so sometimes he *did* state the obvious, Conn thought.

Sairey swallowed but said nothing, whether out of her natural reticence, or out of some budding sense of what was prudent to say around powerful men, Conn couldn't tell. Still, it was the right thing to say, and he credited her for that.

"Mathus," Frank said, looking right at him. His own

dark features showed unmistakable reluctance. But at the least Conn could trust the man not to mince words with him. Otherwise he'd have been no use. Conn could throw a rock blind into the night from here and hit somebody who'd be happy to babble whatever he or she thought Conn wanted to hear, out of fear of the gaudy keeper's monstrous enforcer.

Still, there was no harm in encouraging him. "Speak," he said. "Don't hold back."

"I hear talk," his counselor said, "in the camp. People are beginnin' to mutter. We have failed to bring the coldhearts to justice, just as Wymie did. And even before this latest butcher's bill, at greater cost to the people of the district."

"Tell me who's talkin' loose talk like that." Potar's eyes glittered, with a far different light than Sairey's did, as he leaned his ominous moon face forward. "Me an' the boys'll straighten 'em right out."

"We can't rule by fear!" Frank protested.

Potar produced a chuckle like head-sized granite rocks being rolled downhill in a rain barrel. "What does Mr. Conn pay me for, then?"

Conn raised a hand. "Potar," he said, "you do your job very well. As does Frank. And in this case, Frank's correctly pointin' out that you catch more flies with honey than with vinegar, at the risk of sounding like the late, lamented Vin Bertolli."

"Why'd anybody want to catch fuckin' flies?" Potar asked.

"Figure of speech," Conn said. "In any event, we'll all have a smoother road to travel if we continue to get our people to work with and for us voluntarily."

"Well, they'll volunteer not to get their heads broke," Potar said. He smiled. "Or just disappear."

"I prefer to reserve those actions to enhance their effect."

Frank licked his thin lips. "That's not all they're sayin'. They say it can't be the outlanders who've been doing all the chillin'. At least not the butcherin' and eatin' part. There aren't enough of them, and anyway they don't work that way."

"And who's saying this?"

"Pretty much everybody who's not one of Wymie Berdone's remainin' few diehards. And Wymie herself, of course. She denies the existence of coamers. But they're who everybody else has begun to blame."

"And has anyone actually *seen* one of these red-eyed, white-haired, naked, screamin' ghouls out of legend?" Conn asked. "Much less chilled one and brought in the body?"

"Not as far as I know," Frank said hesitantly.

"Not my boys 'n' girls, that's for nukin' sure," Potar said. "And I've had 'em lookin' for them."

"None of which means there might not be somethin' in the old stories," Frank said, "old half-forgotten legends and campfire tales though they are."

Conn thought a minute, then he looked at his lead scout, who squatted across from the fire on her skinny legs, front and back flaps of her buckskin loincloth trailing to the ground. If anything, her face looked more frightened than it had before.

"Thanks, Sairey," Conn said. "You've done well."

She sat looking at him with huge, silent eyes.

"You can go now, child," Frank said, not unkindly.

She gulped visibly, nodded and vanished into the night in an eyeblink.

"If we can't produce coamers," Conn said, "we have to look elsewhere for the ones who have been assisting the outlanders in their crimes."

"But you yourself are uncertain of their guilt, sir," Frank said.

Conn sighed. "At the least, they're guilty of chillin' many of our people, robbin' families of loved ones and breadwinners. And even if the army's seeking about to fix blame, they're the ones they signed on to hunt down and exterminate."

He looked at Potar. "So they must have assistants. That much is generally agreed on—even if it's not strictly factual, Frank, so you can spare me further objections. So it becomes incumbent upon us to keep our force engaged and at least mollified by producin' some of these accomplice coldhearts and subjecting them to sufficiently exemplary public punishment, of course."

"Uh, where exactly do you expect us to look for these accomplices, boss?" Potar asked.

"Why, around. Known bad actors, the shiftless. The rootless and vagrant. People whose downfall will be publicly welcomed. Or who, in any event, shall not be widely missed."

Potar frowned momentarily, then his vast brow smoothed, and his smile came back, broader and uglier than before.

He may be slow, Conn thought, but he's definitely not a feeb. It would do well to remember that.

"Take out the trash, as it were," he said. "Chill two birds with one stone. My, I really am turnin' into that oldie blowhard Vin. I leave it to your capable hands."

"How many you want?"

"As many as you and your people can lay hands on, for now. We don't need any great number, really. Three or four should suffice. For now."

"But, Mathus," Frank said, "that is dishonest! What about justice?"

"To quote an old saw that Vin likely never would, 'There ain't no justice—there's just us!' But seriously. Until we can find the real perpetrators, whoever they are, the mob demands blood. And think about it—if we lose them, what happens? Do you want Wymie back in charge? Or mebbe someone less delusional but also less scrupulous? Or do you want them runnin' wild, mere anarchy loosed upon the land?"

At that last, his adviser's dark features paled. Frank was a big believer in order.

Which is well for us all, old friend, Conn thought. Since much as I need and value your candor, there are still limits.

"You see?" he asked, deliberately gentling his tone. "It's not as if we're preyin' on the innocent, after all. And in tryin' times like these, sacrifices must be made by all of us—for the greater good."

"So that's how they obtain their light," Doc said. "The walls in their passageways are dotted with some manner of phosphorescent moss or fungus. I wondered why the cannies, though obviously primarily troglodytic in their habits, had not evolved to be blind, as so many cave-dwellers do."

"But how do they recharge the stuff down here?" Mildred asked. "It's as dark as a baron's heart in these caves. And the growths, whatever they are, need to absorb light at some point to give any off."

Despite her forced calm, Krysty grimaced as one of the five albino cannies holding her above their matted-hair heads jostled her kidneys. Otherwise, it was a remarkably smooth ride; though not much larger than children, the creatures were surprisingly strong.

It's a good thing my friends can keep their spirits up enough for discussions like that, she thought. Or is it their way of dealing with the fear?

They had had no chance. Even though they had to have chilled at least a dozen of the stinking, naked white creatures, the cannies never faltered. They swarmed the companions and powered them down by weight of numbers and ferocity. Krysty heard Ryan calling her name, and steeled herself for the first kiss of fangs.

Instead her Glock was wrenched away, her arms yanked behind her back and her wrists bound with something that felt like rough vegetable-fiber rope. Despite the strength and fury with which she kicked them away, caving in at least one snouted, red-eyed face in the process, they managed to tie her ankles together, too. She might have summoned the strength of Gaia, who felt so near to her as Krysty was here in the Earth Mother's bosom, but the onslaught just happened too quickly.

And it was just as well. As she was hoisted aloft and saw her friends raised up likewise, she saw they were surrounded by what looked like a throng of hundreds of the slight, stooped, yet deadly creatures. Even had she fought them with all the mad strength Gaia sometimes gave her, she would still probably have been overwhelmed after the Gaia power left her, as she would have been depleted and helpless.

There's not much reason to think they're letting us live out of kindness, she thought.

She was as stunned by the fact their animalistic attackers had tied them, and with brisk efficiency, as that they refrained from eating them alive. It seemed so... human.

They were being carried along a relatively straight and oddly uniform passageway about fifteen feet in diameter. On both sides Krysty glimpsed small groups of coamers, mostly female, taking clumps of blue-green glowing moss from a piece of plank on one side, and what had to have been a scavvied cast-iron kettle on the other, and somehow sticking them to the walls.

They looked somehow different from the cannies they'd seen before, including the unwashed horde that carried them now to an uncertain but no doubt unpleasant fate. But she didn't get an ace look at them. She had other matters on her mind, much as she would have liked to drown her fears in detail.

"Why haven't they chilled us yet?" she heard Ricky ask. He sounded as if he was trying to be brave.

Evidently their captors didn't mind them talking.

"They got plans for us," Ryan said gruffly.

"Wh-what sort of plans?"

"We'll know it when we find out."

The walls and ceiling fell abruptly away, and they were bundled into a vast subterranean chamber awash with light from a thousand fragrant pine-scent torches.

Chapter Twenty

"Too bad the smell's not enough to drown out the stink of these bastards," Ryan commented.

"Aren't you afraid you'll piss them off?" Mildred said.

"Do they understand speech?" Doc asked.

"We didn't think they used rope, either," Mildred pointed out. "Or tactics."

"I don't care if I piss them off," Ryan said. "They're pissing *me* off."

He was mostly mad at his own powerlessness. He wasted not a second on regret, and less feeling guilt at them all being captured so quickly. They hadn't even had the chance to fall on their swords, so to speak, much less fight to the death. It had been that sudden and complete.

Despite himself, he was impressed at their surroundings. Turning his head this way and that, he could see the chamber was a good two or three hundred feet across, with big clumps of pillow-like flow rock and thick stalagmites sticking up from a mostly level floor. The ceiling was high enough even the tips of the longest stalactites were lost in the impenetrable shadows beyond the reach of even so many torches.

But mostly he was impressed by the fact there were hundreds of the unwashed, red-eyed cannies thronging the place. From the midst of the bad-smelling crowd rose a hump of melted-looking stone that had had a sort of seat carved out of the middle of the top of it, and on it sat a single figure who looked, even at this distance, far more human than the rest.

Their bearers carried them beeline toward the stone throne. The hordes of cannies melted away on either side before them. Looking down past his boots—Ryan was being carried on his back and headfirst—he saw that many of the huge but lesser horde that had swarmed them were spreading out to join the assemblage.

As they were borne into the avenue of living, death-reeking flesh, the cannies threw their clawed fists into the air and began to chant: "Muh-tha! Muh-tha! Muh-tha!"

Even the ultra-laconic J.B. was moved to shout, "I thought they couldn't talk!"

"They're just full of surprises," Ryan called back.

Still, he thought they were barely a step above animals, and not a long one. But that they had some degree of human intelligence was becoming more and more obvious.

As, he thought, was the fact they followed direction from some single, greater intelligence. He hung his head back to get a better, if inverted, look at the solitary person on the throne.

Even with her sitting down, Ryan could tell she was tall, gaunt to the point of emaciation, and though dead pale, and though the hair piled in a swirl atop her head was also white, it wasn't clear to him that she was an albino. She was definitely old, he thought, as the lines of her narrow, high-cheekboned face came into monocular focus.

Her eyes, which regarded him steadily, were of a pale color, green or blue or even white. But one thing they surely weren't was *red*.

"Down," she called in a clear, sharp voice as the captives were carried near her throne. The rock was a good ten feet tall, without steps in the front. Ryan briefly wondered how the nuke she got up in it. "Put them down!"

The reverential chant died away. Hundreds of cannies went to their knees all around, in a ripple effect that emanated from the smooth rock as if it had just been thrown into a pond. As Ryan was lowered to his feet with precision and gentleness, alike amazing, it occurred to him she could get them to form a human—or cannie—pyramid and climb up them to her seat, if she ordered them to.

He shook his shaggy, sweaty black hair from his face and stared at her with defiant arrogance. He realized that around her skinny neck she wore a bracelet of strung-together finger bones, adult-human-sized. As a pendant, she wore a small, bizarre skull, with a cranium like a human's, if lower and longer, but a snout like a baboon's. He realized it had to have belonged to a coamer infant.

That's cold, he thought.

"You're not a coamer," he told her.

"Ah, but you're wrong," she said. "I am Angela Mc-Comb. I am, you might say, *the* coamer. And these—" she spread elegant, spider-leg hands "—are my children!"

"Mutha!" the cannies cried, surging to their feet as one, each thrusting his or her right fist in the air.

Do they *practice* this shit? Ryan wondered.

"And you," she said, leaning forward with her hands on skinny thighs covered in a mostly clean white linen gown, "are Ryan Cawdor, and these are your friends."

"How do you know my name?"

"I know many things," she said. "I have eyes and ears

throughout the region. You have reason to know how stealthy my children can be."

"But they scarcely seem capable of forming coherent speech, madam," Doc said. "Hardly enough to convey even the rudiments of such intelligence—to call it that—as they gather in their reconnaissance. Much less convey our names and descriptions in detail."

"It's true they do not speak frequently, nor well. Much of the power of speech was lost in the…changes that have made them as they are today. As to how I know what I know…" She smiled thinly at him. "You will allow me my secrets, surely, Dr. Theophilus Tanner? Especially since you don't have any choice."

"You don't talk like most people in the Pennyrile," Ryan said. "Much less these things."

"I am different than they," she said with a haughty sniff. "I am above them, as befits a queen."

That brought out another joint shout of "Mutha!" so out-of-nowhere that it was all Ryan could do to keep himself from jumping in surprise.

She's got some means of signaling them, that's for sure, he thought. Or, more likely, she's got helpers who do. He suspected the caste system of this bizarre cave society had more layers and complexity than was apparent. On admittedly short observation.

"So they aren't actually your children," Krysty said.

"Goodness, no," McComb the Mother said. "Not of body. Figuratively, yes. They are actually birthed by specially chosen breeders in dorm caves below."

Ryan frowned. Krysty was usually too sensible to waste what might yet prove to be some of the last of her air yapping about random bits of information with this demented freak, who was somehow all the more freakish for looking so normal, here surrounded by her "children," with their stooped postures and their fang-filled, doglike muzzles.

Then he pushed the thought aside. While Krysty had a sentimental streak Ryan mostly lacked, and definitely her own perspective, at base she was no more likely to talk to hear the sound of her own voice than Ryan was. He realized such information did have value—any fact about how these twisted creatures lived, and more to the point kept living, could prove vital to their survival. Potentially.

"I brought them into being," McComb the Mother said. "So naturally, I rule them."

"How old are you, anyway?" Mildred asked.

"The knowledge that created my children sustains me," the queen said. "That is all you need know. More, perhaps."

"You didn't chill us," Ryan said, before Mildred and Doc could ask the questions he could hear them drawing breath to ask. "Or, you didn't have your children do it. That means you got plans for us."

"Perhaps I mean to have you killed before my eyes to amuse me."

"I don't reckon so."

"Your reckoning about me and my people does not have a conspicuous record of success, Mr. Cawdor. Make few assumptions."

He felt someone step up beside him. From the scent and sense of presence, he knew it was Krysty.

"But he's right," she said forthrightly.

McComb the Mother nodded. "I have a task for you."

Ryan uttered a grunt that his companions would know

to take for a short, wry laugh. "What kind of deal are you offering us?"

"I need make no deal," she said, "beyond refraining from killing you as a reward for your success."

"But you'll chill us if we fail!" Ricky piped up.

The kid's got balls, Ryan thought. Unfortunately, they tend to overcome his brain at the worst bastard times. He reassured himself with the knowledge that this crazy cannie queen and her brood had to need him and his companions bad. She'd have to be far crazier than she'd shown so far to have them chilled for saying the wrong thing.

"If you fail, young Master Morales," McComb the Mother said, "I shall have no need to punish you at all. Nor indeed the ability to do so, unless you believe in an afterlife. I do not."

She sat back up erect in her chair.

"I believe in what I can see, and hear and touch!" she declared.

"Mutha!" shouted the naked multitude.

"I am prepared to offer you a substantial reward for your assistance, however," she said.

"What kind and how much, exactly?" Mildred asked.

"Substantial," McComb the Mother repeated. "My children bring many treasures down from the surface. Others make their way here in…other ways. Much of that we have little use for. You shall have it—if you do what I demand."

"Ace," Ryan said. "We accept."

"But, Ryan—" Mildred began.

The one-eyed man didn't so much as glance her way. She was out of his field of view, as it happened, some-where behind his left shoulder. He merely extended the forefinger of his right hand, whose wrist was tied crossed over his left. Merely a flick.

Mildred abruptly shut up.

McComb the Mother nodded. "Of course you do. We sized you up well."

"So that's why your folks kept shadowing us, and occasionally throwing stuff at us," J.B. said. Ryan knew that wasn't a rhetorical question.

"Indeed."

"Testing us," Ryan said.

She nodded. "You demonstrate the sort of facility for which you have been chosen to serve. And—potentially—to walk out of here alive."

"You seem to have spent liberally of your 'children's' lives in these tests," Doc pointed out.

"Their lives are short and lived only to serve the community, which means, for all practical purposes, me. Even in all our numbers, we lack the strength to save ourselves from the doom that rapidly overtakes us. You have proved, by the very hurt you inflicted upon our flesh, that you may have the ability to succeed where we have failed."

Ryan rubbed his chin.

"I probably shouldn't say this, but you got the better of us triple quick there, a little while ago. What makes you think we can do what your people can't?"

"You and your people possess not just skills but tools that we lack," the cannie queen said. "Bluntly, if throwing bodies at the menace could end it, it would have. It didn't. So here we are."

"So that last cann—uh, wave attack was just, like, a final test?" Ricky asked.

The cannie queen nodded.

Ricky said no more, which wasn't exactly characteristic of him. But Ryan heard him make a "whoo" sound through pursed lips.

"So if we failed—" Mildred said.

"You would have proved unworthy, and my people would have enjoyed special meats at the ensuing feast."

"Uh, yeah," Ryan said. "So what is it you want killed?"

McComb the Mother laughed. "You come so easily to the conclusion that is what we require?"

"I don't reckon you selected us for our digging and scavvy-trading skills. Those and fighting were pretty much the ones you would've seen us display." Well, not including certain partnered nocturnal activities, on the part of him and Krysty, and Mildred and J.B., but he didn't want to pursue that line of thought.

"You're correct, Ryan Cawdor. As I have told you, we face a terrible menace. Something evil and huge, long forgotten except in our whispered legend, has awakened in the depths far below. It now seeks to come—up."

"The Balrog?" Mildred and Ricky asked simultaneously.

"Nothing so fanciful," the cannie queen said. "But no less terrifying. Or formidable."

"What is it, then?" asked Ryan, who'd read those books, too. The baronial palace in Front Royal where he'd grown up had a well-stocked library and as a baron's son, Ryan had been taught to read.

She shook her fine head. The pendants of human finger bones hung from either pierced earlobe tinkled like dull chimes. Somehow Ryan knew they were norm-human bones, not those of coamers.

"It's big," she said. "It digs great tunnels. It eats. It destroys. And it reappeared months ago.

"Our people have spread far and wide. Not merely down, though we have done that, too. The caves are vastly more extensive than we—than was ever guessed at, even by whitecoats, before the Nuke War. The monster first showed itself miles to the east of here, driving our people before it. Those who survived."

She paused for a moment and passed a hand wearily across her eyes. Even by the light of torches, abundant but not bright, Ryan almost thought he could see the bones of her hand through her age-thinned white skin.

I can almost believe she's as old as she claims to be, he thought. Sort of.

"The thing dived deep when it reached our heartland, here in these caves," she continued. "We are not without defenses, but it is as if it toys with us. It has been working its way up, slowly, slowly, devouring our breeders and devastating our grub farms."

"Wait," Ricky said. "Grub farms? You mean you raise food?"

"It is not a rare practice, after all. Even in this brutal, desiccated world of today."

"But I thought your, uh, children ate people."

"Don't be stupe, son," J.B. said matter-of-factly. "They can't very well live off eating each other. And if they hunted humans for their main food, they'd have been at war with the surface years ago."

"You are correct, Mr. Dix. The flesh of norm humans is a delicacy among us, you might say. Its taste and texture highly prized. It is a consequence of their creation."

Ryan noticed she didn't say "accidental" or "unintended."

"Yet we refrained from foraging aboveground, except on the rarest occasions, until the monster left us no choice. And as for dining on one another, it's true that tradition calls upon us to return our flesh to the family when we are dead. But we could no more subsist by that than you and Mr. Dix could build a perpetual-motion machine."

"So why didn't you try to recruit the locals, instead of us?" Mildred asked.

"You made a quick impression upon me. You possessed an air of competence, especially with weapons, the inhabitants of the district do not generally possess. And your weapons are much superior to theirs. You've fought them. Would *you* have faith in them as champions against a monster that's a force of nature?"

"They saw us off quick there, last time we ran into them," Ryan said. "Or, rather, they ran into us."

"They prevailed by sheer force of numbers. Surely you did not forget I said what little use mass attacks have already proved against our great enemy? We can bring far greater numbers against it than were assembled against you. And their crude black-powder firearms lack power to do our enemy any great harm."

"You judge ours have the power, though," J.B. said.

"I have faith in your ability to use them," the cannie queen said. "And in your resourcefulness. But if those are not enough to defeat our great enemy after all…"

For the first time her smile widened to show her teeth. They looked surprisingly normal. Except, perhaps by a trick of the light, or even Ryan's imagination, her eye-teeth—her fangs. These looked as long and unnaturally wicked-sharp as those of her canine-snouted children.

"Then we'll know when you fail to return and claim your reward, then, won't we?"

Chapter Twenty-One

"We need action!" the man with the food-stained beard hanging well down the front of his shabby overalls declared. "Somethin's gotta be done!"

His crowd of a dozen or so listeners nodded sagely. "Yeah," one of them shouted from the rear of the clump. "Somebody's gotta do somethin'!"

"But we hunted down like half a dozen collaborators already," insisted a sturdy middle-aged woman with a greasy bandanna around her mouse-colored cap of curls.

"And the attacks ain't stopped yet," the bearded orator declared. "We need to do something that works."

The group had gathered on the fringes of Mathus Conn's camp, near the excavation site. The sun was low, though it had not yet dropped behind the rise whose crest had fallen in on itself to swallow what was proving to be a still-unexhausted treasure trove of scavvy. Conn halted his small party, returning from a walk near the camp, in the deep shadows gathered in the bushes between a pair of red maples, at the clearing's edge.

Potar growled low in his throat. "Henry Harkens," he said, then spit. "Want me to put a stop to that stupe-talk?"

"Not yet." Conn considered briefly. The unsuspecting men nearby continued to gripe about the ongoing cannie attacks—and their own fear.

"It wasn't these drifters from over by Sanders Gap

we hanged yesterday done it," said a short, squat man whose features were totally obscured by a floppy hat and bristling facial hair. "No loss, 'cause they was just petty thieves and robbers. But they didn't have nothin' to do with all the cannie killin' and eatin' people. That's them coamers, sure."

"Wymie says it's all them outlanders," a second woman said. "Them and their helpers. And there ain't no such thing as coamers."

"Wymie did a great job of gettin' us massacred," someone else said.

"We're not doin' nothin' now that works," the woman said. "Chillin's still goin' on."

"It's gotta be the coamers," the hidden-faced man insisted. "What the outlanders said they looked like was right out of the old stories. And they only come out at night—just like the stories."

"They are just stories!"

"They stole the chills straight off the gallows, soon as nobody was lookin'!" a gaunt man said. He looked nervously around as if the fabled cannies might jump out of the bushes at any moment. "It's gotta be the coamers!"

"Does not!"

"Does too!"

As arguments broke out, Conn gestured with a raised forefinger. The group started to move again, swinging wide back into the woods a short distance to approach Conn's tent without passing through the camp proper.

"Been a lot of talk like that the last couple days," Frank said. "All over the camp."

"They were eager enough to see the last set of ne'er-do-wells swing, and the ones before."

Frank wrung his hands in a worried gesture.

"But it was true what they were saying, that the cannibal attacks have not stopped," he said. "That has people antsy and wantin' more action. And more and more are blamin' the coamers, in spite of Wymie and her holdouts."

He scratched his head. "I wonder sometimes if we're on the wrong track, chasing the outlanders at all."

"Coamers're real," Chad insisted. The bouncer's right arm was tied against his chest in a sling. Gator Malloan's ax to the chest had been more gory than actually damaging; it had done little more than break his right clavicle. He and his pal Tony had both attached themselves to Conn as bodyguards, which worked out fine, as Potar, while seldom leaving his master's side, was growing more and more preoccupied with playing sec boss, spying on Conn's army and keeping order in it.

Tony said nothing. He was busy eyeing the surrounding brush nervously with a replica .44 Henry repeating longblaster in his hands, unnerved by the rapid onset of darkness. The sun had dropped below the rise while everybody was engrossed in the camp gossip.

"Every night we see their red eyes glowin' in the firelight of the camp," Chad said. "Watchin' us from the bushes."

Conn waved a hand dismissively. "At this point it doesn't much matter whether the coamers are real or not," he said. "At least as regards the fate of the outlanders. We have no choice but to continue our pursuit of them, gentlemen. It's mere self-preservation."

"But if the coamers are responsible for the attacks," Frank said, "the attacks will continue until we deal with them. That requires us to find a way to come to grips with them. We don't even have any direct evidence they exist. And the mob, as you point out, is demanding action now."

"You should let me do something about that loud-mouth Harkens. He's been a troublemaker all along," Potar said.

Conn stopped. Then he smiled. "You're right, Potar. I should and I will. Now let me tell you *how* you're going to handle him…"

"IT STRIKES ME," Doc said, "that these creatures into whose service we find ourselves so involuntarily pressed are rather more sophisticated than we imagined."

With a grateful grunt Ryan swung first his Steyr on its sling and then his heavy rucksack off his back and lowered them to stand propped against the stone. The coamers had given them all their gear and weapons back *after* they had escorted them well away from the immense royal cavern, and formed a solid white-skinned phalanx between the surface-dwellers and their queen.

He sat beside the pack and blaster on a knee of flowstone protruding from the passageway wall at an appropriate height and uncapped his water bottle. At least they had access to abundant freshwater down here. Even if it tasted a mite strange, and both Mildred and Doc fretted about possible ill effects of its unknown mineral content on their health.

He took a long swallow anyway. The stuff hadn't given anybody the pukes or the runs, nor any pains yet. So any bad effects were in the long run, which they didn't seem likely to live to see.

The passageway descended at a gentle angle deeper into the earth. By the light of the glowing moss the coamers set out everywhere to illuminate their living spaces, he could see several of the cannies carrying what looked like human infants with oddly pearlescent skins and no limbs visible at this distance. From having seen the things up close, he knew that was because their limbs were more like an unknown number of paired black hooks along their bellies. They were in fact infants, though. Just not human ones.

Nor mammalian ones. He'd been wrong to think "grub farms" was a figure of speech.

"You and I have very different definitions of sophisticated, Doc," Mildred said.

"It is a relative term," the old man stated loftily. "Consider the workers down there. They conform in general to a rather different somatotype from the ghouls we first encountered on the surface, do they not? While they are superficially similar, with the same symptoms of albinism—with apologies to Jak…"

Hunkered nearby, a little farther down from the rest as if to stand guard in the direction, Jak just nodded.

"They possess sturdier builds, shorter limbs and blunter physiognomies."

"Physio-whats?" asked J.B., who was clearly interested despite himself.

"Faces," Mildred said. "Theirs are more like ours."

"I propose that the differences are more than incidental," Doc said. "It seems to me that the two types have been born into distinct castes, each bred for a different line of work."

"They're like ants!" Ricky exclaimed.

"In a manner of speaking, yes."

"Working the same way bugs do doesn't strike me as sophisticated," Ryan said. To him, here and now, discussing even the finer points of cannie society did not constitute indulging in abstract knowledge. They were grasping at straws, and their lives were at stake.

By J.B.'s wrist chron, they'd been working their way through a slowly and irregularly descending network of caves and tunnels for three days now. They had so far seen nothing that looked like a sign of this giant menacing *thing* they'd been sent to hunt and chill, which was lucky in a way. If the creature was that scary, none of the companions were in a hurry to come face-to-face with it. But there was no way of knowing when that crazy old coldheart McComb the Mother would decide time was up and send a swarm of her wicked brood to put an end to them all.

As was often the case, if Krysty's thoughts weren't the same as his, they resonated. "This caste system of yours," she asked Doc, "how does that fit with their queen? She doesn't look like any of the others, except for her pale skin and hair. And the hair is probably whitened by age."

Doc shook his head ruefully. "I cannot account for her. She is an anomaly."

"That seems like kind of an understatement," J.B. said. "Then again, this whole setup seems pretty anomalous. Even compared to what we're used to."

"Hey," Ricky called. "Check this out, guys."

He had a hand buried to the elbow in a crevice in the wall. It was so narrow not even Ryan's eye, lone but keen, had picked it out of the smoothly irregular surface.

"Don't stick your hand in there!" he and J.B. said simultaneously.

"It's all right," the youth replied. "I scoped it with my butane lighter first."

He pulled his hand back and waved what was in it triumphantly over his head.

"It's a book," Mildred said.

"Some kind of diary, by the looks of it," Krysty observed.

"Hand it here," Ryan ordered.

Though he was obviously beyond reluctant to let go of his newfound treasure, Ricky instantly complied. Ryan turned it over in his hand, squinting at it. It seemed to have been bound in leather—expensive even for its time—which was either black to begin with or blackened by age and possibly accreted human grease. The pages were warped by ages of moisture. He experimentally opened it and thumbed through a few pages.

Ricky lit one of their lanterns and held it up helpfully near Ryan's face. Their stock of turpentine oil was dwindling despite efforts to conserve it, making use of the ubiquitous luminous moss. But he didn't complain.

"Handwritten," he said, squinting at the fussily precise blue lines of cursive. "But some of it's blotted out by water. Some of the pages are stuck together, too."

He looked up at Ricky, who was shifting his weight from one foot to another and trying not to look stricken at the idea of someone else being the one to make use of his uncovered treasure.

"Here, kid," Ryan said. He tossed Ricky the old book. "You look through it. Read us anything that sounds good."

He pushed up off his seat on the smooth rock.

"All right, everybody," he said, shouldering his pack again. "Time to move."

He led them on down the passage. The workers and their unappetizing cargo had vanished.

"The diary seems to belong to a man named Alton J. Foxton," Ricky said. He was trying to hold the lamp closed with one hand while carrying the diary in the other, turning the pages with his thumb. "Whitecoat. He seems to have been in charge of some kind of lab. Listen to this. 'Our cover as a mining-exploration company in search of uranium deposits deep in the caves seems to be satisfying the curiosity of the locals as to what we are doing underground. They also seem to be convinced our small prefabricated office complex on the surface constitutes the majority of our operation. Little do they know that it isn't even the tip of the iceberg, compared to our subterr—' Sorta blurs out there."

"Huh," Mildred said. "Sounds like he's talking about our secret scavvy mine."

She and Krysty walked side by side behind Ryan. Jak ranged out ahead of them like a scout dog.

"If it was really the headquarters for some kind of secret project, it would certainly explain why there was so much worthwhile gear and supplies to recover," Krysty said.

"Especially the ammo and explosives," J.B. added.

"So why didn't the coamers find this stash before?" Ryan wondered. "I judge they've long since found and picked through every hidey-hole down here. Especially so close to their main digs."

"Observe the workers closely," Doc said. "While their appearance differs markedly from those of what I think we might term the 'soldiers,' they are no taller. And the tallest is still shorter than young Ricky."

"Shorter than me," Jak said, emphasizing his point not just by jabbing his own skinny chest with a forefinger, but by speaking in a more or less complete phrase, with an actual conjunction, and even a pronoun. Ryan was impressed.

"So they didn't ever notice it in that cleft there," Ryan said. "They always walked right by because it's over their heads."

Doc shrugged. "Or they lack interest in written matter, inasmuch as they almost certainly lack letters."

"I'd bet you dollars to doughnuts that creepy-ass queen of theirs reads," Mildred said. "And I would be surprised if she hasn't ordered her kiddies to bring her any books or journals or similar stuff they find."

"Why would that be?" Krysty asked.

"She seems like a type who wants to suck up all the information she can. She had her people watching us take dumps in the frigging woods, for cripes' sake. Plus, it doesn't strike me that these coamers have much conversation. All we've seen of the rank and file makes Jak look like Doc here."

Jak looked narrowly at her, unsure whether that was a compliment or not.

"So think how nuking bored she must be. If they brought her an old cereal box, she'd probably read it all the way through every day, fine print and all."

Krysty pulled a face and nodded. "I think you're right."

They entered the cavern where the grub-carriers had passed through earlier. It was lit in places by the luminescent moss. Even in the poor and patchy light Ryan could see that it had a low, fanged ceiling. On closer appraisal he reckoned there was ample headroom for him and even Doc to walk upright, at least mostly.

Three exits gaped out of the chamber. A group of workers was clustered by the one away to the left. A muted but oddly musical *thump-thump-thumping* sound came from that direction.

Mildred squinted. "Why are they beating the walls with rocks?"

"Widening the passage, probably," J.B. replied.

"By hitting it with rocks?"

"It's not like they got better tools. Much less dynamite." He allowed his thin lips a twitch of a smile. "Not like us."

"Doesn't that take forever?" Krysty asked.

"They're not pressed for time down here," Ryan said.

"That reminds me," Doc stated with an air of a man awakening. Ryan suspected he'd been starting to zone out again. "Did it strike anyone else that the final tunnel they carried us along before we reached Mother McComb in her royal cavern seemed unusually uniform? It seemed almost perfectly circular in section, and the walls did not show the marked corrugation characteristic of most of them, carved as they are by the limestone being dissolved away, with other limestone from higher above carried down and deposited along them."

"Not my department," Ryan said, "but now that you mention it… J.B.? You're our engineer. Or can pass for one in bad light, which this is."

J.B. pushed his fedora back and scratched his forehead.

"Not that kind of engineer," he said, "in any kind of light. But for what it's worth, I agree. I don't know if it struck me as unnatural or not. But it was different."

"So which way do we go from here, kemo sabe?" Mildred asked.

Ryan shrugged. "Straight ahead. It looks to go down. We know this Big Ugly we're on the trail of likes down. Until and unless we raise some actual traces of it, that's all we got to go on."

He set out walking toward the cave mouth roughly opposite the one they had come in by. Jak, who was prowling a circuit among the stalagmites and columns surrounding the rest of them, silently glided to scout the way ahead. The others followed.

"Hey, guys!" Ricky exclaimed. He had doused the lantern, thankfully, and hung it back from his overstuffed pack. Instead his round face was spookily underlit by the blue-green-white glow of clump of the illuminating moss, sticking out the top of his shirt like the chest hair he so conspicuously didn't have.

Ryan thought the kid was being more brave than smart. The stuff was radioactive. Ryan's and J.B.'s lapel rad counters told them as much.

"Listen to this. 'Sadly, owing to the fact that our research entails similar genetic manipulation—although theirs does not involve integrating cybernetic controls systems into the organisms they create—the Totality Concept forces us—'"

Doc, whose expression had settled back to that dreamy blankness that indicated he was mentally wandering off in the fog again, stiffened and almost stumbled. His blue eyes snapped open. The soulless, dispassionate whitecoats of the late nineties had destroyed his life.

"If those damned whitecoats were involved," Mildred said, "we know whatever was going on here was evil."

"Wait," Ricky said. "'—forces us to share our underground primary facility with a human-modification project, whose codename COMB appears to have been chosen to flatter the ego of its unreasonable and subcompetent head, the so-called Dr. Angela McComb.'"

"Ho-lee shit," Mildred said. "That explains a lot."

"Does it?" Krysty asked.

"It sure gives us a clue as to where the coamers came from. We already knew how they got their name."

"Does it mean that the Mother McComb actually created the coamers?" Krysty asked.

It was Mildred's turn to frown. "Do you think she's actually more than a century old? I mean, she's no spring chicken, sure, but still, that seems a little bit extreme."

"The diary does say Project COMB was involved in human modification," said Ricky, who was leafing further along in the book, evidently in search of either nonblurred writing, or something else worth sharing. "Maybe along with a whole race of cannies, she came up with a way to make herself immortal?"

"There's a comforting thought," Mildred said.

"Perhaps she inherited the name," Doc suggested. "And with it both the mantle of authority over the wretches, and a superior education by the standards of today."

"I don't see how that loads any blasters for us," Ryan growled. "Immortal bitch-queen or just Angela the Fifth or whatever number, she's still got us staring down both barrels of a scattergun with her finger on both triggers."

Something snagged the edge of his attention. His eye automatically tracked to that which had initially tweaked its peripheral vision: Jak, who crouched by the tunnel entrance they were coming up on, frowning and looking as if he was sniffing the air.

"What's up, Jak?" Mildred called. "You look like somebody farted."

To Ryan's surprise Jak nodded vigorously.

"Did," he said. "Big-time!"

Chapter Twenty-Two

"Rad waste!"

As soon as the words left his mouth, Alfie Kayde turned away. Wymie heard him heaving his guts out on the bare-trampled soil, but she refused to turn her own eyes away from the terrible sight.

The nude figures nailed on the crudely hewn quartet of ten-foot-tall crosses had all been partially torn apart and devoured. Some of the legs had been eaten down to expose the bones of shin and thigh, with shreds of their skin hanging over their feet and down to the ground. Others had had their bellies torn open, organs ripped out by the handful, intestines unspooled the way poor Buffort's had been.

She could do nothing other than pity Alfie in her heart, rather than reproach him. Mebbe he had a queasy stomach for the man who had succeeded her murdered cousin Mance as her chief bodyguard.

But then again, mebbe he didn't. The looks on the four faces—or the three who *had* faces, or enough to make anything of—left no doubt the rending and the tearing and the flaying and the eating had taken place while they were still alive. The stink of rotting meat was thicker than the buzzing fly-clouds that surrounded the tortured chills.

At her other elbow Angus said, "They made the mistake of complaining too loudly about being worked to death digging scavvy out of the cave-in to make Mathus Conn a richer man," he said. "Some of Potar's snitches heard, and Conn decided to make examples."

"Conn loves to make examples," Alfie said, straightening and wiping the back of his mouth with his hand. His tone was almost normal. Wymie guessed he was trying to act as if the vomiting episode had never happened. "First one to get that treatment was Henry Harkens."

"He questioned Conn one too many times," Angus said. As the hotheaded Alfie had taken Mance's place protecting her, Angus had taken over as chief adviser for Dorden Fitzyoo. That smelly old bag of wind and farts Vin Bertolli didn't count, even though Wymie was still sad he'd died. "He always was a loudmouth."

Conn had moved his personal tent and those of Potar, Frank and a couple of this other—Wymie didn't want to think "chief toadies," but couldn't quite stop herself—progressively farther away from the main camp as his army grew, and closer to the dig site where the outlanders had gone to ground. The crosses had been pounded into the earth beside the path between the encampments, on the outskirts of the larger one.

"I heard that Conn had started crucifyin' the outlander coldhearts' accomplices and leaving them for the others to eat," Wymie said. "I never saw it before."

Maintain, she told herself. You owe Blinda that. Just hold it together. Do what you came to do. You didn't know these people. Or—not double well, anyway. They weren't your blood.

"Conn never says it's for talkin' back to him," Alfie said, "but so far it always seems to be the ones who do that get ratted out for collaboration."

He shook his head. "Wymie, you need to take back command. Conn's dirty. No more than a stoneheart himself!"

"It might prove more easily said than done," Angus said.

It was Wymie's turn to shake her head, more emphatically than Alfie had, and with a different meaning to it.

"I don't want power," she said. "I just want justice for poor murdered Blinda, is all."

"You really think you can talk Conn into changin' course?" Angus asked.

"I don't rightly know, but it's what I come here intendin' to do."

"But why would he listen to you?"

Alfie growled low in his throat. Wymie waved him off with a quick hand gesture. Angus had a point, she knew. Conn had taken completely over right away, and nowadays seemed intent on following his own designs. It was exactly what she meant to talk to him about.

At last she tore her eyes away from the scene of frozen suffering. She had punished herself enough. She didn't even know what for. Only that she had had to.

She gave her two companions a smile. "And while I don't *want* to be in charge of this shootin' match," she said, "I reckon a power of people'd feel double relieved to see me do so. And mebbe that gives me leverage."

"I SMELL SULFUR," Ricky said, at just about the same time Doc stated, "By the Three Kennedys—brimstone!"

"Hold up," Ryan commanded, raising his hand for emphasis. "We don't yet know if there's danger. Jak, come with me." He headed toward the cave mouth.

"Air warmer," Jak announced, still hunkered like a cautious animal by the hole.

Ryan felt the truth of that on his face as he came up to where the albino squatted. The sulfur stench was clearly perceptible.

"Doc," Ryan said, making a summoning gesture with two fingers of his right hand and not looking back. He could see the characteristic glows from down the passageway, which descended more steeply than any they'd traversed so far, that showed the coamer workers had been busy with their baskets of glow-moss.

"They must have whole huge farms devoted to that stuff," he muttered. "And how the hell they keep the bastard stuff charged is a mystery to me."

"It is likely by exposing it to sunlight that spills into sinkholes and cracks that lead to the surface," Doc said, approaching Ryan.

Ryan cocked a brow at him. "You started reading my mind, Doc? Wouldn't think you could've held back a mutie trait from us for all these years."

The old man smiled wanly. "Simple deduction. We are all curious about the moss. I could see traces of its illumination from below as I approached. And inasmuch as we know they farm those singularly unappetizing giant-insect larvae for food, your muttering made it abundantly obvious what was on your mind."

"Ace," Ryan said, with an open grin. "So either I'm transparent, or we should start calling you Sherlock. I read stories about him when I was a kid."

"I cannot claim such acute powers of observation, I am afraid." He frowned in concentration as he sniffed at the air, his nostrils flaring. "It is indeed a strong sulfurous odor that emanates from the tunnel."

"Does the cave run through some kind of deposit, you think?"

Doc gingerly touched the wall by the opening, then slid his hand around the rippled yet glossy surface into the passageway.

"It is not just the air that is warmer," he said. "The stone itself is perceptibly warm to the touch here. More so than any we have encountered before."

He took his hand away and looked at Ryan. "It appears clear to me that we are near a magma tube."

"Magma?" Ricky asked, joining them. The others had apparently decided that, if the unknown monster that had the cannie queen and her awful children so upset was about to spring out of the tunnel and eat their faces, it had not just Ryan but Jak fooled. Ryan hadn't specifically rescinded his order to halt to anyone but Doc, but it was clear this wasn't one of those situations where absolute obedience was called for. "Isn't that like lava?"

"Lava's what you call magma that's come out of a volcano," Mildred said. "What? I read a book, too, you know."

"How likely is it to bust out on us?" asked the ever-practical J.B.

Doc shrugged. "It has not so far. Of course, much depends on whether its presence is a recent development."

Ryan's ears perked up. He could hear the doubt and worry creep into Doc's voice as he thought aloud.

"Here, guys," Ricky said. "Listen to this. 'Unfortunately problems have arisen with our power supply. Owing to ill-advised and irrational allocation of all the rumored fusion-power generators to other Totality Concept projects, we are forced to make do with geothermal energy extractors as our primary power source. And for some unknown reason that frightful harridan McComb insists on hogging more than her share for her bizarre glass tubes and vat farms.'"

He looked up from the diary. "Do you want me to see if there's more about the lava? Er, magma?"

"We get the gist," Ryan said. "So, not recent."

"Well, in geological terms—" Doc began.

Ryan waved him to silence. "Yeah. In geological terms the dinosaurs were recent."

"But we've—"

"There's been magma around since sometime before the Big Nuke. That's enough to reassure me we're not about to get a sudden bath in it or anything."

"So do we continue down, lover?" Krysty asked.

"The operative word being *down*," Ryan said. "Sure. It still seems our best shot to find this thing. So off we go."

Mildred hung back. "I have a bad feeling about this," she said.

"If you haven't had a bad feeling about *everything* since you woke out of cryosleep," Ryan said, walking down the slope without looking back, "you haven't been paying attention."

"WYMIE!" MATHUS CONN exclaimed, rising from his folding chair outside his command tent. "What a pleasant surprise to see you."

With an effort, he winched his face into a smile and stepped forward with hand extended as Wymie stepped into the yellow circle of campfire light. Angus, her right-hand man, and Alfie, her sec boss in all but name, followed a pace behind.

Conn didn't need to take his eyes off Wymie's wary blue ones to know that as soon as they entered the light some of Potar Baggart's most trusted sec men had silently stepped in to block the way behind them. They completed the circle that ringed Conn's headquarters.

Potar himself stood a bit to one side, gigantic arms crossed over his ox-like chest. His face showed an expression of smug contempt. But Conn doubted there was anything there to make the uninvited, but not wholly unexpected, guests wary. He usually looked like that, since becoming Conn's sec boss.

Frank Ramakrishnan was not present. When one of Potar's spies reported that Wymie was on her way through the camp to see him, Conn had sent him into the big camp on an invited errand to check the stores of supplies extorted from the surrounding countryside. Only Conn and his sec men remained.

She stopped. Her mouth and brows were set in lines of grim disapproval.

"You won't find it so pleasant when you hear what I've come to say, I reckon, Mr. Conn," she said.

Around the camp fireflies frolicked, crickets sang. Somewhere a nightjar called. As if in reply came the bass-fiddle sawing croak of a bullfrog from the bottoms nearby.

"I'm all ears."

"To start, I passed by the latest poor souls you tacked up outside the camp. The cannies had been at them. Ate them alive."

He shrugged elaborately. "Some might call that justice playin' out. They were collaboratin' with your sister's killers, after all. So what could possibly be more appropriate that their own former friends puttin' an end to them?"

"It looks more like puttin' on a cruel show to make

people think you're makin' progress," she said. "And to keep the ones as don't in line. But you're no closer to runnin' down those coldheart taints than you were when you were standin' back behind your bar, are you?"

"At least we're draining the swamp," he said, forcing his tone to stay level and his face affable. It was good he had plenty of practice in those things from running a gaudy. "You yourself acknowledge the outlanders who murdered your sister had help. Is it so surprising, really, that some of that help came from known malcontents?"

"How do you know they were guilty?"

He allowed himself the luxury of a quick smirk. "Privileged information," he said. "Rest assured, my dear—they were observed having dealin's with the coldhearts' coamer allies."

"See?" she flared. Her eyes seemed to become self-luminous with growing rage. Though he was far from weak nor incapable himself, he was glad to have Potar nearby. Wymie was as strong as an elk for all her beauty, and had never had the tightest grip on her temper. "There's that monkey talk again, even coming from your own lips, Mathus Conn! Our real enemies are these outlanders you let slip through your grip. Not even their traitor allies. And least of all a bunch of made-up graverobbin' boogeymen!"

Potar made a sound low in his thick throat like a volcano getting ready to cut one. "Show more respect to Mr. Conn."

"There, there, Potar," Conn said. "Let Wymie speak her mind."

"We're getting off-course," she said. "Sure, you whipped the bunch I scraped together into line. And you've made 'em grow by leaps and bounds, and a power of good on you. But they seem to be turnin' more and more into your personal, private army, day by day. There's even talk you're fixin' to lead them off to war on the Corners, just for failin' to join up under you!"

"Well, wasn't it you, yourself, who said that those who weren't with us were against us? I resisted that at first, as you know. But I came around to your view. So now we need to make others do so as well, until we've rooted out this evil from all the Pennyrile."

"While vengeance—*justice*—for my murdered baby sister just seems to keep gettin' further and further away."

He spread his hands, palms up. "What would you have me do?"

"You need to take all your high-and-mighty army," she said, leaning forward and saying the words with a fury that surprised him despite her evident anger, "and not send it gallivantin' off to the west, nor the east, nor even the south. You need to send them right straight down into that hole in the ground, and tell them not to come out until they bring back the coldhearts who killed Blinda and lay them at your feet!"

He sighed theatrically. "But we've moved beyond that now, Wymie. Don't you see? Your sister's death was regrettable, sure, but by now, just one out of many. You need to step back and look at the bigger pictu—"

She drew herself up to her full, imposing height, but with her flamboyantly black-haired head lowered like an angry bull's.

"Did you just say my sister's death didn't mean nothin'?"

"Well, to you personally, of course it did. And to many of your followers. But in the greater scope of events that have overtaken our homeland, a single death just doesn't have much meanin', after all."

With a single tearing scream of, "You *bastard*!" she launched herself at him. So furious was her onslaught that Conn feared he would be battered to the ground before his security team could respond.

But while Potar Baggart was built like a mountain, he could move like the wind. At least in short spurts. Even as she got close enough to slam him in the head with her powerful fists, Potar whipped up next to her, and flung her aside with an even more powerful blow to the side of her head.

Angus and Alfie called out in outrage. Alfie flung himself forward, ignoring the Remington cap-and-ball revolver stuck through his belt to reach for the vastly larger Potar with both hands. At least a touch cooler-headed, Angus flashed out his own Ruger Old Army.

Blaster shots cracked from the darkness.

Chapter Twenty-Three

"Take five, everybody," Ryan said.

With relief, Ricky slipped his pack and longblaster off his shoulder and lowered them to the mostly level stretch of cavern floor. A moment later he lowered his butt alongside them. The stone felt smooth and cool through his jeans. He recognized by now that the path had been made, or at least improved, by the patient, unspeaking, incessant labor of the coamer worker-drones.

The first thing he did was break out his water bottle and take a hefty drink. It was lucky that, at the very least, freshwater was readily available everywhere they'd been, so far. If you didn't mind weird chemical tastes, which Ricky did not.

Mildred griped about the water some. She was more squeamish than the rest of them. Even Doc.

Of course, it helped when drinking the water not to think too deeply about the cannie sanitary arrangements, which, given Ricky's naturally inquisitive mind, and almost obsessive need to know how things worked, was not easy for him. But they had to have sanitary arrangements. Not just the cannie queen's giant audience chamber but everywhere they'd been—including more than slightly unnerving glimpses into breeder dorms and feeding halls—and the passages themselves were all spotless. That was especially surprising given what they all knew about the coamers' taste. Clearly, cannie inbreds or not, they knew not to shit where they ate. Ricky suspected that some of the working caste had the job of clearing waste. The others all sat down around him and likewise drank in the low, small chamber, which was really more a widening of the passageway than anything else. Even Jak squatted on his haunches near Ricky. Ryan had taken on the task of prowling around, peering down the two tunnels that led to and from the place and keeping watch.

Krysty would probably upbraid him later about ignoring his own needs. He would nod and ignore her protests. The usual.

After draining his bottle and stuffing it into his pack, Ricky's next move was to dig out the diary and keep reading. He lit his lantern to do so, immediately filling the air with pine tang. Though their oil stocks were low, Ryan had given him permission to use the lamp when absolutely necessary to read. Their leader thought what they'd learned from the diary had some prospect of upping their chances of getting out of this mess alive, and hoped that maybe even a hint to dealing with whatever they were looking for—and still hadn't found—might yet lurk in the water-warped pages. The glow-moss here was clearly getting near exhaustion, and gave off only a feeble illumination. Not enough by which to read the precise but tiny handwriting.

"'Our Digging Leviathan is progressing beyond our wildest expectations,'" he read aloud. "'Its growth is remarkably rapid, even given its gene engineering, and its development remains within parameters. If anything, it almost grows too fas—' It ends, in several more pages so soaked together I can't even pull them apart. Probably nothing readable on them if I did, so…"

He ended with a shrug. That was the kick. While having been stuffed, somehow, into the hard-to-see crevice in a cave wall by some long-forgotten hand had preserved the diary until its chance discovery, it had done nothing to shield it from the occasional influx of the mineral-rich water whose drips had carved these caverns over endless millennia. He wondered that it had survived as intact, and legible, as it had.

"Interesting," Krysty said.

"Huh, Krysty," Mildred said. "You usually don't take to science-y stuff like that."

The tall, statuesque redhead laughed.

"You're right," she said. "I don't—usually. But I do take interest in my intuition, and that twitched when you spoke the words *Digging Leviathan*."

"Strange," Doc said. "'Leviathan' appears as a sea monster in the Old Testament, and is generally used to refer to such. It would seem to accord oddly with the sobriquet, 'digging.'"

"It gives me the creeps, too, now that you mention it," Mildred said. The sturdy woman, like Ricky, was sitting on the cool stone floor. The others squatted on their haunches the way Jak was.

Ryan approached them. "All right," he said with a nod to Jak. The albino sprang to his feet as eagerly as a puppy freed from its leash. "You can go poke around."

The tall one-eyed man likewise hunkered, took out a water bottle and drank deeply. Then he turned his lone eye to Ricky.

"We've got a couple minutes, by my reckoning," he said, which made Ricky smile. The fact that it was Ryan's reckoning made it that way, regardless of what J.B.'s wrist chron said. "See if you can find something else worth reading to us. I've got to say, tramping around these nuking half-lit caves gets to be wearing, after a spell."

They had been exploring more laterally than vertically since discovering the proximity of live magma. Ryan wanted to get some idea of where the stuff was to be found, for their own safety. Ricky wasn't sure exactly how that was a concern, given—as Ryan himself had said—that if the stuff hadn't flooded into the cannie's cave system yet, it wasn't particularly likely to now. But Ryan had gut feelings, too, and he knew to trust them.

The cannies had a system of marks notched in the walls as navigation aids. Because they clearly weren't particularly bright, except their mother, the system was simple. The companions figured it out in short order. Ricky and J.B. took notes and sketched maps in scavvied notebooks anyway. For his part Jak claimed to know his way around anyplace they'd been, and while this was even more remote from their usual environment than a ruined city was, Ricky was inclined to believe him. He also half suspected Ryan kept a pretty fair map in his own head.

Ricky skimmed over some uninteresting sections of the diary, griping about this delay or that with the program, who was subcompetent—everybody but Foxton, apparently—and repetitive whines about McComb and her rival project, and their incessant war over resources.

"Here we go," he said finally, as Ryan ordered an end to their break and everybody got back to their feet. He paused to pull on his pack and longblaster sling, then picked up the lantern. The oil reservoir hadn't gone down much.

"'We have received a full alert of possible impending

global war,'" he read as he walked. "'Totality Concept leadership informs us this is not a drill. I have ordered the evacuation of the surface facility, and all personnel have taken shelter underground.'"

He raised his head and looked around. "So where *is* this lab, exactly? It should've been right beneath us."

"Nowhere we've been," Ryan said. "They must not have located the office complex directly over the actual laboratory, which makes sense as a cover. They wouldn't want to have a signpost right up in the open announcing We Are Here."

"Maybe they did," Mildred suggested. "But what we first came into down here was just an admin complex—desks, chairs, computers, separated by movable panels. It was a basic, late twentieth-century cube farm. All of which could've easily been looted, destroyed, or just thrown away later."

"Where were the big labs the diary keeps going on about?" J.B. asked.

Ricky knew his mentor was thinking in terms of possible terrain advantage in case they had the need—or even the opportunity—to make some kind of defensive stand. A predark lab could offer all kinds of good cover, depending on what its function had been, and how well its equipment had stood up.

Mildred shrugged. "Somewhere else. Probably not far. But we got grabbed right off the bat, and carried off to Queen Crazy-Ass Bitch, before we had a chance to poke around and find them. So, as Ryan said, nowhere we've been."

The passage widened. The light brightened. The glow-moss here was much fresher, and Ricky gratefully doused his lamp and stuffed another handful down his shirt.

I sure hope the radiation doesn't make me grow a third nipple or a second head or anything, he thought.

"There's an interruption of a couple of days," he reported. "Then we get 'Shocks of terrifying magnitude have at last subsided. If I were given to fits of irrationality, I would ascribe the fact that the caverns were not collapsed on our heads to a miracle. But we seem to have weathered the worst of the storm.'"

A growl from Ricky's stomach interrupted him. It was loud enough that Jak, who had been showing no signs of interest in Ricky's recitation, stopped prowling out front, looked at him sharply and grinned. If water was thankfully no concern, food was another issue. They had managed to bring with them an abundant supply of still-good canned food and even treasured self-heat MRE packs from the scavvy site. But those were still in limited supply, and the companions had been tramping these endless passageways fruitlessly for several days now.

So they were all on tight rations. Even Deathlands-hardened survivors like Ricky's companions, used to scavenging whatever protein they could find to get by, had refrained so far from eating the variety of cave bugs and other vermin that proved fairly common even down this far, once you started to look for them. And the pink cave fish they saw in many of the underground streams they encountered looked too small to pay off the energy spent catching them, metabolically speaking.

Ricky took a deep breath, sighed it out through pursed lips and went on.

"He goes on for pages and pages complaining about how things are going to…pieces. He stops getting any communication from the outside world, not even over the Totality Concept's supersecret setup."

"Huge surprise," Mildred said.

"Then, a few months after the war during skydark, we get 'We have suffered repeated incidents of pilferage of stocks, primarily foodstuffs. I blame McComb and her twisted freaks. I know she's started letting some of them off the leash, though she denies it.'"

He flipped some pages and stopped abruptly, then turned back a few pages. "Whoa," he said. "Listen to this. 'Awakened by a terrible tumult during my sleeping period. It appears the containment unit's integrity was compromised by the series of severe earthquakes that followed the global thermonuclear exchange. The Digging Leviathan has escaped. It managed to batter and burrow its way through the reinforced walls into the caverns. We have no prospect of tracing it, far less the means of restoring it to captivity if we should locate it. This is a disaster of unprecedented proportion—'"

"Whitecoats," Doc said, as if he'd just accidentally stepped on a dog turd.

"'We can only hope against hope that the entity does not return here,' Foxton says, 'either by choice or by blind accident.'"

J.B. halted, blinked at Ricky, then took off his glasses and began polishing them with his handkerchief. Ryan called another brief halt.

"Reckon that giant digging thing of theirs could be the same as the thing we're supposed to be hunting?" he asked.

Ryan grunted. "Be a triple-nuking huge coincidence if it wasn't."

As if on cue, a rumble shook its way through their boots and up their legs from the floor, accompanied by a deep roar like an angry volcano.

Chapter Twenty-Four

"The monster!" Ryan heard Ricky yell over the rumble and the roar. Both went on and on until it felt as if the marrow was being rattled loose from his bones.

"Or one of the magma intrusions erupting into the cave system proper," Doc suggested.

"I'm not loving either of those alternatives!" Mildred shouted.

"Hear screaming," Jak called back from the far side of a cluster of short, needle-tipped stalagmites.

"Other than us?" Mildred yelled.

"Lead us to it," Ryan called. The terrible sub-basso noise and accompanying vibrations began to dwindle, and now he could hear shrieks, tiny and thin with distance, echoing up the passageway that lay before them.

Unslinging his Steyr as he ran, he led them along a passageway with a well-worn floor. The glow-moss was sparse here, and Ryan had to bend over or risk his head to a sudden impact with a stalactite. But it had clearly been carefully cleared to the specifications of the coamers, and was easy going. That was fortunate, because the slope accelerated until running would have been tricky even without obstacles.

The screams and roaring rose to crescendos, accompanied by the crashing of splintering stone. Something big was going on, and something big was causing it.

"Cannies!" Jak yelled as he approached the barely visible entrance to another sizable room. Figures broader and even shorter than the albino scout were suddenly crowding into the tunnel and rushing at them.

"Ryan—" Krysty called.

"Hold fire!"

He saw at once those weren't cannie warriors, but workers—mostly female, but not all, carrying white-skinned, red-eyes babies as naked as they were, and all squalling up a storm. Unlike Krysty, Ryan wasn't motivated by compassion, but by the fact they'd no doubt be needing every cartridge and every scrap of physical energy they had in one hell of a hurry. He wasn't about to waste either on noncombatants.

"Packs on!" Ryan barked over the tumult. He left unspoken the obvious: that they might need to get out of there a lot faster than they came down.

Panicked though they were, the coamer nurses parted to go around point man Jak without touching him. Likely he looked terrifying to them, despite his skin, eyes and hair, in his camo jacket and his jeans. And the rest of his band looked even worse, such that when they reached Ryan the fleeing workers were almost rubbing the walls to both sides, almost as eager to avoid contact with these scary invaders as to get away from the bigger one below.

The bigger, *louder* one. Bouncing off the walls and ceiling, its roars and banging pounded on Ryan's skull like hammers.

Jak, brave but no fool, knelt just shy of the widening of the way and peered inside. He had his big Magnum revolver in his hand.

"What do you see?" Ryan yelled, pounding up behind him.

"Not much," Jak replied, not turning his head. "But big!"

Halting right behind him, Ryan looked into the chamber. It was wide with a floor flat and mostly free of stalagmites or columns, suggesting the coamers had cleared and leveled it.

Workers must be as fanatic as the warriors, in their way, he thought. The roof, spiked with stalactites as per usual, arched to about twenty feet at the highest. The glow-moss light was so faint it was hard to tell.

The floor was still strewed with hundred of infants, squalling in carefully constructed nests of what looked at a distance like scraps of vegetation, cave-moss of the nonluminous variety, and scavvied clothes scraps. A throng of nurse-workers was desperately trying to scoop them up and escape into one of the several tunnels leaving off it.

For a moment Ryan didn't even see the source of all the commotion. Then some sort of shadow lunged forward and blotted out a big area of the floor. Ryan couldn't even tell what exactly it did to a couple dozen infants and maybe a dozen nurses that it hid, but he doubted they survived. He got an impression of rounded immensity, and furious powerful motion. It heaved up and swung side to side, shattering stalactites as thick as Ryan's torso like matchsticks as it did.

"Blast it!" he yelled.

He threw his own Scout longblaster to his shoulder, took quick aim across the sights below the Leupold scope and fired.

In the abysmal gloom the flare of the powerful 7.62 mm cartridge going off was as huge and dazzling as a nearby lightning strike. He saw yellow reflections glinting off some kind of pallid, hunched surface, getting a flash impression of vast, thick rings.

Jak added the sharp bark of his .357 Magnum blaster to the sound of J.B. cutting loose with a burst from his Uzi as Ryan jacked the action of his carbine and brought the weapon back online. The others had come up and opened fire as well. He paid them no attention; he knew they had set up to stay out of one another's fields of fire. That was one of the lethal edges they had over their opposition, even when it greatly outnumbered him: by virtue of long practice, they fought together like parts of a perfectly designed and well-oiled machine. The combined seven muzzle-flashes still gave Ryan no clearer picture of what it was they were fighting.

They only showed him that if anything, it was bigger than he even thought.

Into one of those sudden lulls in the firing, J.B. shouted, "If that thing finds out we're shooting it, it's going to be hot past nuke re—"

The final *d* was drowned out by a shrill noise like a predark ocean liner's steam whistle going off. It was so sharp, and not just unimaginably loud but huge, that it drove Ryan to his knees, trying to cover his ears with his hand and forearm as best he could without letting go of his longblaster.

It hardly helped. The keening noise went on and on, stabbing his eardrums like hammer-struck spikes, threatening to liquefy the very bones within him.

Then it was replaced by a colossal grinding rumble, like gravel being crushed in a gigantic machine.

Ryan was up again instantly, leveling his Steyr. He could see the dark shape's ill-defined nearer end had turned into a passageway to his left, presenting a curve of colossal body that seemed to consist of giant ribbed segments. The tunnel seemed too small to let it in. The grinding and the cloud of dust and fragments that surrounded its fore-end—he wasn't even sure if it had a head or not—told him it was doing something about that, in no uncertain terms.

He shot again.

"Fire it up! Keep shooting!"

"But it's going!" Mildred cried.

"We want to keep it that way! Shoot, fireblast it!"

They did. Even the terrific clamor of seven powerful modern blasters going off close together in such a confined, stone space was not enough to drown out the monster's rumble and squeal.

Suddenly the shadowy immensity was flowing unimpeded into the passageway. With shocking quickness, it was gone.

Ryan's yell of "Cease fire!" wasn't needed.

"¡Nuestra Señora!" Ricky's exclamation sounded as if it was echoing out of a deep well twenty feet away, through Ryan's deafening tinnitus. "What the hell was *that*?"

"Big," J.B. replied. "Dark night, it was big."

"My friends," Doc said, pausing in the midst of reloading his giant beast of a LeMat revolver to execute an elegant bow and sweep of his long arm, "permit me to present to you the fabled Digging Leviathan!"

"Are you sure it's—" Mildred stopped herself. "What am I saying? Of course it is."

Ryan had the partially depleted 10-round box magazine out of the well and was swapping it out for a fresh one. He was suddenly extremely glad that they'd loaded down with as much extra ammo from the sunken offices as they could possibly carry.

Krysty shook her head. Her sentient red hair had curled itself to her head in an almost skintight cap. By the barely present illumination, Ryan couldn't see the emerald color of her eyes, but he could see they were as wide as a startled alley cat's.

No sign of life remained out on the floor of the ravaged nursery.

"The widening of the entrance looks surprisingly rough," Doc commented, squinting to see through the near-darkness. "Perhaps we were mistaken about the source of the unusually uniform tunnels we've passed through?"

"The thing was in a bit of a hurry for close work, Doc," J.B. observed. He straightened his fedora, which had worked itself slightly askew on his head in all the excitement.

"Do you think we hurt it?" Ricky asked.

"You're joking, right?" Mildred said.

"Depends what you mean by *hurt*," Ryan said, slamming the fresh mag home with his palm and feeling the satisfying click of the catch. "If you mean, did we do it any harm, then nuke, no. But it felt our fire, sure enough, and didn't like it."

"And exactly what does that mean, Ryan?" Mildred asked.

A rumble shook the walls of the passageway beneath them, and the floor beneath their feet. Frowning, Ryan stepped first toward the right-hand wall, across the passage from him, felt the cool, smooth stone with quick fingertips, then he moved back to press a palm against the other wall.

"It's moving," he said. "This side of us."

As he spoke, the giant thunder-sound grew perceptibly louder.

"It means," he said, turning back up the steep way they had just come, "that we pissed it off. And now it's coming for us. *Run!*"

"SHE'S STILL BREATHIN'," Potar said. He himself wasn't breathing easy, bent over his profound belly as he was to examine the fallen woman with a giant paw. "Just out cold. I hit her a good one."

"These two ain't," reported one of the sec men who were hunkered down beside Angus and Alfie.

Or rather their corpses, Conn reckoned.

He didn't know either sec man's name. They came from somewhere away off east. He didn't know any of the detail his sec boss had handpicked for this night's business, which had turned ugly, as Conn had instantly foreseen would happen when he heard the volatile, raven-haired rabble-rouser was on her way to see him.

He judged that for the best. He didn't know most of Potar's sec men, not even as casual customers of his Stenson's Creek gaudy, and he had a good memory for faces as well as names. He thought it better that way, because he didn't want them hanging back from doing their jobs out of sympathy for fellow Sinkhole-district locals, and so they'd fret less about possible reprisals taken against their own kin by families of men and women they'd been forced to deal with.

"I'm glad your men shot true, Potar," Conn said with some asperity. "It would have been a nukin' poor twist to be struck down by a ball from one of my own body-guard's blasters."

With a vast grunt of effort Potar put a hand on his knee and shoved his massive torso upright. "I'll talk to them if you want, Mr. Conn."

"Not needful," Conn said. He shied away from the prospect of having his enormous, bullying sec boss "talk to" one of his men the way he did to dissidents and troublemakers. Not all of them had wound up tacked to crosses by railway spikes through wrists and feet, like the taints who had got poor Wymie so worked up.

"What should we do with the chills?" asked the sec man who'd announced the woman's two escorts were dead.

"Drag them a distance away from camp and dump them in some brambles," Conn said. "We'll let the coamers clean up after us."

He shared knowing smiles with Potar. "Not for the first time."

"Is that—is that true, Mr. Conn?" the sec man asked nervously.

"Is what true?"

"You believe in them coamers, then? I mean, my old gram used to scare me when I was a toddler and she didn't want me to grab the cook pot off the fire with my bare hands. Said that if I didn't do like she said the ghouls'd get me."

"Of course I believe in coamers. I've seen their red eyes glowin' in brush outside camp with the firelight myself. You don't really think those stupe bastards from the outlands had anything to do with the killings, do you? At least not until this feeb Wymie had to go and stir them up?"

The man fell silent. Conn's brow furrowed. He could tolerate doubt among his own bodyguard far less than he could tolerate intramural violence within it. He looked to Potar.

"No worries, Mr. Conn," the giant said. "Liam's solid as they come."

Conn nodded once, briskly.

Potar opened a huge hand toward the still-unconscious Wymie.

"It time, boss?" he asked.

Conn lowered his chest to his collarbone and creased his brow in thought. For a fact, things had not broken this night as he'd anticipated. He'd sent off his number-one adviser, Frank, because the tall dark scarecrow still had a conscience, one that Conn did not care to encumber by making him a witness if he had to take stern measures. But mostly he'd had Potar ensure only his most trusted bully-boys were anywhere nearby as a precaution. And in case the troublesome Wymea Berdone needed to be persuaded.

But things had powered right past that point. So be it, Conn thought.

He raised his head and smiled at Potar. He thought he saw the barest flicker of fear in the man's boar-hog eyes.

"Yes, Potar," he said gently. "It's time."

Chapter Twenty-Five

"'We found Watts and Dorkins partially dismembered and devoured, their bones gnawed,'" Ricky read out loud.

Krysty could clearly hear the youth panting as he spoke. They were all winded, after their sprint through the cave network, up and away from the terrible rushing roar that pursued them. But they seemed to have lost it, or at least put some distance between them and its vengeful fury. For now.

At the higher end of a huge cavern, Ryan had called a halt to drink and catch their wind. A stream of cold, freshwater, relatively sweet-tasting, ran from a crack high up in one wall, through a well-defined channel it had cut in the floor, to vanish into the echoing but impenetrably dark depths beyond a shoulder-high opening in the farther wall. Ricky had shouted into it from a few feet, which got him barked at by Ryan for taking the risk that whatever was chasing them might hear. None of them had felt like venturing closer.

They had not been there before, but the notches the coamers had struck by the entrances showed which direction was which, and that was enough for Ryan and Jak to orient themselves. Or so they said, and neither was of a frame of mind to shade the truth to humor the others.

"'It can only be McComb's albino monsters, with

their blood-colored eyes and horrid dog faces. She's let them off the leash and set them on us for certain. And now the time has come to put an end to this threat and this perversion of science. I have ordered an all-out attack…'"

Ricky looked up. He had shadows under his eyes, and his dark brown eyes were large in his face. Despite the fact the big chamber showed little sign of alteration for use by the coamers, there was enough recently charged glow-moss available for him to do the trick of stuffing a clump in his shirt for light to read by. He seemed almost obsessed by the task.

"There's just one more entry," he said.

"Well, don't tease us," Mildred grumped. "Read the damn thing."

Ricky looked at Ryan, who nodded.

"What?" Mildred prodded, clearly feeling out of sorts. She was, as she frequently pointed out, built for comfort, not speed, with her short legs and generous hips. She wasn't fat; years of tramping over the same countless miles of Deathlands and beyond had melted pretty much all of them to muscle and bone. She was just sturdily built. "How many magazines will hearing that last bit load for us, anyway?"

"Back up off the trigger of the blaster, Mildred," Ryan growled. He was sitting on a rounded stump of stalagmite. Krysty hated how haggard he looked, and not just from exertion. "I've got curiosity, too. I'm not made of stone."

"Sometimes it's kind of hard to tell."

"Well?" Ryan said to Ricky. "Get on with it, kid."

"'I am the last,' Foxton writes. 'I am wounded and bleeding and out of ammunition, and my time is near. I know. I write this final entry by the shine of clumps of some manner of self-luminous moss or fungus, clearly developed by the madwoman McComb's labs.

"'I must hide this account for future generations, if anyone survives the cold and the dark outside to reproduce. Has the world fallen to these naked Morlocks? I cannot know. But in spite of all, I can hope. Yes, and pray.

"'I hear them now, closing in. My right leg will not carry me another step. They're com—'"

Ricky shut the book with a reverence Doc did not think the evil whitecoat author deserved.

"That's how it ends. Guess he made his last stand right by the place where I found this."

Ryan sighed. "At least we've got some idea of what we're facing," he said. "Both sides—the cannies and the creature. I don't know how much it'll help, but I know it feels better than knowing nothing."

"So what now?" Krysty asked. She hated to put any weight back on her lover's overburdened shoulders, but she felt no less responsible for the survival of her companions than he did. She knew time pressed. And she was eager to *know*.

"Perhaps the monster's wrath has cooled off, and it has forgotten all about us," Doc suggested. "I doubt its vast size houses any commensurate mentality."

"Like we're ever that lucky," J.B. said with a dry chuckle.

"As the great, and presumably long-late, Samuel L. Jackson said in the movie *The Long Kiss Goodnight*," Mildred said, "'When you make an assumption, you make an ass out of you—and umption!'"

Krysty looked blankly at her friend. So did all the others.

"No, Millie," J.B. explained patiently, "it's 'when you assume, you make an *ass* out of *u* and *me*.'"

"I know that," she said. "It was a joke way of putting it. That was the point. It was a movie. You know what? Never mind."

"I for one am eager to hear an answer to the estimable Krysty's question," Doc said.

Ryan was rubbing his chin, the way he did when he got thoughtful.

"Jak, J.B.," he said. "Gather round. You still got a working pen on you, Ricky?"

"I have a pencil. Those usually don't stop working no matter—"

"Shut it. How many empty pages left in that diary?"

Ricky thumbed through the warped pages of the cracked-covered book. "About half," he said. Then he raised his face to give Ryan a stricken look. "But you can't mean to write in this! It's a priceless artifact."

"Nuke that," Ryan said. "What's priceless to me is my own personal ass. Yours, too. At least in comparison to a bunch of water-soaked pages written by some long-chilled coldheart of a whitecoat. Though don't go getting cocky, because that's relative."

Chagrined, Ricky handed over the book when the one-eyed man stuck out a palm. When Ryan had his face turned where the boy couldn't, he flashed a quick wink at Krysty.

"Ace," he said. "We've got sketch maps of some of the places we've been. Let's bring those out."

Doc and the Armorer dutifully produced their own notebooks.

"Of course we had no opportunity to map the ways

we took to get here," Doc pointed out, "being in somewhat of a hurry as we were."

"That's why we're going to pool our memories and fill in the blanks," Ryan said. "Especially where we found the magma ducts."

"Mildred and I will keep watch," Krysty said. "You got a plan, lover?"

He showed her his wolf grin.

"Not yet," he said. "But I got some ideas. We—"

Krysty frowned as something jarred the cavern floor.

With no more warning than that, the cave floor fifty yards away, toward the far end of the chamber, erupted. With a cataclysmic roar, a giant, elongated shape shot upward until it struck the actual ceiling of the cave, shattering massive stalagmites as it went.

Showering dust and rock splinters as it did, the creature turned its head down to look at them. Or at least, turned its forward end down to point at them. Krysty could see no eyes, just a round, perpetually open mouth big enough to swallow a predark sedan, ringed with sharp, inward-pointing teeth. Their bases, it turn, were fringed with what could only be stone-cutters: still pointed, but wider than they were long, looking impossibly sturdy.

Only when she could tear her eyes away from the swaying, crumbled-stone-drooling maw did Krysty fully realize what the creature was: a kind of immense worm, as big around as a railway car or more.

"Well, that's not something you see every day," Mildred said.

"It's hunting for us," J.B. said softly. "It doesn't see us."

"Why didn't we hear it digging up through the floor?" Mildred asked quietly.

"No doubt the roof of the chamber beneath is especially thin," Doc said. "It presumably can sense such things, though how it senses anything at all is entirely beyond me—"

"Here it comes!" Ricky shouted.

There was clearly no reason to keep their voices down any longer. Whether it had actually spotted them or not, it was launching itself to the attack. Fortunately, a creature that size took a while to get moving.

"Run!" Krysty yelled, just because it felt as if someone had to.

They ran.

She started scrambling over a litter of columns and stalactites that had broken free of the ceiling somehow and fallen among some low stalagmites. As she did, she couldn't help looking back over her shoulder.

The creature's head smashed down on the cave floor not ten yards behind them. The shock might have thrown her off her feet had she been upright. As it was, she was knocked sideways, banging her right knee painfully against a stalagmite stub.

Rock exploded away from the impact. The creature kept on going—down through the rock floor.

They were making for a large exit with a flattened floor, but Ryan shouted, "No! Right! Go now!" He led off at an abrupt angle toward a passage mouth that looked like barely more than a crack in the chamber wall.

For a moment Krysty doubted her lover's judgment. As brilliant a tactician, a survivor and a man as Ryan Cawdor was, he was not infallible. She knew it; he never tried to hide it. He was human, not a god.

Her whole body burned with the urge to flee that unspeakable atrocity, as far and fast as possible. Yet here her lover was, turning them away from the highest-speed route available, so tantalizingly near to hand, to move a greater, obstacle-strewed distance toward a passageway that itself might not even be passable to them at all.

"Come on, Krysty!" Mildred shouted, grabbing her left elbow and towing her forward like the stocky tugboat she rather resembled. "No time to commune with your Earth Mother now!"

That snapped her out of it. Of all of her companions, her best friend Mildred was by far the most inclined to be skeptical of Ryan's choices—and to voice that skepticism. That she was obeying and following without question told Krysty it was likely her mistake to doubt him.

Of course they all might be wrong. But Krysty started to run. Mildred let her arm go as soon as she felt the taller woman start to move of her own accord.

Ahead and to their left, Doc caught a toe beneath a fallen chunk of limestone cylinder and took a header, sprawling dangerously close to some thin and pointy knee-high baby stalagmites that jutted like spikes. Mildred broke wider left, Krysty right. They came up either side of the tall, thin man even as he came up on all fours.

He waved a long arm after Ryan and the others as they scrambled into the crack. They were clearly having a hard time navigating into it with their packs on their backs, but they were motivated.

"Go on!" Doc shouted. "Leave me! I've had my run!"

"Oh, bullshit," Mildred said.

Both of them quite strong to start with, and their bodies pulsing with adrenaline, the two women picked him up bodily, yanked him upright and hauled him toward the crevice. He had just started to get his feet beneath him and helping to move him forward when they propelled him into the narrow black opening in the tan-and-yellow-striated wall.

Krysty felt the shaking commence again, up through her feet and her legs. "Go ahead!" she yelled at Mildred.

The black woman started to talk back. Krysty pushed her into the crevice ahead of her. Then she sprang over the projections that fanged the very entrance, praying she didn't land on something that would break her leg, or even twist her ankle. Anything that slowed her now would as good as chill her.

She plunged into darkness. Her left foot landed on a rock and she lurched that way, slamming into the unseen wall of the crevice. Fortunately it wasn't far enough away to build up momentum.

Ahead of her yellow light appeared as someone struck a lighter. She felt a strong hand grab her right arm and begin to pull. She made out the distinctive curve of Mildred's forehead by the feeble gleam.

The Digging Leviathan shattered its way through the cave floor not sixty feet shy of the crevice. It plunged its eternal toothy gape of death toward the crack down which its presumptuous prey was trying to flee.

It seemed the whole Earth shook at the impact as the monster tried to ram its head down an opening far less than half as wide.

And it seemed the universe shook to the whistling scream of frustrated fury that vented from the monster.

The light expanded into lantern gleam. As the grinding teeth began to work at the rock around the crevice with an ear-torturing squeal, she heard Ryan shout, "Don't just stand there admiring the view, Krysty. Move your ass!"

She did.

WHY IS MY NOSE in the dirt? Wymie wondered.

She had awakened lying on her belly, she quickly realized. A light rain was falling on her back. She opened her eyes to see that it was nighttime. Enough moonlight filtered through the clouds so that she could see the serviceberry bushes, branches heavy with new fruit, fringing the arc of the edge of the clearing before her eyes, and dense woods beyond.

She tried to put her hands down to hoist herself off the cool earth. Her flannel shirt had soaked through, and she could feel that wet had soaked into the crack of her butt through her jeans. She was liable to get chafed down there something fierce if she didn't do something fast.

But she couldn't move her hands. They were held behind her back by an unyielding pressure. It flexed slightly when she tried to pull loose, but it showed no sign of loosening, much less letting go.

Wymie tried pulling her right knee under her, but her ankles were held together, too. She realized she was tied. The smells of green grass and wet dirt were heady in her nostrils.

She rolled over. The rain caressed her face. She blinked at it.

Motion caught her eye.

The black-haired young woman craned her head back, rolled her eyes up. Was that a branch quivering? Perhaps it was the rain doing that.

But the other branches around it weren't moving.

She heard a soft rustle from somewhere past her left boot. With a wrench of effort she sat up. She had reason to be thankful a lifetime of hard work chopping and hauling had strengthened her back and belly muscles, and kept them strong.

Nothing. She looked around.

Flitting motion continued to snatch at the corners of her vision. She turned her head rapidly this way and that, trying to see what was moving in the darkness around her.

The rain grew heavier, beginning to hit so hard she felt it on her scalp through her heavy hair.

And then they were there, appearing within the tiny glade, all around her, as if suddenly coming into being.

They were staring at her with hypnotic fixation. In the gloom their eyes looked black, but she knew them. Those strange distorted faces, the skin beyond chill-pale. The long and matted white hair.

"Coamers!" she gasped aloud, as they advanced slowly on her. "But that can't be true! You ain't real! *I know what I saw!*"

They pounced on her, grabbing her hair and wrenching her head back, tearing her durable work clothes from her bound and helpless body as if they were rotten cheesecloth.

And then her world became a final infinity of yellow fangs, black claws and pain.

Chapter Twenty-Six

Feeling as alone as he ever had at any point in his eventful life—which seemed longer than it had really been, but also shorter than he wanted it to be—Ryan descended the steeply ramped passageway by himself.

Below him the screams had ceased. They had been what drew the companions' attention this way to begin with. The coamer marking system indicated it was a workers' dorm. That system managed to be both simple and remarkably sophisticated, they'd discovered. Mildred, who was familiar with the specialized disciplines of her time, reckoned McComb had to have employed the services of anthropologists, linguists and even cryptographers to create it for her home-brewed race of man-eating subhuman troglodytes. Doc had assured them from personal experience that the top secret Totality Concept leadership could command specialists of any kind, in any number.

Now Ryan heard a sound that he could only compare to munching and a curious deep gurgling that had to be the Digging Leviathan digesting its prey.

The one-eyed man was moving light. No pack or coat, just his weapons, holstered and slung. And the objects he carried in his hands.

In the time since they had encountered the monstrous worm, they had been scrupulously pussyfooting around and talking in soft murmurs. They already by long practice employed good noise discipline, with no random buckles or other dangly metal bits to clink at inopportune moments and give them away to the bad guys. Or worse, monsters. Krysty intuited that the Digging Leviathan had to be sensitive to vibrations, especially through the cave rock. They had to stay constantly alert to avoid tipping off the monster to their locations.

It had worked so far. Up until now. Ryan Cawdor was about to go do the absolute opposite, as hard as a hard man like Ryan Cawdor could do it.

Why did I think this was a good idea, again? Ryan mused.

Oh, right. Because if we don't chill this thing, Mother McComb and her endless horde of cannie children will eat us.

As he neared the bottom, the slope slowed and bottomed out to near-level. He crouched and crept up behind a convenient jut of flowstone right at the opening to the large cave beyond. The noise had grown deafening.

Ryan looked around. He kept it a standard three-second glance, then slid back out of sight without jerking. They had no evidence the monster had eyes, but then, they had no evidence it *didn't*. Ryan reckoned, better safe than swallowed whole.

From the sad jumbles that were clearly the remains of adult-coamer-sized versions of the detritus nests they used for their babies, it was clear this was indeed a dormitory of sorts. What kind of coamer it had in fact been meant for was not so clear. All that remained of the former occupants were some lurid purple-red smears on the stone floor and a couple of turdy columns, plus a sparse scatter of dissociated body parts. The lower half of a male coamer looked to have the stockier build of the worker caste, anyway.

And there in the middle for the floor, like a maggot magnified a billion times and given a round combination circular saw and pincushion for a mouth, lay the Digging Leviathan. Its gray body gleamed in the light of glow-moss. A slurry of blood mixed with what Ryan guessed was crumbs of chewed-up stone drooled from the bottom of the needle-edged maw. The horrific gurgling noises continued, at wall-shaking volume, but the munching sounds had stopped.

As far as he could tell, the monster was enjoying a postprandial nap.

Time to change that, he thought. He straightened and readied the objects he carried in his hands.

"Hey, asshole with teeth," he bellowed at the top of his lungs. The words echoed away down the large chamber.

"Time to wake up!"

The enormous flabby bulk stirred. Or at least a quiver rippled along its ring-segmented body. It looked even more disgusting than Ryan had anticipated it would. Using the butane lighter he'd borrowed from J.B., he lit the fuel-soaked handkerchief fuse of the makeshift Molotov they'd cobbled together out of one of their last remaining clay jugs of turpentine-based lamp oil. When it was burning with black-smoking, pine-reeking blue flame, he cocked back his arm and hurled it as far as he could toward the stirring monstrosity.

Though it was a large target, his aim was true. Or his luck was in. Trailing fire and smoke, the projectile arced between a pair of particularly low-hanging stalactites to smash to pieces against a thick story-high stalagmite that had been cracked at the base and pushed to a fifteen-degree angle by the blubbery-looking flank of the horror. A rooster tail of fire, shockingly bright in the faint light, sprayed right over the thing's "head."

With speed shocking for its freight-train size, the beast reared right up, splintering the two stalactites the Molotov had missed plus a whole lot more with its blazing head. It vented a whistling scream that seemed to shatter rock. It was so loud and intense it not only threatened to implode Ryan's eardrums, but made it hard to breathe.

"Fireblast!" he yelled. He could barely hear the syllables conducted through the bones of his own skull for the terrible noise.

Still blinking to clear floating orange blobs of afterimage from a gloom-accustomed eye dazzled by the fire, Ryan drew his SIG P226. Pointing it with one hand but getting a flash picture over the front sight out of sheer habit, which he preferred not to mess with, he squeezed off six quick shots at the howling hulk.

"That's right, you overgrown bastard earthworm!" he shouted, though the creature certainly couldn't hear him over the racket of its screeching and the constant cracking and crashing of stone as it whipped its still-burning head this way and that. "Come get me!"

It might not have heard him, but it obeyed. The creature lowered its front end, cascading with rubble and still drooling the odd strand of still-burning pine oil, as if to look right at the one-eyed man. Then it lunged at him.

He stuffed the handblaster back in its holster, turned and sprinted back up the sloping passage as fast as his long, lean-muscled legs would carry him.

So much for the easy part, he told himself as he powered up the smoothed-stone ramp. Now he had two things to concentrate on: keeping the horror following him at all costs and not dying.

He reckoned it was the second one that was going to be a problem.

He didn't look back. That slowed a person. Also, although the stone had been smoothed flat by generations of naked coamer feet, if not patient hammering by coamers with rocks, he did not want to risk turning his ankle on some random piece of debris shaken free by the monster's thrashing.

The rock beneath his flying feet shuddered so violently he almost took a header. He threw down a hand to keep from planting his face on stone, but fortunately he was able to lever himself upright again, without risking snapping his forearm from landing wrong. The crash of the worm hitting the tunnel mouth off-center momentarily silenced its steam-whistling of pain and fury. But it instantly reared back and squealed twice as loud as before.

He reckoned the creature wasn't used to running into things it didn't intend to. Having your face on fire could do that to you.

But even as he was hoping like thermonuclear hell that his eardrums wouldn't simply shatter—if not his entire skull—it struck him that this was now a problem for him.

The whole point of this crazy exercise was for him to get the creature to follow him. Specifically, up this very tunnel, calculated by Doc, and J.B.'s myopic but experienced eyes, to be *just* wide enough to accommodate its tremendous girth. That was one of the factors that had kept them stalking the creature, while their rations ran ever lower, and they lived in constant fear of causing some unavoidable sound or vibration that would make the monster worm turn.

They'd finally pinned down its location in a place where they could implement their scheme. And the nuking thing above all required that the Leviathan follow Ryan.

The one-eyed man stopped. He was going so hard it took a couple steps to actually arrest his upward progress. The end of his exertion made him abruptly aware of how it was making his chest pump like a bellows.

"Fuck," he said, and actually heard it with his ears. A little. The terrible whistle had stopped, as if the monster was concentrating on trying to figure out where the little meat morsel who had so impudently caused it pain had got to. He turned back around, unslinging his Steyr Scout longblaster as he did so. It was time to bring out the big blasters. Or the biggest one he had.

Sure enough, he could see some of the creature's pallid belly, off to his left of the tunnel mouth and arching up clear out sight. It was casting about for his scent. "This way," he yelled as he shouldered the longblaster, punishing his poor throat even more. "I'm *here*, you triple-stupe mutie tapeworm!" Ryan punctuated his taunts with shots from the Steyr.

He didn't think anything could make his ears ring worse than the racket the monster had made once he nuked its face, but the reports of the powerful 7.62 mm cartridges going off in this stone echo chamber proved him wrong.

He could actually see the monster's flesh ripple away from the high-speed impacts like pond water from a rock. He wondered how it could be so blubbery yet apparently chew its way through solid stone. But *he* wasn't one of the army of crazy whitecoats who had genetically designed the thing to be the way it was.

He was thankful to have something to be thankful for, here and now.

The worm froze momentarily, then it bent down with what seemed like caution. Abruptly its tooth-rimmed mouth appeared at the entrance, almost filling it. Light from the glow-moss inside the passageway glinted on its teeth. Each was easily as long as one of Ryan's arms.

He fired a shot right down its throat.

As he recovered from the recoil, chambering a fresh cartridge, he saw the body behind the head seem to swell. Then the creature lunged into the tunnel, almost to where Ryan stood. Reflexively he flung himself backward, landing on his butt. The wedge-toothed fringes of the great mouth worked angrily. Peristaltic waves surged down the fang-lined tunnel of its gullet.

Ryan sprang up, turned. At every pounding step he expected to hear the rustling rumble of the monster sliding forward, to feel the inward-slanting teeth catch him and engulf him, thrusting him into darkness and pain. But either disoriented by its leap, or not fitting the tunnel as comfortably as it expected, the monster had to wiggle its enormous bloated body in to pursue its prey.

Then Ryan did hear it sliding after him. He risked a glance back. It propelled itself forward with a curious turning motion, as if *screwing* itself up the tunnel.

The symbolism of that did not escape him. The humor of it did, at the moment. He'd laugh later. If he lived.

Hoping his memory was as sharp as he thought it was, he took a hard left, sprinted across a small chamber, along another passage. A rising thunder followed him.

He glanced back. The monster was picking up speed,

smashing aeons-old stone spikes and pillars to fragments with too little awareness to call it *contemptuous* ease.

He had gotten, somehow, roughly a forty-yard head start on the thing, but now it was rapidly making up the distance.

Another turn right into a side tunnel. Ryan heard the Digging Leviathan crash into the intersection, with what he could only think of as frustrated grumbling as it had to maneuver its way around the turn. But it was clearly not going to stop. It sensed its tormentor, however it did that, and it seemed determined to finish him.

The passage widened up to perhaps twice as wide as the worm. The air grew warm and stank of sulfur. Heat began to pound against Ryan's sweat-flooded cheek from the wall to his right.

For just a single trip-hammer beat of Ryan's heart the monster hesitated. Then, with a sinister sound like a hurricane blasting through a dense forest, it charged after him, picking up speed as it came.

With all the wind he could spare, Ryan began to holler, "Blow it! *Blow it!*"

"NUKE THAT," J.B. MUTTERED, as if his best friend could hear him, fifty yards down the gently sloping chamber and running flat out, while a monster pursued him with a locomotive sound. "Dark night, you're not going to kill yourself on my watch!"

"Go, Ryan!" Mildred yelled from behind.

"Hurry, lover!" Krysty called.

Against the Armorer's better judgment, the others were clustered right behind where he knelt watching down the tunnel as the colossal worm ate up the distance between its toothy circular gape and Ryan, spinning like a huge, fat drill bit. Then again, he could hardly blame them. *He* wouldn't have missed the show for the world.

Doc and Ricky added their voices to the encouragement, cheering themselves hoarse. Ryan put on a visible burst of speed.

"Clear!" the one-eyed man roared. "Blow it, nuke you!"

But J.B. was focused on the broad stripe of pebble-sized rubble fragments strewed side to side across the wide floor. He drew in a deep breath, then let half of it out.

Ryan vaulted over the line. Grinning like a hyena. J.B. twisted the initiator plunger in his hands to unlock it, then rammed it home.

A spark shot along the high-speed fuse, and a line of C-4 charges he'd stuck along the left-hand wall—from his viewpoint—cracked off in almost a single, head-shatteringly sharp crack.

For a moment nothing happened. The worm did pause, as if startled by the blaster. Caught by the fringes, Ryan stumbled wildly toward them.

Krysty ran to meet him, and he caught her in her strong arms as he finally lost his fight with gravity and started to pitch forward on his face.

Behind him the cavern wall erupted, with a surge of glowing-red lava that shot almost to the far side of the chamber before hitting and splashing the limestone wall right in front of the corkscrewing monstrosity.

A scream pealed from the creature louder than the plas-ex charges going off. A wave of intolerable heat washed over them, instantly making J.B.'s face feel sunburned.

Ryan had his feet under him again. Hand in hand he and Krysty dashed upward, racing by the others even as they turned to flee the killing heat. The backs of their clothes and hair were smoking.

They were a hundred yards away, well up into a passageway, before it cooled down enough to be merely uncomfortable. Then they turned to view their handiwork.

The big chamber had filled side to side with orange-glowing, molten stone to just above the height of the breaches J.B.'s charges had knocked in the thin stretch of the wall that separated the caverns from the interwoven tubes where magma ran. It was still flowing, presumably rolling back down the route Ryan had traveled and various side passages. It would roll downhill, scorching and burying all it encountered at once, until it cooled enough to dam itself.

Mildred was fussing over the back of Krysty's head. She'd doused her smoldering red hair with a full canteen of water. It had stopped smoking, but the strands were writhing in obvious pain.

"You have no idea how much that stings," Krysty said through gritted teeth.

Ryan sprawled on his butt and elbow, with his long legs stuck out before him. He was panting like a dog, although the air was filled with sulfur, smoke and an oddly tainted barbecue tang.

"Is it dead?" Ricky asked.

"It's seen better days," J.B. said with quiet satisfaction. "That's for sure."

"Far as we know it's chilled," Ryan rasped. "Also, far as Mother McComb will be able to find out."

"I wonder how many of the coamers got caught by the lava surge," Doc said thoughtfully. "Or simply trapped below, to die of whatever form of privation they succumb to first."

"I know their crazy queen won't waste any tears on them," Ryan said. "So I don't propose to, either. Here, give me a hand up."

He held out his arm. He and J.B. gripped each other's, forearm to forearm. For a moment they held that pose, grinning. Then J.B. hauled his friend to his feet. Ryan was a bigger, heavier man, but the Armorer raised him easily enough.

"So now we go collect our reward?" Ricky asked Ricky.

J.B. saw Ryan look at the kid, saw his look turn thoughtful. Then he grinned.

"First," their leader said, "we haul our butts someplace where we can breathe without poisoning ourselves, and where we can catch our breath and rest a spell."

He grinned.

"Then we go and pay a visit home to dear old Angela McComb."

Chapter Twenty-Seven

"I see five of you," the Mother of All Coamers said, leaning forward on her carven-flowstone throne and squinting through the light of myriad torches. "You were seven when I sent you off."

Through the lane left open through a vast crowd of silent cannies, crouching like coyotes and smelling no better than usual, Ryan strode boldly up to the foot of her dais. Krysty, Doc, Mildred and Ricky followed. They had their packs on their backs, and all their weapons, though stashed away. No one had raised a claw to interfere with them since they'd entered the gigantic royal chamber.

"J. B. Dix and Jak Lauren didn't make it," Ryan said heavily. "The worm got them."

The cannie queen straightened in her chair. "So that is what it was. A worm."

"A triple-big one the size of a bunch of buses strung together, with a mouth that could bite through solid rock and swallow that boulder you're sitting on whole."

"Impressive. And you have dispatched it?"

"We did. It's dead."

"And how did you accomplish this feat?"

"Decisively."

She smiled thinly. "Do not toy with me, Mr. Cawdor," she said. "I, the all-powerful ruler of the subterranean domain in which you find yourself, the Mother of the

Nation of Perpetual Night, have granted you the privilege of doing me a service. I believe my largess entitles me to a certain candor."

Does this hoity-toity psycho think she can throw me off using big words? Ryan wondered.

Though the diary Ricky had read to them was written by what would turn out to be her literal mortal enemy—or rather, she turned out to be his—Ryan suspected she wasn't too different in reality from the way she was portrayed. And that sounded like the sort of thing Angela McComb might try, for no better reason than to display her own assumed superiority.

Ryan was no more interested in playing ego games with her than he was about to be disconcerted by hers. He knew what the nuking words meant.

It also didn't mean he was *buying* that she was Angela McComb for a single, solitary minute. That sort of snootiness was the kind of bad habit that often did get passed along in powerful families. He should know, having been born and raised in one.

"You got magma tubes running through a lot of this underground domain of yours," he said. "We had a handful of plas-ex charges we scavenged from those sunken office buildings. We found a place where one of the magma ducts ran close to a chamber, lured the worm into it, blew the wall with the charges. No more giant worm."

She nodded. "You have done well," she said. "Not least of which was providing me a truthful account. It may surprise you to know that my own spies have already brought substantial corroborative evidence to me."

"Not particularly. You had people creepy-crawling us outside. I reckoned you had spies all around this nation of yours, too." She tipped her head back as if she were considering.

"So," she said. "What shall I give you as your reward?"

"Why did you, uh, create the coamers?" Ricky blurted.

Ryan frowned, but did not speak up to intervene. It was too late, in any event. And he didn't see what harm the kid could do, at this point.

"I mean, they couldn't have been good as soldiers," Ricky went on, "not using weapons and all. And they're too wild to make decent assassins. Why?"

The cannie queen smiled.

"Why, for the pleasure of doing it, boy. Why else? Haven't you experienced the joy of making something no one else has, with your own mind and hands? What my spies saw tells me that you do relish that. I'm no different."

Glancing over his shoulder, Ryan saw Ricky visibly shivering at the comparison. He wondered, not for the first time, how the inarticulate, bestial coamer soldiers had relayed such detail about his band's daily activities to their crazy queen. It was one of those mysteries they would never know the answer to.

"Anything else you would like to know?" she asked.

"Are we free to go?" Ryan asked.

She laughed. It was a surprisingly pleasant laugh. He doubted her sense of humor was half as nice as the sound of her laughter.

"Are you not eager to claim your prize, which you have so richly earned?"

"What we want most is out of here," Ryan said. "But sure. Go ahead and tell us what we've won."

He felt Krysty's hand slip into his.

McComb the Mother brought a hand to her chin and tapped a finger against her withered cheek.

"Let me see. You have performed a heroic service in destroying the great enemy of my children. And—you have also destroyed a great many of my children yourselves. Not least the ones chilled when the lava broke through into our home."

She smiled sweetly and snapped her fingers. "I know what I shall give you!" she declared. "I give you—death!"

"Death!" echoed a thousand cannies with a single voice.

So they got a two-word vocabulary, Ryan thought. Aren't they just full of surprises.

Suddenly Ryan's Steyr longblaster was in his hands, shouldered and aimed at the cannie queen, likewise with Krysty's Glock, Mildred's ZKR 551, Doc's LeMat replica and Ricky's trusty DeLisle.

And just as suddenly, a score of naked white bodies swarmed over the throne rock from behind to wall her off from their blasterfire.

The cannie queen's musical laughter rang from behind the phalanx of dangling white dicks.

"Oh, do twist on the hook!" she exclaimed. "I do love it so! It's too rare to have a good show down here."

"The show hasn't even begun!" Krysty's voice rang with challenge.

"Oh, you mean you can shoot down my human shields? More stand ready to replace them the second they start to fall. And then the others will swarm you. Kill as many of us as you like. My breeders will make more, until we overrun the Pennyrile and the world! And they won't stop coming until I watch them strip your living flesh from your bones with their teeth!" Then, screaming, "Now, my children! Kill the intruders!"

Around them Ryan could feel a thousand pale cannie bodies coiling themselves to spring.

From somewhere rang out a loud, flat *bang*. The coamers froze in place.

From both sides of the cavern came arcing, smoking comets. They fell amid the ranks of cannies and immediately began to billow gray smoke.

"Watch out!" Krysty screamed at the top of her lungs.

"Poison gas!" Mildred added her voice to the warning cries.

The response was electric: the coamers began screeching in unmistakable fear. Those near the dense smoke cloud, which was heavier than air and rapidly spreading, fled in all directions as fast as they could. They jostled those in their way, shoving them aside, throwing them to the stone floor, or simply clambering over them in their panic. The panic spread outward from the two smoke fountains as more smoking objects were hurled into the cannibal throng.

The jostled coamers either starting trying to escape themselves, or turned snarling on their assailants with snapping jaws and slashing nails. Blood flew. Ryan and his people were forgotten in the instantaneous riot.

Ryan took a shot toward where he had last seen the cannie queen. It struck one of her guards right at the arch where his lean belly met his prominent sternum. That one slumped, his heart blasted apart, an instant chill. He slid down the face of the humped rock. Another fell wheezing and kicking, lung-shot by the blow through. It rolled down the stone after the first one with pink froth welling from his nostrils and bloody slobber drooling from his mouth. All Ryan saw of Mother McComb was a swirl of the skirts of her elegant gown as some of her better-focused bodyguards bundled her to safety down the throne rock's far side.

She had clearly lied about what would happen if the companions opened fire, which came as no surprise. For a flash Ryan wondered again if there was at least a third, somewhat more intellectually capable caste of coamer.

He was already turning and slinging his longblaster. Doc fired his under-barrel shotgun into the mob between them and the passageway by which they'd originally been carried by their captors—the way back to the surface, and freedom—if *freedom* was what lay waiting for them back at their former dig site, and not another form of death…

Pallid bodies cringed from the flame and blast of the LeMat's shotgun blast. A fusillade of lead balls lanced into them, bringing red flowers into bloom on white skins.

Ryan charged in among them, swinging his panga diagonally. It bit through a white shoulder and flung the owner, arm flapping loosely, into several of the others. As Ryan waded forward, clearing coamers from his path as he might dense bush, Ricky joined him on his right, using his stoutly built DeLisle carbine as a riot baton. He levered cannies from the path with barrel jabs, staving in ribs and faces with savage strokes of the steel-shod butt, crushing larynxes with two-handed thrusts of the weapon held horizontally before him.

Behind Ryan's left shoulder came Doc, the slim steel blade of his rapier darting like a rattlesnake's tongue to elicit shrieks and sprays of blood. His other hand fended off clawed cannie hands with the sheath.

They had unearthed a store of short-handled, Swiss-made entrenching tools in the sunken buildings. Fol-

lowing the men, Krysty and Mildred each held one of
the tools, spade blades honed sharp. The women swung
them one-handed in vicious arcs. They did almost as
much damage as Ryan's broad-bladed panga to cannie
limbs and faces.

Still, the exit they were running for seemed impossibly far away, across a sea of churning, screeching, snapping bodies. Smoke erupted in their path. Coamers flew
away from it like panicked birds. Whether they had understood Krysty and Mildred's cries of "gas!"—whether
they even knew what poison gas was—they instinctively
feared the thick, choking smoke that blossomed among
them and quickly spread.

The smoke-spewing comets were just smoke bombs
homemade by J.B. and Ricky, using the same black powder the locals burned in their blasters. They were basically harmless, but they stung eyes and throats and were
as alien as opera down here in the torch-lit depths of the
royal cave.

As fear-ignited confusion spread through the cannies, short full-auto bursts of 9 mm slugs sleeted through
coamer bodies. Thunderous shots from a .357 Magnum
blaster blew out chunks of flesh and bone and fans of
blood when they struck.

The black powder in J.B.'s bombs put out a prodigious
quantity of smoke in a dazzlingly short amount of time—
it was how black powder weapons worked, the explosive
release of the smoke being enough to propel bullets. And
the heavy smoke stayed low.

The coamers did not know how to deal with it—such
profane intrusion into the holy sanctum of their queen.
For all their usual savage ferocity, they broke and fled
from the advancing party.

"Took your time," J.B. said laconically as his companions joined him, almost overwhelmed from exertion and smoke exhalation. Across the cave mouth from him Jak stood grinning and looking highly pleased with himself as he twisted a speed-loader off the six fresh cartridges he'd stuck into his Python and snapped the cylinder shut.

"Enjoying the view," Ryan said.

From behind them rose a chilling howl of rage. They looked back as it echoed throughout the enormous cavern.

It was the cannie queen, rallying her people to vengeance. She stood surrounded and shielded by her bodyguards, off past the boulder throne. Heartened by her unswaying courage, many of the coamers were evidently finding their terror turning to anger. White bodies were congregating around their monarch as if drawn by a powerful magnet.

"The blackguards will be after us in no time," Doc gasped. He had sheathed his sword, stuck his cane through his belt, and now stood bent over with hands on his knees, sucking air. Higher than most of the cave floor as the portal was, the air here was clearer than below, and it was better-smelling even before the charcoal-sulfur-saltpeter mix in the bombs had started cooking off.

Ryan's eye narrowed. "I could take the shot," he said.

"But why bother?" J.B. asked. "I've got us covered."

"After them!" they heard the shrill, thin voice of Mother McComb scream, the words throbbing with hate. "We shall devour them by inches, my children!"

The mob surged forward like a wave, baying. Cannies who had scrambled to get out of the invaders' way now snarled and turned back to the attack.

J.B. drove home the plunger of his handheld detonator. The impulse traveled along the last of their high-speed fuse at twenty thousand feet per second.

At the apex of the royal chamber, the ceiling was punched in as if by a giant hand. Hundreds of tons of rock tumbled down in an inverted funnel of dust. The coamers froze in place, staring upward with their queen at the doom descending on them.

Dust obscured the scene as the almost unitary crack of the last of their plas-ex charges reached their ears from the cavern directly above the throne room. The time the party had spent dodging coamer patrols to reconnoiter the area had paid off with a jackpot.

The cannies had gotten complacent, over the decades alone and dominant down there. The only real threat they'd known was their old nemesis, the Digging Leviathan, returned for reasons known only to itself to wage war from below upon them. But it never occurred to them that there in the very heart of their nation they might face a threat from a surface world that didn't even acknowledge their existence except in whispered, half-believed horror stories, even though the royal cavern did not lie that far from the surface itself.

The rumble of a huge chunk of ceiling falling in on the cannie queen and her brood went on and on.

J.B. stuck out his chin and nodded. "I didn't think the C-4'd be that effective," he admitted.

"You did well, John," Mildred said.

"Yeah, well, there's still a horde of the red-eyed bastards in these caverns," Ryan said, his voice roughened by the smoke that had been their salvation. "And they're all going to be lusting after our blood in short order.

"You can gloat on the move."

KRYSTY WAS LOST, but Jak, carrying a lantern burning the last of their turpentine oil, was confident he was leading the way toward freedom. And in fact Krysty did summon vague memories suggesting this might be the route by which their cannie captors first carried them to meet their queen.

"So she was really over a century old," Ricky said wonderingly. "She was well preserved."

"Just because she knew some of the same stuff we got out of your book," Ryan said, "that still doesn't prove she was *the* Angela McComb."

"But she said—" Ricky protested.

"Crazy people say crazy things."

"If she had kept her end of the deal, would you have dropped the ceiling on her?" Ricky asked.

"We'd have no reason to," Krysty said.

Ryan glanced at J.B. "There never was a chance that McComb, whichever one she was, was aiming to keep her end."

"But why did you make the deal, then?"

J.B. chuckled. "Got us our weapons and gear back. Plus freedom of movement."

"She never did have eyes on us tight as she claimed," Ryan said. "If she had, she'd have known Jak and J.B. were still among the living—and they'd never been able to plant the charges above her throne."

"But there was no way we could just walk out, either," Krysty said. "And speaking of which—"

From below the sounds of wrath came echoing after them: howls, screams, chitterings of rage. Ryan had been right, Krysty knew. Regardless of their queen's fate, the majority of the cannie nation survived the fall of the cavern's ceiling. And now they were coming, fast.

"Better mosey," J.B. suggested.

"What's waiting for us up above?" Ricky asked.

"Nothing good," Mildred said.

"But better than what's coming," Ryan stated dryly.

Chapter Twenty-Eight

"Conn! Conn! Conn!"

Tonight is the night I achieve my destiny, Mathus Conn thought as his army chanted his name.

Standing on a dais made of log pilings hammered into the ground, with a platform of split logs to top it, he raised his hands with palms beneficently opened toward the throng.

"Conn! Conn! Conn!"

All of his life, he now realized, with the waves of sound beating on cheeks flushed with adulation of the multitude, had been leading up to this. It had been preamble. The decades spent working his way from the bottom of the gaudy trade to its top: preparation. He knew what motivated men. He knew their hearts—they'd spilled them to him across his own countertop for years, after all.

"Conn! Conn! Conn!"

And what did it matter that the chant had first been raised and was being led by Potar's bully-boys, dotted among the crowd? And that many of those who had first taken it up with the shills had done so for fear of getting a sound beating, or worse, if they did not? The chanting was infectious. More and more of those who hadn't been chanting were caught up as it went along, and joined their voices to the rest. And those who were chanting found themselves swept up by their own emotions, and carried forward—

Toward the man on the platform and his destiny, which now was theirs.

It didn't matter at all whether the enthusiasm he saw growing on so many faces by the light of pine-splint torches had started out authentic or not. When the stories were written of this night—or if no one read anymore, then the songs that were sung by campfires, the tales passed on by wrinklie grandparents to their rapt descendants—all that would be remembered was the passion and the acclamation that had greeted the launch of Mathus Conn's campaign of conquest.

He reached down, picked up a funnel-shaped megaphone made out of papier-mâché and held it to his mouth.

"My friends," he said.

The chant continued. Forcing himself to smile through his agony of impatience, he raised both hands and made tamping-down gestures with his palm and the megaphone.

The crowd began to pipe down on command. A few overenthusiastic types tried to continue on their own. Conn saw knots of brief convulsive activity dotted here and there throughout the mob as Potar's sec men beat down the ones who wouldn't take a hint fast enough.

"My friends," he began again, and this time his words prevailed. "Tonight I announce the beginnin' of our real campaign of vengeance for the blood of our murdered loved ones—the war against the traitors of Maccum Corners, who sell us out to the cannie coldhearts and have refused to join our cause!"

A moment of silence followed the announcement. The upturned, fire-tinted orange faces went blank.

From somewhere in the middle of the army a voice was raised. "But they ain't done nothin' to us! The cannies are chillin' us right here! This is where we signed up to fight! This is—"

His words ended in a flurry of club blows delivered from behind by a flying squad of sec men, cutting through the crowd like a wolf pack through sheep.

"Their hands are red with the blood of our friends, our children!" Conn cried, as a limp, bloody figure was hoisted off the ground by wrists and ankles and bundled off into the night. "They help those who chill us. So what shall we do to them?"

He paused, pretending to listen. From the front row of the mob Potar Baggart bellowed like a buffalo bull, "Chill them!"

A dozen of his goons, well-briefed, instantly picked up the new chant: "Chill them! Chill them!"

Conn turned his head to one side, held his hand to cup his ear, miming as if he couldn't hear.

And hundreds of voices began to roar at him.

"Chill them! Chill them! *Chill them!*"

"Not what I signed up for," Frank Ramakrishnan heard one laborer mutter to his companions as they dug at dirt piled up in the bottom end of the small-frame annex. "Signed up to fight the cannies that're chillin' us, not this shit. Not to grub around in this stuffy old hole in the ground looking for loot to make Conn richer!"

"I know," another man said. His eyes shifted nervously left and right in a ratlike face. "My wife needs me. My kids. I—"

As if casually, the cloth-maker looked around. His team of two sec men were standing just outside the door of the wildly canted room, talking to one of their comrades who had come in on some pretext.

"Hey, boys," he called to them, "why don't you head topside for a breath of air, a quick smoke break."

One frowned. "You know we can't do that, Mr. R. Potar told us to stick right by you. These bastards would hit you over the head and light out for the hills, soon as look at you."

Frank looked at the half-dozen workers, who were stripped to the waist. Their bodies glistened with sweat and dirt streaks in the lamplight.

"You wouldn't do that, would you?"

"No, sir!" they answered fervently.

The second member of Frank's detail grabbed his partner's sleeve. "Come on, Quint. Don't be a dickwad."

Quint shrugged. The three picked their way back up to the humid but fresher nighttime air.

"Now, listen up," Frank told the conscript workers. "You can't let a sec man overhear that kind of talk, or Potar will make an example of you. Am I clear? Be careful."

Their shadowed faces went ashy under their coatings of grime.

"Thanks, boss," both men said in unison.

Frank nodded. "Excellent. Now—"

He heard a footstep behind him and turned. "Back so soon—?" he began.

Then he stopped. Instead of the sec man he expected to see, he was face-to-face with a black woman a head shorter than he, with her hair wound into beaded plaits. She stuck a blocky revolver almost up his left nostril and clicked back the hammer.

"Think I found an important one," she called without taking her brown eyes off his.

"Ace on the line," a male voice responded from outside. "Bring him."

"Come along, you." She grabbed his arm and tugged him into motion. She was stronger than she looked.

"Don't hurt him," one of the conscripts urged.

"Yeah," his partner said. "He's a good one." He turned his head and spit. "The only one."

There was a knot of people clustered in the corridor outside the annex. With a shock, Frank realized two things: they had emerged from the hole to the underworld, and they were the outlanders first Wymie and then Conn had been so hot to find.

They bristled with weapons.

"Who are you?" demanded the tall, rangy man with shaggy black hair, his left eye covered by a patch.

"Frank Ramakrishnan." He swallowed. "I'm chief adviser to Mathus Conn."

"Is he the one straw-bossing this outfit?" asked a short man in a battered fedora and a dusty leather jacket. He cradled a shotgun casually in his hands.

Frank nodded. He didn't trust himself to speak.

"Hey!" a harsh voice demanded. It was Quint, the senior of his sec guards. "What's goin' on—"

There was a flash and a tremendous explosion. By the light of the muzzle-flare Frank saw Quint's throat explode as what had to have been a shotgun blast ripped into him at point-blank range.

Silhouetted by the shot was a tall, stork-like man in a dark frock coat. He shifted the huge blaster in his hand and fired another shot. This one, though painfully loud, was not as world shattering as the first. Frank's other guard, Ash, went down with a third eye in his forehead.

Their pal, whose name Frank didn't know, turned to run. The man, who looked to be an oldie, fired two shots with coldheart precision into his back from the revolver. The sec man pitched onto his face.

The one-eyed man nodded. "Any more?" he asked Frank.

"N-not so far as I know."

As silent as a moonbeam, a little albino in a camo jacket appeared among them. "Coming," he said.

"He means cannies," the short man in the hat and jacket said. "Hundreds of them. All hot way beyond nuke red. We best get out of here in a hurry."

Ryan looked at his hostage and smiled. "Take us to your leader," he said.

"—CONQUER MACCUM CORNERS, we shall punish them for their treasons!" Mathus Conn was ranting over a megaphone when they came in sight of his army camp. "And we shall reap the rewards of our labors, yes, we shall!"

"What the hell?" Mildred demanded. "Maccum Corners what?"

Ryan was no less surprised. He was as much startled that they could hear the gaudy owner so clearly at a couple hundreds yards' distance, though he was obviously not using electro-amplification. Whoever his sec boss was, his men were doing an ace job keeping the crowd quiet while Conn was speaking.

Or in this case, getting the crowd to pipe up only on cue. There was a sudden burst of cheering at the implicit promise of loot and presumably other dark treasures, then it cut off quickly as Conn began hollering again.

He looked to their "hostage," Frank. "It's his new fixation," he said, almost guiltily. "He claims to have evidence the people of Maccum Corners refuse to join his crusade because they have made a secret deal with the cannibals. With, uh, you."

"As you'll have noticed, we've been otherwise occupied," J.B. said.

"With the *real* cannibals," Mildred added pointedly.

"What's your role in this exactly, Frank?" Krysty asked. Her tone was pleasant, but Ryan knew her well enough to feel the steel in her words.

"I do my best to talk Mr. Conn out of the…worst excesses."

"And how's that going for you?" J.B. asked. The Armorer was unusually voluble this night. Ryan guessed he was pumped at having pulled off two incredibly demanding demo shots—both technically and tactically—with near-total success in less than forty-eight hours. Even a man as mechanically precise as J.B. had his professional pride.

He thought he heard screams from the cave-in site behind.

Either the workers didn't clear out like we told them to, or they caught more sec men to leave to the coamers, he thought. Either way, time's blood. In this case, pretty literally.

"We have to shake it," he said firmly, trying not to let his anxiety show.

"That's a big mob he's got there," Ricky said dubiously. "Really big."

"That is an army, lad," Doc said. "In intent and size, if not in training."

"And we're going to walk right into the middle of it?" Mildred demanded.

"That's the plan," Ryan said.

"Why, again?"

He tamped down his irritation. This was not the best time to be questioning him. Then again Mildred wasn't hanging back. They were on the verge of walking into the circle of light from a hundred fires, crossing the point of no return.

"We're caught whatever we do," Krysty said. "There're too many of them swarming around, and they know the ground too well. We could never hope to slip past."

"Yeah, but—"

"Are you forgetting recent events, Millie?" J.B. asked blandly.

"What? Oh."

"Put your hands back up, Frank," J.B. said. "It makes it more convincing that way."

The tall man's eyes darted left and right with surprise in his dark face. "Oh, yes. Sorry." He obeyed.

"Walk in side by side with me," Ryan told him. "Blasters out, everybody." He made a show of holding his SIG near Frank's narrow face.

He had to give it to Conn. The former gaudy proprietor—Ryan reckoned he'd gone into a new line of work now—could hold a crowd's attention. Nobody had eyes out on the surrounding night. Of course part of that was plain overconfidence, that no one would dare to challenge such a huge force, for this peaceful region, directly.

It was the second time in not much more than an hour

that Ryan's and his friends' survival depended on some-body powerful's blind overconfidence in that power.

He narrowed his gaze at the sight of all the men and some women wearing red hankie armbands and carry-ing clubs or toting blasters, cruising through the crowd in twos and threes. Conn hadn't just been busy recruit-ing warm bodies to his cause. In a short period, he had acquired a sec force that would do credit to any baron.

But the sec teams were focused mostly on their big boss, looking for clues as to how to prompt the crowd. Instead it was some of the regular grunts who spotted the intruders, who after all were strolling almost casu-ally among them, straight for Conn's dais.

"Hey, wait!" Ryan heard a man's voice yell. The cry was echoed by several others.

And then a woman's scream: "Oh, blind NORAD, *it's the baby-chillers!*"

That got everybody's attention. A nearby sec unit of two men and a crop-haired woman closed in.

Suddenly the companions had blasters leveled in all directions. Krysty menaced the sec team with her Glock.

"Full-auto, folks," she said. "I'd take my hands away from those blasters."

Tied to mostly single-shot, antique-style weapons as they were, the people of the Pennyrile knew about au-tomatic weapons, if mostly through awestruck legends that greatly amplified their power and effectiveness. Men and women of the sec force halted. They didn't raise their hands, exactly, but they sure moved them away from their waists.

Ryan jammed the muzzle of his P226 under the angle of Frank's jawline, with his finger outside the trigger guard. He knew nobody in the throng around him would notice, not even the sec men.

He and his companions kept walking forward, aware of the terrible pressure of what was going to erupt out of their former dig site at any minute.

When the hubbub around them grew loud enough, and the skin between his shoulder blades grew itchy enough about what those behind them might be getting up to, Ryan raised his face.

"Conn!" he shouted.

"What's the meaning of this?" Conn yelled at the disturbance. "Mr. Baggart, see to whoever's disruptin'—"

A gigantic figure who'd been standing near the log platform where his master stood turned and began to lumber toward the intruders.

"The fat bully-boy's his sec boss now?" J.B. asked.

"Oh, yes," Frank replied.

"We're disrupting your little tea party," Ryan said. He didn't shout, just put snap and volume in his words to make them carry about the murmur and occasional startled outcry from the mob. "We are not baby-chillers, and we've come to warn you. The real baby-chillers are following hot on our tails!"

Conn laughed theatrically.

The dude really has a gift for this, Ryan thought. I'll give him that.

"Lies! All lies! A pile of jack to whoever brings the murderers to me. Alive! We all know how to take care of the likes of these stoneheart taints, don't we, boys and girls!"

With at least fifty sec goons converging on the companions, there wasn't anybody left to make sure the crowd responded on cue. Only a couple of gleeful shouts were raised in response.

Frank cupped his hands around his mouth. "Please listen to them, Mathus! They tell the truth! It was the coamers all along, and they are after us! All of them!"

"You, too, Frank?" Conn asked. He sounded sad, but he didn't lower his volume any. "My friends, an additional award to whoever brings Mr. Ramakrishnan to me. The traitor's head will suffice."

Ryan raised his handblaster and fired a shot in the air. Even among the rising tumult of the crowd, the shot rang clear through the night. Instant stillness ensued.

The sec teams closing in on them seemed to really notice the imposing array of blasters being pointed outward by their intended victims. They froze.

"Don't be stupe, Conn," Ryan declared. "You traded with us often enough. You know we deal straight. I don't know what you've been telling these folks, but the truth is, the coamers are real. They took us captive, and we busted out. And now they're on their way right here with bloodlust and fire in their bastard white bellies!"

He wondered what had happened to Wymie, the black-haired girl who'd lost her sister and blamed them. Briefly. Ryan knew firsthand how the game of power was played full-contact. He had the eye patch and the scar down his face to show for it. Conn clearly not only knew how to play the game, but how to win it. But Conn's run was about to come to an abrupt end. Ryan heard more screaming from the path they'd just walked to get here.

"Time's up, Conn," he said, shouting this time, because it was true. "Forget about fighting us and join with us."

Conn laughed showily again. "Forget about fightin'
you?" he said cockily. "Or you'll what? We hugely out-
number you."

"Not us," Ryan answered. "Them."

The night exploded with screaming white bodies.

Chapter Twenty-Nine

"I'd suggest you run, Frank," Ryan said. "Fast as you can."

"Where?"

"Away!" Mildred shouted. Her hands were trembling where they gripped her ZKR in isosceles combat-shooting stance. She kept a cool head under fire—they all did—but this situation was beyond extraordinary.

"West," J.B. said.

With a spastic nod of thanks, Frank took off in that direction as fast as his long, thin legs could carry him. Nobody paid attention to him, not even the sec force who had largely ringed in the little group.

The coamers had not appeared all around the army, but they were attacking in a white wave from at least a full quarter of the perimeter, all from the east.

They were too enraged—and not bright at the best of times—to think tactically enough to spread out underground far enough west that they could surround the camp when they broke out into the night air. But they had sure started swarming out of other bolt-holes than the passage Ryan's crew had unsealed at the bottom of the caved-in site.

Blasters were booming all around. No shots headed the companions' way. The rank and file had no trouble believing Ryan's warning. At least not when the coamers were leaping on top of their friends and neighbors and crunching off their faces right before their eyes. "Git your worthless asses up on stage in front of Mr. Conn," Potar bellowed to his sec team like an angered bull. "Or I'll make you wish we'd hung you on a cross for the cannies!"

This time Ryan had a clear shot at the commander of the enemy throng, but Ryan had no time to unslung his Steyr, much less take aim across a hundred yards or more, because he and his companions were abruptly fighting for their lives.

He heard two shots erupt from Krysty's Glock 18. It took skill to fire in such a controlled way, given the weapon's high cyclic rate. He looked to see a sec woman falling backward with her hands coming up. Her double-barrel shotgun spewed its titanic smoky flame toward the handful of stars visible above the bonfire, torch and lantern light in the trampled-flat clearing.

Whether driven by lust for Conn's promised reward or simply fixated on the prey at hand, some members of the sec team attacked. Even as a double boom rang out, Krysty ripped off another two rounds, then a 3-round burst, crumpling the sec woman's male companions.

Drawing his panga, Ryan charged at a another knot of sec men, half a dozen strong, west, the way they'd sent their erstwhile captive. The screams, getting closer, showed the infuriated coamer horde was overrunning the army camp with shocking speed.

Ryan double-tapped the sec man who raised a single-shot longblaster at him from twenty feet and closing. He took another one down with a left-handed transverse slash across the face with his panga, which left a spurting, bone-crunched ruin in its wake. The man dropped keening to his knees, clutching his smashed-in features with both hands. Blood squeezed between the fingers.

Another sec man caught hold of Ryan's right arm. The one-eyed man jammed the muzzle of his SIG into his adversary's paunch and fired once. The man dropped with his cotton shirt smoking, howling in pain from being gut shot.

Something hard and heavy clipped Ryan at the curve of his skull, above and behind his left ear. He stumbled, then went to his hands and knees. Stars went nova in his brain, red and white and actinic blue, and his stomach suddenly sloshed with nausea. He would have puked up everything he had eaten that day—if he had eaten that day; their rations had at last run out.

Some combination of trouble-honed senses brought Ryan's head left. That made it feel as if his brain had come loose and was spinning inside his cranium. He found himself looking up the bore of a black-powder longblaster. It looked as big around as that cave they'd dropped on the giant worm. Fuzzily beyond it he saw a demonically twisted face leering at him triumphantly over its cap-lock firing mechanism.

"Say good-night, Gracie," the sec man said.

Something thunked hard at the juncture of his neck and his right shoulder. A black liquid sheet shot suddenly up to hide that side of his face. Ryan's still-scrambled wits recognized arterial spray, even as they sent him half diving, half falling flat on the ground.

Launched by the dying sec man's reflex clench on the trigger, the black-powder blaster's dragon breath felt nearly as hot as it blowtorched near his backside as the live lava had been.

Krysty looked down at him as she yanked the sharp-ened blade of her Swiss e-tool out of the neck of the top-pling man. She had holstered her handblaster, and stuck out her freed-up left hand to Ryan.

"Shake it off, lover," she said, keeping her humor even as literal hell broke loose around her, complete with flesh-eating, white-skinned devils. "You're hold-ing up the parade."

Thankfully, he held out his knife hand. She caught his wrist and pulled him to his feet as if he weighed no more than a child. Even without the help of her guiding spirit, Gaia, the redhead was strong.

He swayed. The universe was still rotating rapidly around him, but at least his brain had decided to settle back into place.

The other sec men weren't idle, but neither were Ryan's companions. In an instant he saw Doc backhand one man across the face with his LeMat, sending him sprawling. A bushy-bearded sec man twice Jak's size grabbed him by his collar and started to spin him. Then he instantly yanked his hands away, screaming shrilly at the pain in his fingers and palms, which had been slashed by the razors Jak had sewn there to discourage just such familiarity. The albino had long since emptied his blaster and tucked it away, happy to be able to fight with some of his beloved knives. He drove the brass-knuckle hand guard of his World War I–style trench knife into the screaming bearded mouth in a rattler-quick over-hand right.

To Ryan's left, Ricky doubled over another sec man with a piston drive of his fat longblaster barrel to his op-ponent's solar plexus, then brought the steel-plated butt down hard on the man's exposed nape to shatter his spine.

Ryan recovered enough to shoot a man ten feet ahead

who showed signs of aiming a handblaster. It was a sloppy shot, one-handed, without even a sight picture. Trader would have chewed his ass for hours for taking a rank-ass, triple-stupe amateur shot like that. But the 9 mm bullet hit somewhere, and he knew he hadn't hit one of his companions.

The sec man dropped his Peacemaker revolver, clutched his shattered shoulder with his left hand and turned and ran away, shrieking. The shrieks got louder when a hurtling white shape landed on his back. Then it cut off as doglike jaws crunched through the back of his skull. The sec man fell forward, still ridden by the coamer who'd killed him.

"Just run!" Ryan croaked.

The sec men, and whatever regular army members remained nearby, instead of falling back in some order for the tents to the west, or just lighting out for the hills like sensible folk, suddenly forgot all about the rewards on Ryan and his crew. Instead they were finding ways of dealing with the difficult realization that the stalkers of their childhood nightmares—the dread albino ghouls called the coamers—were absolutely real. And that "dealing with" consisted either of fighting furiously with blaster, farm implement, big rock, boots and bare fists, or dying noisily—and not infrequently both.

J.B.'s Uzi ripped out an unusually long burst. The Armorer wasn't concerned about overheating his weapon, clearly. You had to live longer than seemed likely for that to matter much. Men and women in the path of his copper-jacketed slugs screamed and fled, screamed and fell, screamed and limped or tried to crawl away. Ryan didn't know whether any of them were sec men, or had even been offering resistance. They were in the way. The Armorer was sweeping them out of it. Nothing personal.

As Ryan vaulted a writhing woman with a cloud of pale frizzy hair, he saw a cannie leap at Mildred from the right, claws and jaws spread wide. She shot him through the upper jaw. The bullet punched through the roof of his mouth, out the top of his snout and rammed into his skull right between the blood-hued eyes. The right one popped from its socket.

A weight landed on Ryan's back, or rather, his pack—they were all carrying their gear. They didn't plan to stick around the Pennyrile any longer, one way or another.

He heard frustrated subhuman snarling, felt hot breath on the left side of his face, smelled the knee-loosening stench of rotting human flesh. He felt the creature wiggle on his back, trying to bring its canine jaws within biting range of Ryan's flesh.

Ryan stuck his P226 back over his shoulder and fired blind. The weight and the stink abruptly left him.

The coamers seemed as though they'd lost their laser focus on the surface-dwellers who had chilled their queen and so many of their inbred kin. They hadn't gotten over their rage. They now seemed content to take it out on anyone.

For their part the locals were focused on running away. The ones who had held back to stand and fight were presumably all cannie snacks, for now or later. The ones who retained presence of mind, and weren't just locked in the *flight* part of flight-fight-freeze mode, were making the best speed possible for the defensive phalanx that had formed before the densely packed tents pitched along the northwestern edge of the open campground.

Ryan and company steered a course due west, and a little south, to avoid running into any lines of blasterfire.

At least the cannies behind them had gotten tangled up with locals. Over it all, Ryan realized Conn was still raving over his megaphone. Insanely, it was against them. "Don't let the stonehearts get away!" he shrieked. "They're the ones to blame for all of this! Chill them!"

A quick glance showed that no one paid attention to him. Not even the score or so sec men standing shoulder to shoulder in front of the dais, blasters leveled straight ahead, who looked glumly determined to chill anyone or anything who got close to their master. Apparently they were still, after all of this, more afraid of their monstrous sec boss than an endless swarm of raging cannies.

Suddenly the still mostly human stream of running figures parted ahead of Ryan and his friends, to flow around a single gigantic figure standing as immovable as Mother McComb's throne rock.

"Not so fast, you cannie-lovers!" the sec boss boomed. "I've got you now!"

"Fireblast!" Ryan exclaimed. "Can't you give it up?"

"You and me, One-Eye!" the giant bellowed, beating his chest with fists that looked as large as Ryan's head. "One-on-one. *Mana y mana*. Like men."

"It's *mano a mano*, dickhead," Ryan said. He raised the SIG and fired twice.

With breathtaking speed Potar snatched the two random figures running closest to him. One was a coamer female, and the other was a beanpole man about Ryan's own height. As if they were dolls, the sec boss clapped them together in front of his bulk to take the bullets instead of him.

"Blasters are for pussies!" he said, with a gust of laughter. "Bare hands, or I'll crush you with these losers."

"Fuck that."

Ryan was carrying his Steyr slung muzzle-down for rapid access, the way he usually did when they were headed into known danger. Stuffing his SIG back in its holster beneath his left armpit, he reached back, grabbed the longblaster by its fore-end, whipped it up past his own waist, then let it go. Reaching back, his hand found the rear grip with practiced ease. He fired from the hip.

Against black-powder blasters, even double-potent ones, Potar would have been safe as houses behind his human shields, one limp, one still writhing with some vigor. And Ryan was not inclined to rely even on the renowned penetration of his 9 mm ball handblaster bullets.

But a sharp-nosed, 147-grain, M80, full-metal-jacket round, traveling at upwards of 2700 feet per second, blasted right through the torso of the motionless full-human beanpole without appreciably slowing down.

Big bully Potar Baggart didn't understand about blow-through, but he learned as the bullet lanced right into his capacious belly and introduced him to a whole new world of pain.

He groaned and bent over, but he stayed on his feet and kept the bodies he held in his massive fists up, still shielding him. To the extent they did.

Going against an entire lifetime of training and experience, Ryan let the longblaster fall to hang by its sling without immediately jacking a fresh cartridge into the chamber from its 10-round detachable box magazine. He could not remember a time when he had done that.

But there was no way even he could throw the bolt one-handed now, not without stopping, and he was severely disinclined to so much as break stride. He couldn't currently feel a cannie actually breathing down his neck, and he sure as glowing rad death didn't want to.

Instead he yanked out the SIG and stuck it out ahead of him. He aimed to try to race past the wounded but still-full-of-fight man-mountain and leave him in his dust. If not, he was willing to take any shot he could get.

He could see flashes of the man's enormous face, red-flushed and sweat-sheened in the compound firelight, grinning at him past his victims. But the big man was smarter than Ryan reckoned as well as faster. He kept weaving them before him, spoiling any shot Ryan could hope to take, in no pattern the one-eyed man could figure out in the handful of heartbeats remaining.

The big man was about to toss one or both bodies at him. Ryan planned to dive left and hopefully clear. If one of them took him down, he was dead meat. He'd try to get a shoulder down, roll and come up blasting. Or die trying.

White hair flying behind it like a cavalry pennon, a short, slight figure raced by him at inhuman-seeming speed. But instead of showing nothing but snow-white coamer hide, it was sheathed from the neck down in dark.

Jak Lauren leaped like a monkey, grabbing hold of each of Potar's captive shields. As fast as he was, the giant had no time to react as Jak brought up his sneaker-clad feet, then sprang upward over Potar's sloping left shoulder. As he did, Ryan saw the glimmer of one of his favored balisong knives whip open in his left hand. It darted down and was planted at a forty-five-degree angle in Potar's swollen trapezius muscle. Using that as an anchor, Jak whipped his body around somehow to land astride of his adversary's shoulders.

The sec boss dropped his captives to grab frantically

at the white-faced attacker on his back. Jak's other butterfly knife whirled open in his right palm. He yanked its mate free, then he plunged both with points toward each other into the sides of Potar's massive neck, just in front of his neck bones.

Then the lithe albino pushed them both forward, instantly severing both carotid arteries *and* both jugular veins. Black fans of blood shot up like wings to either side of the sec boss's pain- and rage-distorted face.

His knees gave way beneath him. Plucking his knives free, Jak threw himself into a perfect backward somersault off his victim.

The flab covering the massive muscles of Potar Baggart's chest and belly shook like a bowlful of jelly as Ryan and all his friends fired on him. It was a waste of ammo; the giant's brain, instantly starved of oxygen, had already closed up shop for good. But none of them felt like taking anything for granted.

As Potar hit the ground like a falling skyscraper, the companions split to either side to race around him.

"Trouble!" Ryan heard Ricky call.

Having sheathed his panga to ram a new mag into his SIG, Ryan let himself risk an over-the-shoulder look. Scores of bodies wrestled in the hellish firelight. Others, many others, lay sprawled, some motionless, some not. Demonic white figures squatted over many of them, tearing at them with gore-dripping muzzles.

A dozen or more of the cannies, though, still ran in hot pursuit of the companions. They were no more than twenty yards back and closing fast on Ryan's exhausted band.

J.B. whipped smartly around. "Black dust, don't you

know when you're beat?" he asked in an almost conversational tone.

He whipped the Uzi up to his waist and raked a sustained burst back and forth across the charging pack. Coamers shrieked and fell, spurting blood.

Half of them went down, their bones and internal organs ripped by his merciless slugs. The survivors, at long last, turned their naked backs to their prey and fled back the way they had come.

There was a lot more meat that way, anyway, and much of it was free for the taking.

Wearily, the companions dragged themselves in among the now unoccupied tents along the southeast side of the campground's perimeter. As they did, Ryan realized Conn was still on his platform, and still hollering. And this time, his wails of rage were directed at them.

"Cawdor!" he heard him screech. "You cannot escape our justice! I will follow you wherever you go, to the ends of the Earth and beyond. And then I— Wait! Stop! What are you doin'? Get away from me! You can't do this—this is my destin-*EEEEEEEEEE*!"

Panting hard, Ryan turned and looked. Conn's sec men were all buried beneath a pyramid of coamers—the ones who hadn't gotten smart and run away, anyway. As Ryan watched, the cannies swarmed over Conn. The former gaudy owner had been so wound up he never even took the megaphone away from his face when he abruptly found himself confronted on his own bully pulpit by a pack of rabid, dog-faced horrors.

The horn went cartwheeling away from a wildly flailing hand. But Mathus Conn didn't need it anymore.

His screams as those inhumanly long muzzles ripped

mouthfuls out of his face and flesh could likely be heard clear to Sinkhole, Ryan reckoned.

"Your destiny, huh?" Ryan said grimly. "Truest thing you said all day."

He turned to his friends, all of whom were drinking air in the biggest gulps they could. Mildred and Ricky were sitting on the ground. He saw no reason to do anything other than let them—for a moment.

"Anybody see any reason why we should stick around this hellhole any longer?" he asked.

A ragged, weary, but fervent chorus of "noes" answered him.

Krysty stepped up to him. She raised her face and planted a kiss on his cheek, despite the stubble, and the coating of sweat, blood, cannie spittle and dirt that covered it.

"No reason at all, lover," she said. "Let's leave this place before the cannies figure out there's more fresh meat."

After a quick backward glance, they started to jog to the west.

* * * * *

COMING SOON FROM

GOLD EAGLE ®

Available June 2, 2015

THE EXECUTIONER #439
BLOOD RITES – *Don Pendleton*
When rival gangs terrorize Miami, Mack Bolan is called in to clean up the city, but the mess in Florida is just the beginning. The drug trafficking business is flourishing in Jamaica...along with the practice of voodoo and human sacrifice.

STONY MAN® #137
CITADEL OF FEAR – *Don Pendleton*
Able Team discovers that Liberty City, an economic free zone in Grenada, is a haven for building homemade missiles. Phoenix Force arrives just in time to provide backup, but the missiles have already been shipped to a rogue group with their sights set on the California coast...

SUPERBOLAN® #174
DESERT FALCONS – *Don Pendleton*
In the Kingdom of Saudi Arabia, a secret group is plotting to oust the royal family. Their next move: kidnapping the prince from a desert warfare training session outside Las Vegas. Mack Bolan must keep the prince safe—but someone in the heir's inner circle is a traitor.

CNMGE0515

Available July 7, 2015

THE EXECUTIONER® #440
KILLPATH – *Don Pendleton*

After a DEA agent is tortured and killed by a powerful Colombian cartel, Bolan teams up with a former cocaine queen in Cali to obliterate the entire operation.

SUPERBOLAN® #175
NINJA ASSAULT – *Don Pendleton*

Ninjas attack an American casino, and Bolan follows the gangsters behind the crime back to Japan—where he intends to take them out on their home turf.

DEATHLANDS® #123
IRON RAGE – *James Axler*

Ryan and the companions are caught in a battle for survival against crocs, snakes and makeshift ironclads on the great Sippi river.

ROGUE ANGEL™ #55
BENEATH STILL WATERS – *Alex Archer*

Annja uncovers Nazi secrets—and treasure—in the wreckage of a submerged German bomber shot down at the end of WWII.

"I'd say it's just about ready to get serious," J.B. said, sounding more interested than alarmed.

Krysty looked back. The people who had gone on board the barge to fight the fire in the fabric bales were scrambling back across the thick hawser that connected the hulls. She was relieved and pleased to see Doc trotting right across, as spry as a kid goat, holding his arms out to his sides with his black coattails flapping. Despite his aged appearance, he was chronologically a few years younger than Ryan. The bizarre abuse and rigors the evil whitecoats of Operation Chronos had subjected him to had aged him prematurely, and damaged his fine, highly educated mind. But he could still muster the agility and energy of a man much younger than he appeared to be.

Ricky came last, straddling the thick woven hemp able and inch-worming along. But he did so at speed.

Avery had vanished. "You and Mildred best head for cover," Ryan said.

"They'll only hit us by accident," Mildred said, "shooting oversize muskets at us."

"They're going to have a dozen or two shots at us next round," J.B. said. "That's a lot of chances to get lucky."

"Looks like some smaller fry are heading this way," Ryan reported. "Krysty, Mildred—*git!*"

"Come on." Krysty grabbed the other woman's wrist and began running for the cabin. Though Mildred was about as heavy as she was, Krysty barely slowed, towing Mildred as if she were a river barge. She was strong, motivated and full of adrenaline.

Krysty heard Ryan open fire. Given the range, the bobbing of the approaching lesser war craft, and the complex movement of the *Queen*—pitching fore and aft as well as heeling over to her right from the centrifugal force of the fastest left turn the vessel could manage, she doubted he'd be lucky enough to hit anything significant.

The women had almost reached the cabin when the next salvo hit, roaring like an angry dragon. Krysty saw stout planks suddenly spreading into fragments almost in her face.

And then the world vanished in a soundless white flash.

Don't miss
IRON RAGE by James Axler,
available July 2015 wherever
Gold Eagle® books and ebooks are sold.

James Axler
Outlanders®

"You can't hide from the truth because it will always find you."

Almost two centuries after the nuclear catastrophe that led to Deathlands, the truth comes out: aliens were behind the nukecaust that reshaped, remolded and forever changed the face of the earth and its inhabitants. One hundred years after Deathlands, anarchy is in retreat in the newly renamed Outlands. A rigid and punishing hierarchy of barons rules the oppressed populations of the fortified villes. Now the baronies have been consolidated in a Program of Unification and are protected by highly trained and well-armed enforcers. Kane, once a trained enforcer for the barons, finds a new destiny thrust upon him, pitting him against the powerful alien forces directing the world's fate.

**Available wherever Gold Eagle®
books and ebooks are sold.**

**GOLD
EAGLE**®

GEO2015

Joan of Arc's long-lost sword. A heroine reborn. The quest to protect humanity's sacred secrets from falling into the wrong hands.

Rogue Angel is sophisticated escapism and high adventure rooted in the excitement of history's most fabled eras. Each book provides a unique combination of arcane history, mystery, action, adventure and limited supernatural elements (mainly the sword). The series details a young woman's transition from an independent archaeologist who hosts an American cable television show to an action heroine with a surprising connection to Joan of Arc and a role in French mythology.

Available wherever Gold Eagle® books and ebooks are sold.

GOLD EAGLE®